"Can books be better than television? You bet they can—when Lee Gol........ ........... ........... .......child

"This is probably the best *Monk* novel that Lee Goldberg has written. . . . Plain and simple, it's flat-out awesome!"     —Gelati's Scoop Blog

"Readers will enjoy *Mr. Monk on the Road* as much as, or more than, any of the *Monk* books that have preceded it. Heartily recommended!"     —Gumshoe

### Mr. Monk Is Cleaned Out

"What's left to say about Lee Goldberg's *Monk* books? You already know they're some of the very best TV tie-in books being published today. More than that, they're some of the very best mystery novels being published today, period."     —Rough Edges

"For a lighthearted, enjoyable whodunit with an old friend, read *Mr. Monk Is Cleaned Out*—you'll thank me later!"     —San Francisco Book Review

"The latest hilariously funny and devilishly clever novel about TV's obsessive-compulsive sleuth Adrian Monk is an impossible-crime lover's delight."
     —Ellery Queen Mystery Magazine

"Goldberg weaves a tale that is fun, entertaining as hell, and totally satisfying."     —CrimeSpree Magazine

### Mr. Monk in Trouble

"Once again, Goldberg expertly sails along the fine line of character quirks that make Monk so infuriating, and yet so endearing."     —Bookgasm

*continued . . .*

"Lee Goldberg knows that the richest humor veers close to pathos, and that is one reason the novel succeeds so well. This is much more than entertainment."
—Richard S. Wheeler, author of *Snowbound*

### *Mr. Monk and the Dirty Cop*

"Sharp character comedy combines with ingenious . . . puzzle spinning."     —*Ellery Queen Mystery Magazine*

"You'd be hard-pressed to find another recent work that provides so many hip and humorous moments. *Monk* series fans have another winner here to enjoy."
—Bookgasm

### *Mr. Monk Is Miserable*

"Fans of the show are in for a treat. Goldberg does a stunning job capturing Natalie's voice."
—Roundtable Reviews

"Full of snippets of slapstick humor and Monk's special talents for observation."     —*Library Journal*

### *Mr. Monk Goes to Germany*

"The story flows so smoothly, it's effortless to read."
—*CrimeSpree Magazine*

"A great escape. Lee Goldberg has written another wonderful novel."
—*Futures Mystery Anthology Magazine*

### *Mr. Monk in Outer Space*

"You say you don't read tie-in novels? You should give the *Monk* books a try and find out what you've been missing. They're funny, they're well-written, they're carefully plotted, and they're poignant."
—Bill Crider, author of *Murder in the Air*

### Mr. Monk and the Two Assistants

"Even if you aren't familiar with the TV series *Monk*, this book is too funny to not be read."
—The Weekly Journal (TX)

### Mr. Monk and the Blue Flu

"A must read if you enjoy Monk's mysteries on the tube." —Bookgasm

"A very funny and inventively plotted book."
—*Ellery Queen Mystery Magazine*

### Mr. Monk Goes to Hawaii

"An entertaining and ruefully funny diversion that stars one of television's best-loved characters."
—*Honolulu Star-Bulletin*

### Mr. Monk Goes to the Firehouse

"The first in a new series is always an occasion to celebrate, but Lee Goldberg's TV adaptations double your pleasure. . . . *Mr. Monk Goes to the Firehouse* brings everyone's favorite OCD detective to print. Hooray!"
—*Mystery Scene*

"It is laugh-out-loud funny from the get-go. For *Monk* fans, this is a must. Totally enjoyable. Lee Goldberg has expertly captured the nuances of what makes Monk, well, Monk."
—Robin Burcell, author of *The Bone Chamber*

"Lee has found the perfect voice for Natalie's first-person narration—sweet, exhausted, frustrated, exasperated, and sweet again. None of these feelings has to do with the mystery. They're all reactions to Monk's standard behavior as he wars with all the ways nature is trying to kill him. Lee Goldberg has managed to concoct a novel that's as good as any of the *Monk* episodes I've seen on the tube." —Ed Gorman, author of *Stranglehold*

# The Monk Series

*Mr. Monk on the Couch*

*Mr. Monk on the Road*

*Mr. Monk Is Cleaned Out*

*Mr. Monk in Trouble*

*Mr. Monk and the Dirty Cop*

*Mr. Monk Is Miserable*

*Mr. Monk Goes to Germany*

*Mr. Monk in Outer Space*

*Mr. Monk and the Two Assistants*

*Mr. Monk and the Blue Flu*

*Mr. Monk Goes to Hawaii*

*Mr. Monk Goes to the Firehouse*

# MR. MONK
## ON THE COUCH

A Novel by
**Lee Goldberg**

Based on the USA Network television series created by
**Andy Breckman**

AN OBSIDIAN MYSTERY

OBSIDIAN
Published by New American Library, a division of
Penguin Group (USA) Inc., 375 Hudson Street,
New York, New York 10014, USA
Penguin Group (Canada), 90 Eglinton Avenue East, Suite 700, Toronto,
Ontario M4P 2Y3, Canada (a division of Pearson Penguin Canada Inc.)
Penguin Books Ltd., 80 Strand, London WC2R 0RL, England
Penguin Ireland, 25 St. Stephen's Green, Dublin 2,
Ireland (a division of Penguin Books Ltd.)
Penguin Group (Australia), 250 Camberwell Road, Camberwell, Victoria 3124,
Australia (a division of Pearson Australia Group Pty. Ltd.)
Penguin Books India Pvt. Ltd., 11 Community Centre, Panchsheel Park,
New Delhi - 110 017, India
Penguin Group (NZ), 67 Apollo Drive, Rosedale, Auckland 0632,
New Zealand (a division of Pearson New Zealand Ltd.)
Penguin Books (South Africa) (Pty.) Ltd., 24 Sturdee Avenue,
Rosebank, Johannesburg 2196, South Africa

Penguin Books Ltd., Registered Offices:
80 Strand, London WC2R 0RL, England

Published by Obsidian, an imprint of New American Library, a division of
Penguin Group (USA) Inc. Previously published in an Obsidian hardcover
edition.

First Obsidian Mass Market Printing, December 2011
10  9  8  7  6  5  4  3  2

# MR. MONK
## ON THE COUCH

A Novel by
## Lee Goldberg

Based on the USA Network television series created by
## Andy Breckman

AN OBSIDIAN MYSTERY

OBSIDIAN
Published by New American Library, a division of
Penguin Group (USA) Inc., 375 Hudson Street,
New York, New York 10014, USA
Penguin Group (Canada), 90 Eglinton Avenue East, Suite 700, Toronto,
Ontario M4P 2Y3, Canada (a division of Pearson Penguin Canada Inc.)
Penguin Books Ltd., 80 Strand, London WC2R 0RL, England
Penguin Ireland, 25 St. Stephen's Green, Dublin 2,
Ireland (a division of Penguin Books Ltd.)
Penguin Group (Australia), 250 Camberwell Road, Camberwell, Victoria 3124,
Australia (a division of Pearson Australia Group Pty. Ltd.)
Penguin Books India Pvt. Ltd., 11 Community Centre, Panchsheel Park,
New Delhi - 110 017, India
Penguin Group (NZ), 67 Apollo Drive, Rosedale, Auckland 0632,
New Zealand (a division of Pearson New Zealand Ltd.)
Penguin Books (South Africa) (Pty.) Ltd., 24 Sturdee Avenue,
Rosebank, Johannesburg 2196, South Africa

Penguin Books Ltd., Registered Offices:
80 Strand, London WC2R 0RL, England

Published by Obsidian, an imprint of New American Library, a division of
Penguin Group (USA) Inc. Previously published in an Obsidian hardcover
edition.

First Obsidian Mass Market Printing, December 2011
10 9 8 7 6 5 4 3 2

*To Valerie and Madison*

## AUTHOR'S NOTE AND ACKNOWLEDGMENTS

This story takes place a few months after the final episode of the *Monk* TV series and not long after the events in my book *Mr. Monk on the Road*.

This book was written mostly in Los Angeles and a little bit in Owensboro, Kentucky (those are the pages stained with BBQ sauce).

I am indebted to Bruce Frazier at Bushnell Outdoor Products and Eric Lane for their knowledge of old binoculars, to Simon Wood and Sharon DeVita for their assistance regarding Mexican immigration documents, to Brenda Holcomb and Lois Hirt for their enormous help on a path I ultimately didn't take, and, as always, to Dr. Doug Lyle for his counsel on medical matters.

Finally, this book would not have been possible without the continued support and enthusiasm of Andy Breckman, Kerry Donovan, and Gina Maccoby.

I look forward to hearing from you at www.lee goldberg.com.

# 1

# Mr. Monk and the Sunday Paper

There is never a day off from death.

I was sitting at my kitchen table in my bathrobe and slippers, eating a cream cheese–slathered bagel for breakfast and reading the massive Sunday editions of the *San Francisco Chronicle* and the *New York Times*, when I got a phone call from Captain Leland Stottlemeyer of the San Francisco Police Department, notifying me of a homicide.

I'm not a cop, but I'm on call 24/7 to the police department anyway. That's because I'm the personal assistant, driver, secretary, shopper, and all-around beast of burden for Adrian Monk, the brilliant detective and the SFPD's only paid consultant (though he isn't paid nearly enough for one person, let alone two, if you ask me).

I'd received well over a hundred such calls from Captain Stottlemeyer over the years, so starting my day with a corpse was as routine for me as a breakfast bagel.

There was a time when seeing the dead really bothered me. It wasn't so much the bloodshed as it was my firsthand knowledge of the grief and lasting heartache the victim's loved ones would soon experience. Each murder reminded me of what it felt like when I learned that my husband had been shot down over Kosovo.

I also felt like an intruder, not on the death, but on the crime scene.

I didn't belong there. I was extraneous, irrelevant, a tourist.

Even worse, I was unskilled, untrained, unofficial, and uninterested.

I was useless to anyone but Adrian Monk, and even then, my duties were minimal. My job was to make sure nothing distracted him (and he could be distracted by something as innocuous as a stain on someone's tie or the creak of a loose floorboard) and to supply him with disinfectant wipes (which he needed constantly).

But as time went on and I got caught up in the investigations, all of that changed.

I learned how to read a crime scene, how to process evidence, and how to question witnesses and suspects.

I also picked up some deductive skills and crime-solving instincts of my own, enough that I felt not only comfortable at a crime scene, but entitled to share my thoughts on a case and expect them to be taken seriously.

I wasn't just a reluctant observer anymore.

I began to *like* participating at crime scenes.

I looked forward to the puzzle, to the challenge of solving a crime, and to the satisfaction of learning the solution, something Monk always discovered, even when it seemed like an impossible feat.

But the biggest change in my attitude toward homicide was more recent and profound, arising out of my experiences on Monk's past few big cases.

I'd begun to think of myself as a pretty good detective in my own right, not that I'd shared that opinion with anyone else yet. I'd barely admitted it to myself.

Being a detective was certainly not something I'd ever aspired to or a field that I had any interest in (beyond my childhood desire to be one of Charlie's Angels, but that had more to do with their clothes, their independence, and their sassy attitudes). Becoming interested in detecting myself evolved slowly and unconsciously out of my relationship with Monk and, to a lesser degree, with Captain Stottlemeyer and his former lieutenant Randy Disher, who'd recently left the department to become the police chief in Summit, New Jersey.

But it had happened, and now I was eager to somehow put myself to the test, which I knew wouldn't be easy, or perhaps even possible, with Adrian Monk around. His powers of observation and deduction are as astounding as they are irritating, so much so that he often solves cases within minutes of arriving at a crime scene. It doesn't leave much room for anyone else to shine, much less a novice like me.

Monk has an uncanny ability to spot the slightest thing—whether it's an object, a behavior, or an event—that's uneven, odd, lopsided, or out of place, and when it comes to homicide investigation, that's usually the piece that solves the crime.

He's able to spot that telling detail because he obsesses over little things that are invisible to most of us. We don't see them because they are ridiculously mundane or irrelevant, except when they are not, which is any time there's a dead body involved.

It's a personality quirk that works great for Monk when it comes to solving crimes but not so well when it comes to functioning in normal society.

That's mostly where I came in. I facilitated his interaction with others and with his environment.

In other words, I tried to keep people from driving him crazy and vice versa, while at the same time trying to hold on to my own sanity.

But it wasn't enough for me anymore just to stand there, straightening things and handing out wipes.

After getting Stottlemeyer's call that Sunday morning, I quickly dressed in a T-shirt, V-neck pullover, and jeans, hurried out of my little Victorian house in the Noe Valley area of the city, and drove north to Pine Street, where Adrian Monk lived in an even-numbered second-floor apartment that measured exactly eight hundred square feet in an art deco building with four floors.

When I arrived, he was in the kitchen, in the middle of his Sunday morning ritual of cleaning his cleaning supplies.

There was a time not so long ago when I found it odd to see him spraying a can of Lysol with a can of Lysol, but not anymore.

It's amazing what you can become accustomed to.

Monk was wearing a white apron and yellow rubber dish gloves and was happily humming one of his favorite songs: Tommy Tutone's annoying 1982 hit "867-5309," aka "Jenny." He liked the song because the phone number adds up to thirty-eight, an even number, and it was released in an even-numbered year, and it hit number four, also an even number, on the Billboard charts.

"Just give me a moment to finish up," Monk said, buffing the can of Lysol until it gleamed.

"It's Sunday morning, I'm double-parked out front, and there's a bunch of cops and crime scene investigators waiting on us who've locked down an entire block in the Marina District. But there's no hurry."

My sarcasm was wasted on Monk, who didn't understand it and wouldn't care even if he did. I knew that but it didn't stop me from indulging myself anyway.

"When was the last time you cleaned your cleaning supplies?" he asked.

"Um, let me think." I looked at my feet as I pretended to ponder the question, then, after a long moment, I raised my head. "Never."

"You've *never* cleaned your cleansers?"

"They're cleansers, Mr. Monk. How much cleaner can they get?"

"Do you clean your vacuum?"

"I empty the bag."

"That's not the same thing," he said. "Do you clean your broom?"

"When my broom gets dirty, I throw it out and buy a new one."

I thought he'd appreciate that. But he didn't.

"It gets dirty every time you sweep."

"I'm talking about when it gets really dirty."

"That is when it gets really dirty. When was the last time you threw out a broom?"

I had to think about that for a moment. He grimaced and looked up to the heavens. "Oh, dear God. She has to think about it."

"A year or two," I said.

Monk marched over to his huge utility closet and took out one of his many brooms, the brush wrapped in plastic. He held it out to me. "I want you to have this."

"I have a broom," I said.

"Cleaning your home with filthy equipment is like washing your hands with dung. It's a miracle you're still alive." He thrust the broom at me again. "In the name of all that's holy, take the broom."

I took it just to shut him up. "Thank you. Can we go now?"

He put his cleansers in a plastic box, placed it on a shelf in his utility closet, then took off his apron and neatly folded it.

"Promise me that you'll throw out your old broom the instant you get home."

"I'll throw it out."

"In an incinerator," he said.

"I don't have an incinerator."

"You, of all people, should get one." He went down the hall and got his coat.

I followed him. "*You* don't have one."

"Because I'm careful to keep myself and my belongings free from dirt and disease," he said and held the front door open for me. "You wallow in it."

I walked past him outside. "Then I must have a terrific immune system."

"You're being selfish," Monk said, closing the door and locking it behind him. "You aren't considering the danger your filthy conduct poses to the people around you."

"You mean yourself."

"Of course I do," he said as we walked side by side to my car.

"You don't think *that's* selfish?"

"I represent all of humanity," Monk said.

"How do you know?"

"Because there are only two of us in this conversation," Monk said. "And humanity wouldn't pick the filthy one."

# 2

## Mr. Monk Battles Willy-nilly

The homes in the Marina District looked like birthday cakes. The bright colors and the smooth texture of their stucco looked so much like frosting that I almost wanted to lick them. The effect was only heightened by the yellow crime scene tape that closed off both ends of the street and fluttered in the brisk bay breeze like party streamers.

The block was cluttered with the usual array of official vehicles, parked every which way in the center of the street, resembling a freeway pileup, only without the collisions.

"I don't understand why Captain Stottlemeyer lets them do that," Monk said. "How can he concentrate on anything with that going on?"

"I don't know," I said.

I parked in a red zone, parallel to the curb, and put my police parking permit on the dash. We got out of the car and had to weave our way around all the official vehicles to get to the police line, which only increased Monk's irritation.

"It's impossible to walk from point A to point B in a straight line with the cars parked this way," Monk said. "It's taking us twice as long as it should to cover the distance between our car and our destination."

"We can use the exercise," I said.

"Speak for yourself," Monk said. "I'm not the one who has gained two pounds and four point eight ounces in the last eight weeks."

I stopped. "I've gained two pounds?"

Monk turned around. "And four point eight ounces. Don't worry, no one will notice."

"You did," I said.

"I notice lots of things that other people don't."

"Where is it?"

"Where is what?"

"The two pounds and four point eight ounces, Mr. Monk."

"On your body, of course," Monk said, turning his back on me and continuing toward the yellow tape that demarked the police line. "It's insignificant, except for that extra ounce. You really must lose that."

Captain Stottlemeyer, bundled up in a wrinkled coat over a sweatshirt and jeans, met us at the corner of Avila Street and Capra Way and lifted the tape for us.

"Good morning, Monk, Natalie," he said. "Thanks for coming down."

His hair, which he kept a bit too long, to compensate for his receding hairline, was askew and his bushy mustache was in need of a trim.

"Did you get dragged out of bed for this?" I asked.

He nodded. "The one day I get to sleep in. I look

forward to it all week. You'd think even murderers could use a day off."

I stepped under the tape, but Monk didn't move from the other side. Stottlemeyer looked at him.

"Aren't you joining us?"

"Not until you have someone take care of this mess," Monk said, pointing at the parked cars.

"They were in a hurry, Monk. They were responding to a homicide."

"It doesn't take any extra time to park straight and in rows that are parallel with the sidewalks. The police are supposed to establish and maintain order, not create disorder. It sets a very bad example and creates a huge distraction."

Stottlemeyer sighed. He knew as well as I did that it was an argument he couldn't win. "I'll send some uniforms over to repark the vehicles, okay? Will you come with us now, please?"

"I could direct the operation," Monk said.

"I would prefer you investigated the murder," Stottlemeyer said.

"It won't be easy to do with all of that going on," Monk said, waving his hand toward the cars.

"You'll just draw on your vast reserve of inner strength and deal with it," Stottlemeyer said, holding up the tape and waving Monk over. "Come on already, we got a body on the street here and the medical examiner is anxious to take it to the morgue."

"How about if we compromise?" Monk said. "I'll oversee the parking of the cars and then investigate the murder."

"How about this," Stottlemeyer said. "You get over here right now or I'll spit on the sidewalk."

"You wouldn't dare," Monk said.

"Try me," Stottlemeyer said and looked him right in the eye.

Monk squared his shoulders, took a deep breath, and stepped under the police tape.

"I'm only doing this to save you from doing something you'd regret for the rest of your life," Monk said.

"Thanks," Stottlemeyer said, and motioned over a young uniformed officer. "See to it that those vehicles over there are parked in an orderly manner."

"Right away, sir," the officer said with a grin.

"He means it," Monk said.

The officer looked at Stottlemeyer, who nodded in agreement. "I do. Make sure they are parked in nice rows."

"And by size," Monk said. "And model."

"Don't push it, Monk," Stottlemeyer said as he led us to a house midway down the street.

The victim was a Caucasian man sprawled on the driveway beside a black Audi with slashed tires and broken headlights. The man looked to me to be about forty, six feet tall, and a little pudgy, wearing a blue bathrobe and long pajama bottoms covered with the Ralph Lauren logo. His head was in a pool of blood.

I tried to focus my awesome powers of deduction, but I kept thinking about my extra tonnage. It was true that ever since my daughter Julie went off to college, I'd been hitting the Oreos pretty hard at night. Now I was paying the price.

I forced the Oreos out of my mind and tried to concentrate on the scene in front of me. Dead man in a bathrobe. Trashed car. Nice house, nice car, designer jammies. What did all of that tell me?

The guy was probably a professional of some kind, like a doctor, lawyer, or banker, and made someone angry enough to trash his car and kill him.

Lieutenant Amy Devlin squatted beside the body, arms resting on her knees, head down in thought. She was a former undercover cop who'd recently transferred into the homicide division to fill the vacancy left by Randy Disher.

Devlin was thin and wiry, her dark hair cut raggedly short, as if she'd done it herself in a fit of anger with a pair of desk scissors. With the exception of her leather jacket, we were dressed exactly the same: T-shirt, V-neck sweater, jeans.

She looked up as we approached but directed her gaze at Stottlemeyer.

"I thought you only called Monk in on the murders we can't figure out," she said. "We just got here, but this one strikes me as pretty routine and not particularly complex."

"That's because you're looking at it as a cop," Stottlemeyer said, "not as a politician."

"Because that's what I am," Devlin said. "Aren't you?"

"If you want to reach my lofty heights in the department, you have to be both. The dead man is Garson Dach, a deputy district attorney. So we needed to solve this case an hour ago."

My guess was that Dach ran outside to confront whoever was trashing his car and got beat up. The only questions left to answer were who the killer was and why he did it.

"Dead is dead," Devlin said. "What makes his murder a higher priority than any other?"

Stottlemeyer sighed. "Not knowing the answer to that question is what will keep you at the same pay grade for the rest of your career."

"Fine by me," she said. "I didn't become a cop to kiss asses."

"Then you are succeeding brilliantly," Stottlemeyer said, then looked around. "Where's Monk?"

I turned, expecting to find him back among the parked cars, but he was standing in front of the neighbor's juniper hedge, staring at the Sunday edition of the *San Francisco Chronicle* that was lying on top of it.

"What are you doing?" Stottlemeyer asked.

"Securing the crime scene," Monk said.

"The murder is over here." The captain gestured to the body on the driveway.

"I'm talking about this," Monk said, pointing at the newspaper.

"That's not a crime, Monk."

"Look at where the paperboy has tossed his newspapers," Monk continued. "It's on the hedge here, the sidewalk there, the lawn over there, the driveway there, on the hood of a car over there—it's criminal."

"He's tossing newspapers out of a car," Stottlemeyer said. "It's not an exact science."

"If he can't toss accurately, then he should get out of the car, walk up to the house, and place the newspaper on the front porch. The fact that he doesn't care where the paper lands suggests that he has sociopathic tendencies."

"I'd shoot the bastard on sight," Devlin said, but her sarcasm was completely lost on Monk.

"I know how you feel, Lieutenant," Monk said. "But I think apprehending him and giving him a strong warning would be enough at this stage. Maybe we can scare him straight."

"Let's deal with the murder first, shall we?" Stottlemeyer said.

"That paperboy could still be out there, throwing newspapers willy-nilly," Monk said. "There's a chance we can stop him before he causes more harm."

"There's also a murderer out there, Monk, who could start killing willy-nilly if we don't stop him. *That's* the willy-nilly I'm worried about."

"There's too much willy-nilly going on," Monk said. "It's a scourge."

"It certainly is, and this guy was trying to stop it," Stottlemeyer said, turning to the corpse. "Garson Dach put a lot of very bad people in prison, many of them engaged in the most heinous of willy-nilly behavior. It looks like one of those people got him back for it this morning. Are you going to do something about that?"

I admired Stottlemeyer's not-very-subtle effort to manipulate Monk and get him invested in the case. And it appeared to work.

Monk turned his back on the juniper hedge and walked slowly around the car, his hands out in front of him, framing the scene like a director.

"This is an easy one," Devlin said. "All we have to do is get a list of guys Dach put away, see which ones got out lately, and track their movements this morning. Give me a day, maybe two, and I'll have the killer locked up."

"So what do you think happened here?" I asked.

"It's obvious," she replied, sighing impatiently. "Dach saw a guy trashing his car, stupidly ran out to confront him, and got himself smacked in the head with a baseball bat or some other blunt object for his trouble."

We had essentially the same theory about what happened, but hearing her tell it, I realized that it didn't quite add up.

"I take it Dach was a smart guy," I said, "so why didn't he call the police? Or at least come outside with a weapon of some kind to defend himself with?"

"I didn't say he was a smart guy," Devlin said.

"You don't become an ADA if you're an imbecile," I said.

"Being smart in the courtroom and smart on the street are two different things. Maybe he didn't see the distinction and thought he was as tough out here as he was in there," she said. "I think the bad guy only wanted to trash the car, but when Dach marched outside with a baseball bat, things got out of hand. The bad guy took the bat away from the smug bastard and beat him with it."

"Did you know Dach?" Stottlemeyer asked Devlin.

"This is the first time I've met him," she said, glancing at the corpse.

"So what makes you think he was a smug bastard?"

"He's a man and he's a lawyer," she said. "Which is enough on its own, but throw in a European car and Ralph Lauren jammies, and what more do you need to know?"

She made a convincing argument, not that I'm big on generalities and stereotypes.

"Who found the body?" Monk asked.

"A woman on her morning jog," Stottlemeyer said.

Monk leaned from side to side and began to walk slowly around the car, looking at it from various angles.

"Maybe she did it," I said. "Maybe she's a crazed ex-lover or the relative of someone he put away."

"Why do you say that?" Stottlemeyer asked.

"It just seems to me that pretending to discover the body would be a good way to throw off suspicion and hide in plain sight. Who would ever suspect the jogger?"

"Good point," Stottlemeyer said. "We'll look into it."

But I saw the quick look that passed between Stottlemeyer and Devlin and felt my face flush with embarrassment.

"You already were," I said. "Weren't you?"

"It's routine," Devlin said. "We always check out the person who discovered the body and corroborate their story."

"So why didn't you say that?" I said to Stottlemeyer.

"I wanted to hear your reasoning," he said. "I wanted to see if you came up with the idea because of something you saw that we missed."

"But you didn't," Devlin said.

"That's right," I said. "I didn't."

I was more aware than either of them that my theory was nothing more than a desperate guess. In my eagerness to prove my chops as a detective, all I'd done was underscore that, despite all of my time on crime scenes, I was still an amateur.

"It's okay, Natalie," Stottlemeyer said. "I welcome your perspective."

"Don't we all," Devlin said.

I knew she resented two civilians intruding on her investigation, but I thought Monk had proven himself to her the last time that we'd met and that she and I had even bonded a bit. Apparently, I was wrong.

Monk joined us again, rolled his shoulders, and looked past us to the house.

"Was the front door open when the officers got here?" he asked.

"Yes," Devlin replied. "But Dach lived alone and there's no sign that anything inside was disturbed."

Monk headed for the house.

"The crime scene is out here," Devlin said, calling after him.

"He knows that," Stottlemeyer said.

"So what's he expect to find in the house?"

"I have no idea," Stottlemeyer said. "But I am eager to find out."

We followed Monk into the house. We stepped into a short entry hall with a living room to our right, the kitchen to our left, and a family room and a steep staircase in front of us.

The ceilings were low, the doorways were arched, the fireplace was white brick, and the floors were hardwood. The furniture was contemporary and practical, not the least bit comfy-looking or inviting. The house had all the personality and warmth of the waiting room of an accountant's office.

Monk cocked his head from side to side, held his hands up in front of him, and moved slowly and deliberately into the kitchen, weaving and dipping and swaying with almost balletic grace.

Devlin watched him, frowning with disapproval. "What is he doing?"

"Monk tai chi," Stottlemeyer said.

"He's trying to spot anything that's uneven, odd, or out of balance," I said.

"That's what we think," Stottlemeyer said. "But we aren't entirely sure."

The kitchen was small and neat, with linoleum floors, a cottage-style table, and white tiled countertops with a floral tile backsplash. The coffeemaker, toaster, and other countertop appliances were metallic and sleek and were all the same brand. There was a row of spice jars on the counter near the gas stove, but they were just for show. I deduced that because the labels were yellowed and the jars were all full.

That conclusion didn't reveal anything about the murder, at least not to me. I was just trying to keep my detecting senses sharp. But being in the kitchen made me think of the leftover pizza and ice cream in my refrigerator and the blubber I'd packed on in the past few weeks.

I sucked in my gut.

"It really isn't noticeable," Monk said as he walked around the kitchen table.

"What isn't?" Stottlemeyer asked.

"The weight Natalie has gained," Monk said.

How did he know what I was thinking? But the instant I had that thought, I realized it was a simple deduction. We were in the kitchen and I was sucking in my gut. I might as well have announced what was on my mind.

"Could we please not discuss my weight?"

Stottlemeyer gave me a quick once-over. "You look great to me."

"That's because you've gained even more weight than her," Monk said. "So much that you've had to buy new clothes."

"That's not why I bought them. My clothes were old," Stottlemeyer said. "I'm updating my look."

"And your waist size," Monk said, scrutinizing the table. "You're wearing your belt two notches looser."

There was an empty cereal bowl, a plate, and a coffee cup on the table. A box of granola was out, as was a carton of milk. Coffee was warming in the pot on the coffeemaker.

"Forget about my belt and concentrate on the crime scene," Stottlemeyer said.

"Which is outside," Devlin said. "You know, where the body is."

But Monk wasn't listening to her. He moved to the back of the kitchen, where a doorway led to a tiny laundry room. Right inside the doorway were two trash cans. I presumed that one was for trash, the other one for recyclables. Monk studied them for a moment.

Stottlemeyer leaned toward me and whispered, "It's my wife and all that home cooking. I can't stop eating.

It's like I'm making up for all those microwave dinners I had when I was single."

"Without my microwave," I said, "I'd starve."

"This is a waste of time," Devlin said. "While we're standing around here talking about diets, I've got a corpse decomposing on the sidewalk and there's a killer out there who is covering his tracks."

Stottlemeyer ignored her and kept his eye on Monk, who took out a pen from his pocket and lifted the lid of each can. Monk closed the lid of the trash can quickly, as if something might leap out and grab him, but he lingered over the recycle bin for a moment, studying the stack of newspapers inside.

Then Monk took a step back, rolled his shoulders, and gestured to me for a disinfectant wipe, which I gave him from my purse.

We all stood there watching him as he cleaned the edge of his pen, put it back in his pocket, and then threw the wipe out in the trash can.

"Arrest the paperboy," Monk said.

Devlin lowered her head and sighed wearily. Stottlemeyer rubbed his temples with the thumb and index finger of his right hand and then spoke.

"I thought we were past that, Monk. We're trying to solve a murder here."

"I already have," Monk said.

Devlin jerked her head up. "You have?"

"Arrest the paperboy," Monk said.

"I'll make you a deal," Stottlemeyer said. "Tell me who the killer is, and after we arrest him, we'll arrest the paperboy."

"You can do both at once," Monk said. "The paperboy is the killer."

# 3

# Mr. Monk and the Dead Guest

"I didn't see that coming," Stottlemeyer said.

"Because it's insane," Devlin said, and marched up to Monk, getting right in his face. "The paperboy? Really? Is that the best you can come up with?"

Monk took a step back. "You ought to talk with your dentist about gingivitis."

"You ought to talk to your shrink about joining the real world," Devlin said, then turned to Stottlemeyer. "Why do you put up with this, Captain? This is a simple case. You called him down here before I, or anybody else, had a chance to work it. And for what? The paperboy? Not being able to land a newspaper on the porch doesn't make him a killer."

"It does in this case," Monk said.

"How do you figure that?" Devlin asked.

"Dach has yesterday's newspaper in his recycle bin but not today's."

"That's because he hasn't read it yet," Devlin said.

"So where is it?" Monk asked.

"Maybe he liked to read on the toilet," Devlin said, "and the newspaper is in his bathroom."

"It's not," Monk said.

"You haven't checked," she said.

"No, I haven't, but you can," Monk said. "Go ahead, I'll wait."

"Okay, for the sake of argument, let's say you're right, it's not in the house. Maybe it's outside somewhere."

"It's not," Monk said. "It's the only newspaper on the street that wasn't delivered."

"You don't know that," Devlin said.

"I do, but you can confirm it for yourself by going door to door," Monk said. "Go ahead, I'll wait."

Stottlemeyer shot me a smile behind Devlin's back. He was enjoying this. I wasn't, so I glowered at him instead, which only made him smile more, because he enjoyed that, too.

"Okay," she said. "Let's say he never got his paper. So what? Maybe the killer took it so *he'd* have something to read in the can."

"The killer took the newspaper, but not for reading material. Dach liked to read his newspaper with his breakfast. So he set the table and then went outside to get the paper."

And with that, Monk headed out the door, playing the part of Garson Dach. We trailed after him.

"But as soon as he stepped outside, he saw that his car had been vandalized, so he rushed outside and bent down to examine the damage to his tires and headlights," Monk continued, squatting down in front of the car. "That's when the paperboy drove by, tossing out Sunday papers willy-nilly. He didn't see Dach. He

tossed his paper just as Dach stood up and hit him in the head with it."

"The paper was huge this morning," I said. "It would have been like getting hit with a slab of concrete."

Monk nodded. "Dach fell, smacking his head against the pavement, compounding the injury. The paperboy came over, checked Dach's pulse, and realized he was dead. So he snatched the newspaper and drove off, quickly and haphazardly tossing out the rest of his papers as he fled so he wouldn't draw attention to himself by not making his deliveries."

Once again, Monk had solved the case by spotting a detail I'd missed. Not something that was there, but something that *wasn't*.

"So it was just an accident," Stottlemeyer said.

"Until he tried to cover it up," Monk said. "Then it became a crime."

"Oh come on," Devlin said. "It's a guess, that's all it is. An absurd guess based entirely on *one missing newspaper*."

"And a big mess," Monk said. "The newspapers on the other half of the block are at least on the driveways. The paperboy didn't go entirely willy-nilly until after he passed this house."

"It's still just a guess. That doesn't mean you're right," Devlin said, looking to Stottlemeyer for support, which I knew she wasn't going to get.

"Monk's right," he said.

"We don't know that," she said.

"I do and so will you once you bring in the paperboy. If you hurry, maybe he'll still have the bloody newspaper on him when you catch him."

Devlin scowled but acknowledged the captain's order with a nod and hurried off. Monk looked after her.

"I miss Randy," he said.

"As I recall, it took a while for Randy to warm up to you, too," Stottlemeyer said.

"But she scares me," he said.

"I won't let her shoot you," the captain said.

"I'd rather be shot than get gingivitis."

"I won't let her kiss you, either, though I could kiss you myself for solving this case so fast. Thanks to you, I might be able to get back home before lunch."

"You still have to catch whoever vandalized Garson Dach's car," Monk said.

"It can wait," Stottlemeyer said. "I'm sure Lieutenant Devlin will be glad to do it on Monday."

"Maybe I'll get Lieutenant Devlin a toothbrush, toothpaste, and some dental floss and give her instructions on their proper use," Monk said. "That should go a long way toward establishing a cordial working relationship between us."

"I wouldn't give her floss," Stottlemeyer said. "She might try to strangle you with it."

"That's what you did," Monk said.

"That's why I'm warning you," Stottlemeyer said. "Just be patient with her. She's a terrific cop, but all those years in vice working undercover haven't given her a lot of people skills."

"Or patience," I said.

"Or the awareness of the importance of good dental health," Monk said. "She could have a stroke."

"From swollen gums?" Stottlemeyer asked.

"Oral bacteria can seep into the bloodstream and inflame the blood vessels in the brain, causing a massive ischemic stroke."

"You're kidding," Stottlemeyer said.

"It's one of my greatest fears," Monk said.

"Meaning it's in your top hundred," I said.

"Greatest fears are the top one thousand. Mind-numbing, physically paralyzing fears are the top hundred."

"And what are the top ten?" Stottlemeyer asked.

"Instant-death fears," Monk said.

"Meaning?"

"I'd prefer instant death to even the remote possibility of experiencing the possibility of experiencing them."

"So what will you charge the paperboy with?" I asked in a heavy-handed attempt to get Monk's mind off his instant-death fears.

Stottlemeyer shrugged and glanced at the corpse. "I'll leave that to Dach's friends in the DA's office. I'm sure they'll come up with something creative."

"Whatever the charge is, his days tossing newspapers are over," Monk said. "It will be a lesson to paperboys everywhere. Dach's death won't be in vain."

"I'm sure that will be a comfort to him, wherever he is," Stottlemeyer said. That's when his cell phone rang. He waved us off as he answered it, and we started back toward the car.

I turned to Monk and whispered, "So, where is it?"

"Where is what?"

"The blubber. My thighs? My waist? My chin? All of the above?"

"Oh hell," Stottlemeyer said behind us.

Monk and I turned around. And from the crestfallen look on the captain's face as he listened to his caller, I knew that he wouldn't be getting home for lunch.

And neither would we.

The Excelsior Hotel rented rooms by the hour, the day, the week, and the month to the immigrants, drug dealers, prostitutes, and poor people of the Tenderloin, a crime-ridden neighborhood tucked between the Civic Center and Union Square.

The Tenderloin was just as seedy as it had always been, despite the best efforts of developers to turn all the old buildings into upscale lofts, offices, and coffee bars. The Excelsior was on the front lines of the gentrification invasion. The hotel, a dive bar, a shoe repair shop, and a discount cigarette store were on one side of the street. On the other side was a wannabe Starbucks and a renovated old office building that had been turned into "luxury condominiums" but was 70 percent unoccupied, thanks to the financial downturn.

We double-parked in front of the Excelsior behind Captain Stottlemeyer's car and followed him inside.

The lobby was faded and decaying, much like its tenants, who lazed around on the vinyl furniture, smoking cigarettes, napping, and watching *Dr. Phil* on the TV.

The front desk was enclosed in a cage. The squirrelly manager, unshaven and in a sleeveless T-shirt that showed off his tattooed arms, sat behind the iron mesh, reading manga and drinking Red Bull.

As downtrodden as the place was, it was definitely clean. It smelled like the walls and floors had been doused with buckets of chlorine, but I suppose it was better than the alternative.

Monk took a deep breath. "Why can't the whole world smell this fresh?"

"It's not fresh," I said. "You're breathing powerful chemicals."

"It's better than breathing germs," Monk said.

"Chemicals can kill you even faster than germs."

"But you'll die cleaner."

"You're still dead."

"A clean death is much better than a dirty death,"

Monk said, then turned to Stottlemeyer. "What kind do we have here?"

"A natural death, or so the ME told me on the phone. We won't know for sure, of course, until after the autopsy. But there's nothing about the body that screams murder."

"So what are we doing here?" I asked.

"It's standard operating procedure in cases of unattended deaths to treat them like possible homicides, especially when they happen in a place like this," the captain said. "And I figured as long as you were around when I got the call, you might as well come down and make sure we aren't missing something."

"What do we know about the victim?" Monk asked.

"His name is Jack Griffin, he checked in three weeks ago, and paid cash for a month's rent," Stottlemeyer said. "That's all we've got. He's in room 214."

"That's a good room," Monk said.

"You haven't seen it," Stottlemeyer said.

"It's an even-numbered room on the second floor," Monk said. "It has to be one of the best in the building."

"I don't think that's saying much," I said.

We followed Stottlemeyer up the narrow staircase to the second floor. The thin carpet in the hallway was so stained and trampled that it was impossible to tell what the original color once was. The walls were a sickly yellow.

The door to room 214 was open. Two uniformed police officers and two morgue attendants with a collapsible gurney stood outside in the corridor, presumably waiting for us to be done with the body so they could get it out of there. The four men stepped aside so we could go in the room, Monk leading the way, doing his Monk tai chi.

I decided to ignore him and concentrate on my own observation of the room. To our right was a narrow closet half-covered with a tattered curtain. There was a denim jacket with a fake-fur collar hanging inside and a gym bag on the floor.

To our left was a small bathroom, the toilet squeezed between the shower and the sink. A shaving kit and several pill bottles were on the counter. One was Advil, another appeared to contain vitamins, and another was labeled "Apricot Extract."

In front of us was a window that overlooked the street. The thin, moth-eaten curtain did little to keep out the light. I could see through it to the luxury condos across the way.

To the left of the window was a single bed, the scratched headboard screwed to the wall under an adjustable, mounted reading lamp. The bedspread looked like it was made from the same material as the carpet and was just as stained and colorless.

There was a stack of paperback Westerns, a canister of Pringles potato chips, two cans of mixed nuts, and a bunch of bruised bananas on the nightstand and two tall bottles of water and a pair of old, fat binoculars on the floor.

At the foot of the bed, to our right, a small TV was bolted to the top of the four-drawer, wood-laminate dresser, which was nailed to the floor.

There was also a writing desk with a lamp bolted to the desktop. The desk chair, a denim shirt draped over the back, was the only piece of furniture that wasn't bolted in place.

Finally, I focused my attention on the dead man, whom I'd forced myself to ignore while I looked over the room.

He was on his back, wearing a white T-shirt, brown

corduroy shirt, old jeans, and a pair of stained canvas tennis shoes. He was a Caucasian man, but his skin was dark and leathery and clung to his bones. His hair was sun-dried like straw. It was hard to believe he'd been dead only a day. He looked like an unwrapped mummy.

His hands were rough and calloused, covered with tiny scratches and scars. In his right hand, he held a snapshot that was curled against his palm.

As I leaned close to try to get a look at the picture, I picked up the scent of almonds and my pulse quickened.

*Cyanide smells like almonds.*

I glanced over at Monk, who stood on the other side of the bed, to see if he'd picked up the scent, too.

He rolled his shoulders, tipped his head from side to side, and tugged on his sleeves. He'd straightened himself out and now he'd straighten out the world by telling us Griffin's death was murder and maybe even who did it.

"The medical examiner is correct," Monk said. "Let's go home."

# 4

# Mr. Monk States the Obvious

Monk headed for the door but I stayed where I was.

"How do you know it wasn't murder or suicide?" I called after him.

He turned around and looked at me. "Because it's obvious he died of natural causes."

"How is it obvious?"

"That's like asking how I know that he had cancer or that he'd spent years in Mexico crewing on yachts and sportfishing boats."

Stottlemeyer and I shared a look. At least I wasn't the only one in the room who felt like an idiot. Beyond Griffin's leathery skin, which clearly came from a life outdoors, I was at a loss to understand how Monk deduced the rest.

"I don't see that, either," Stottlemeyer said. I think he spoke up mostly out of sympathy for me.

"You should both see an ophthalmologist," Monk

said, and not in a mean-spirited way. He seemed genu-inely concerned.

"Just because we don't see things the same way you do, Monk, doesn't mean we can't see at all," the cap-tain said.

"Yes, it does," Monk said, returning to the bed and looking down at the body. "Do you see him?"

"Of course we do," I said.

"Then surely you've noticed the severe muscle and tissue wasting."

"It's called death," Stottlemeyer said.

"It's called cachexia, which is highly indicative of late-stage cancer. My guess is skin cancer, given the scars on his neck where lesions have been removed."

I leaned down and looked at Griffin's neck. I'd seen the scars on his hands, but I'd missed these. Once again, I was struck by the scent of almonds.

"How do you know he crewed on boats?" Stottle-meyer asked.

"His hands and feet," Monk said.

"You can't see his feet," Stottlemeyer said.

"I can see his shoes, which are spotted with various shades of teak stain and varnish acquired while refin-ishing and maintaining boats," Monk said. "His hands are calloused on the palms and on his fingers from years of working with rope, which you can tell is of the nautical variety by the size of the rope burn on his right arm."

"How do you know he crewed on sportfishing boats, too?" Stottlemeyer asked.

Monk pointed to Griffin's hands. "Do you see all those little scars? Those are from getting snagged, cut, and scratched with hooks, knives, and fishing line, a common occurrence in that profession."

"Okay, maybe we missed all of that," I said.

"You *did* miss all of that," he said.

"But there's something that you missed."

"I doubt it," Monk said.

"This man was poisoned with cyanide," I said. "I can smell the scent of almonds on him."

Stottlemeyer raised his eyebrows. "You can?" He sniffed around the body. "I can't."

"That's because the ability to detect the scent is genetically determined," Monk said. "And only fifty percent of the population has that ability. I, of course, do."

"So how come you didn't say anything about the almond scent?" I asked.

"I did," he said.

"No, you didn't."

"I said he came from Mexico," Monk said.

"What does that have to do with him being poisoned with cyanide?"

"Nothing," Monk said.

Stottlemeyer rubbed his brow. "If this conversation goes on much longer, I may take the cyanide."

"The scent doesn't come from poison," Monk said. "It comes from the apricot-extract pills that Griffin was taking to battle his cancer."

"Wouldn't apricots smell like apricots instead of almonds?" I asked.

"The pills are actually an enzyme that's derived from apricot pits and produces some cyanide as well. It's a quack cancer treatment known as laetrile that is illegal in the United States but not in Mexico, which is how I knew that's where he came from," Monk said. "That and the dental amalgam used in his fillings, the stitching and material used to make his shoes, and the leather and craftsmanship of his belt, of course."

"Of course," Stottlemeyer said wearily.

"He still could have killed himself," I said.

"You are referring to those," Monk said, casting a disgusted glance at the two cans on the nightstand. "Because you'd have to have a death wish, or no longer care about living, to eat mixed nuts."

"I am referring to the cyanide," I said. "He could have overdosed on his meds."

"If he was going to commit suicide, why come here at all? And why wait three weeks to do it?" Monk said. "He must have come here for a reason."

"What was it?" I asked.

Monk shrugged. "I don't know and I don't care. It doesn't matter."

"It did to him," I said.

"Not to me," Monk said.

"It might to someone who cared about him," I said.

"I'll meet you downstairs," Monk said. "I want to get the name of the cleanser they are using."

I stayed where I was and looked down again at poor Jack Griffin. "What happens now, Captain?"

"We'll run his name and prints through our databases and try to track down his next of kin here or in Mexico."

"And if you can't?"

"We'll take his prints, a sample of his DNA, and store his possessions for a time," Stottlemeyer said. "But after six weeks, if his body isn't identified or claimed, he'll be cremated as a John Doe."

I gestured to the photo in Griffin's hand. "May I?"

"Go ahead," he said.

I carefully extracted the photo from Griffin's stiff fingers and uncurled the photograph.

It was a faded, yellowing snapshot of a nurse, perhaps in her late twenties or early thirties, and a young girl, perhaps four or five years old, astride a pink bicycle with training wheels, a white basket in front, and multicolored plastic tassels dangling from the ends of the handlebars.

The two of them were posed in front of a one-story tract home, seemingly freshly built on a corner lot, the dirt staked out for the sprinklers and landscaping to come, the plants in pots lined up on the front walk. There was a car parked in the driveway. I could see enough of it—the distinctive wood paneling on the side and the shape—to identify it as a Ford Country Squire station wagon, mainly because we had one when I was a kid, too.

I turned the photo over. There was no name or date on the back. I handed it to Stottlemeyer, who gave it a cursory glance.

"It's sad," I said.

"It's inevitable," he said.

"Spoken like a cynical cop."

He shrugged. "I see a lot of death."

"You see a lot of murder."

"So do you," he said.

"But we care about them," I said. "We try to solve those deaths."

"Because those are crimes," he said. "We know what happened here. There's nothing to solve."

Maybe so, but that wasn't how it felt to me.

I dropped Monk off at his apartment and went back home. But once I was inside, I couldn't sit still. I couldn't get Jack Griffin and that photo in his hand out of my mind.

So I tried to busy myself by cleaning up the house, doing some laundry, pulling weeds, washing my car, organizing my sock drawer, and emptying the pantry of expired food, which led to my eating the box of Wheat Thins that I kept around for the rare occasions when Monk visited. The Wheat Thins weren't expired—they were just there.

But none of that busywork and busy eating distracted me. I still kept thinking about Jack Griffin, apparently an expat American in Mexico who traveled to San Francisco to die alone in a dive motel. And I couldn't help wondering why he did. His reasons weren't any of my business, and it wouldn't change anything if I knew them, but that's the thing about mysteries, isn't it? They just keep nagging at you.

Or maybe it wasn't the mystery. Maybe the problem was that I had nothing else to think about. With Julie off at school and no man in my life, I didn't have much to do outside of work.

I needed a hobby.

But I wasn't going to begin looking for one that night. So I ordered a pizza from Domino's and an on-demand movie to watch on TV.

The movie was one of those inane, big-budget comic-book adaptations where good-looking people in colorful costumes try to work out their superficial superangst by throwing cars at each other and making as much noise as possible.

All that mayhem didn't get their superminds off their superproblems, and it didn't work for me, either.

On Monday morning, I dragged Monk down to the police station on the pretext of getting the latest news on the paperboy case.

Monk didn't ask me why I didn't simply call the captain for an update instead. That's probably because Monk appreciated any excuse to visit the police station and he didn't want to question his good fortune.

This was the first time we'd been to headquarters since Lieutenant Devlin had replaced Randy Disher, and as we came in, it was strange for me to see her oc-cupying the desk outside of Stottlemeyer's office. I imagine people felt the same way the first time they saw me with Monk after I replaced Sharona Fleming as his assistant.

Monk gasped when he saw the desk, probably more because of the stacks of bulging files and junk-food containers that were piled on top of it than because of the person who was sitting behind it.

Devlin was facing her flat screen, pounding on the keys as if she were trying to beat a report out of the computer rather than write it.

He took a deep breath and approached her desk. "Good morning, Lieutenant Devlin."

Her shoulders sagged with weariness and she slowly turned around in her seat to face us.

"What are you doing here, Monk?"

"We came to bring you this." Monk reached into the pocket of his coat and handed her a gift-wrapped box tied with a perfectly symmetrical ribbon. "It's a pres-ent to welcome you to the team."

"We aren't a team," she said. "You can keep it."

"It would mean a lot to me if you'd accept it," Monk said. "It's a two-part gift."

"What's a two-part gift?" she asked warily.

"The first part is you open the box," Monk said. "The second part is I clean your desk."

"You touch this desk," she said, "and I will break your arms."

Devlin unwrapped the box and opened it, revealing the toothbrush, toothpaste, and dental floss that were inside. She looked up at him, her expression stony.

"You got me a toothbrush?" she said.

"Not just any toothbrush," he said proudly. "It's the Gertler 4000 with the extrasoft polyurethane bristles and the blue rubber handle. It's handmade, the very best there is."

"Are you trying to tell me I have bad breath?"

"No," Monk said. "I'm telling you that you have hideously swollen gums."

"I have a two-part gift for you," she said.

"You're going to let me clean your desk and empty your trash?"

She stood up and shoved the box back into Monk's pocket. "If you leave right now, I won't knock you on your ass and stomp on your testicles."

Monk shuddered and took a deep breath. "Okay, but after the beating could I clean your desk and empty your trash?"

"Mr. Monk!" I said. "Don't you have any self-respect?"

"None at all," he said. "I thought that was common knowledge."

"She insulted you," I said. "You should be outraged."

"*He* should be?" Devlin said. "What about me? The guy walks in here, tells me my mouth is a sewer and that my workplace is a dump, and I'm supposed to just take it?"

"See?" Monk said to me. "We're getting through to her."

I don't know what Devlin might have done if Stottlemeyer hadn't stepped out of his office at that moment and defused the situation.

"Monk, what a nice surprise," Stottlemeyer said. "Did Lieutenant Devlin brief you on the latest developments in the Dach case?"

"No," I said. "She didn't."

Stottlemeyer turned to Devlin. "Go ahead, tell him. I'm sure you can't wait."

Devlin's face tightened, but she did as she was told. "We arrested the newspaper delivery guy yesterday at an Arby's downtown. He still had the bloody newspaper in his car. He started sobbing the moment he saw my badge and confessed to killing Dach."

Monk nodded. "Will the paperboy be tried as a juvenile or an adult?"

"He's forty-seven," Devlin said.

"Isn't that a little old to be a paperboy?" Monk asked.

"This isn't Mayberry," Devlin said. "Kids don't ride around on bikes delivering papers anymore."

"This paperboy used to market subprime home loans at Big Country Mortgage before they went under," Stottlemeyer said. "Now he's working two jobs, delivering newspapers in the morning and manning the fry station at Arby's the rest of the day."

"I almost feel sorry for the guy," I said.

Stottlemeyer waved Monk and me into his office and closed the door behind us after we'd stepped inside. "What did I tell you, Monk, about giving Amy dental floss?"

"She didn't try to strangle me," Monk said.

"What she wanted to do to you was worse," I said.

"I can't say that I blame her," Stottlemeyer said. "Monk has that effect on people."

"I was trying to help her," Monk said. "You can, too, by ordering her to clean her desk."

"It's her personal space. I don't care how she keeps it. Whatever works for her works for me."

"Aren't you concerned about the spread of disease?"

"Nope," Stottlemeyer said.

"You will be when the office is overrun with flesh-eating bacteria," Monk said.

"That's true," Stottlemeyer said.

"But by then it will be too late," Monk said. "You'll be on your hands and knees, looking for your nose or a finger, and I'll be there to say 'I told you so.'"

"I'm sure you will," Stottlemeyer said. "Speaking of diseases, you were right. It was skin cancer that killed the guy in the hotel. And there were trace amounts of cyanide in his system from his laetrile treatments, but it wasn't enough to poison him."

"Have you had any luck locating his next of kin?" I asked.

"No, we haven't," Stottlemeyer said. "His IDs were all fakes and we didn't get any hits on his fingerprints."

"What about DNA?"

"We got a sample, but it will be months, maybe years, before we get any results."

"Why is it going to take so long?" I asked.

"Because we've got a huge backlog of DNA samples that need to be tested for open rape and homicide investigations and cold cases that have been reopened," Stottlemeyer said. "And he died of natural causes, so it's not just low priority, it's no priority. But if he hasn't been arrested, or associated with a crime, we'll hit a wall with the DNA, too."

"Have you contacted the authorities in Mexico?"

"Yeah," Stottlemeyer said. "They've got nothing."

"They could pass around his picture at cancer centers that offer laetrile treatments and see if any of the doctors or staff recognizes him."

"I suppose the authorities could do that, if they cared enough to make the effort and if the clinics would even give them that information. But since law enforcement agencies down there are rife with corruption, strapped for resources, and in the midst of fighting an all-out drug war, they'd need some strong motivation to canvass every cancer clinic in the country asking about this guy. You know, like a major crime of some kind."

"A man is dead," I said.

"Of natural causes," Stottlemeyer said.

"Why did he have or need fake ID, and how did he get across the border with it?" I asked. "I suppose he could have found a way to sneak over, but that just raises even more questions. Why did he want to get back here so badly?"

"None of those questions matter to me," Stottlemeyer said.

"Why not?" I asked.

"Because he's dead," Stottlemeyer said. "Of natural causes."

I turned to Monk, who hadn't said a word. "Tell him, Mr. Monk."

Monk took a step forward. Stottlemeyer sat on the edge of his desk, crossed his arms under his chest, and faced him, braced for the tirade.

"Have you lost your humanity?" Monk said. "Are you so cold inside that you have forgotten what it feels like to care about somebody?"

I nodded in agreement. I appreciated his support and was encouraged by the surprising passion of Monk's argument.

"He's right, Captain," I said.

"If you still have a heart, if you have any feelings left at all for your fellow man, I implore you, I beseech you, to do the right thing," Monk said. "Command Lieutenant Devlin to clean her desk."

"Mr. Monk!" I said.

"What?" he said, turning to me.

"I'm talking about Jack Griffin."

"Who?" Monk said.

"The man with the fake identity who came all the way here from Mexico to die in some squalid hotel room," I said. "Don't you want to know why?"

Monk frowned and shook his head. "Nope, not really." He glanced at Stottlemeyer. "Do you?"

"Nope," the captain said and shifted his gaze to me. "Are we done here?"

"I'm not," I said.

**5**
_____

# Mr. Monk Cleans Up

I don't know when I actually decided I was going to solve the mystery of Jack Griffin's identity and why he'd come to San Francisco to die. But at that moment in Captain Stottlemeyer's office, I'd committed myself to it and there was no going back. So I asked the captain if I could have Jack Griffin's personal effects. He had no problem with that and sent Amy Devlin down to the property room with me to take care of it.

The captain didn't ask me why I wanted Griffin's things. Nobody did. I hadn't even asked myself, perhaps because I was busy thinking about what I intended to say to Amy Devlin once we were alone.

As soon as the two of us entered the stairwell to go down to the basement, I confronted her, blocking her path.

"What the hell is your problem?" I said.

"Wrong question," Devlin said. "What you should be asking is *who*, not *what*."

"I know better than anybody how difficult and infuriating Mr. Monk can be, but when it comes to homicide investigation, he's the best there is. And you know it, too. So the least you can do is to show him some courtesy and respect."

"Like he shows me?"

"He does, in his own way," I said, feeling the moral high ground disintegrating beneath my feet. "He gave you a toothbrush."

"Because he thinks I'm disgusting."

"That's one way to look at it. But the gift takes on an entirely different meaning if you look at it from his perspective."

"What about *my* perspective? Have you or Monk ever considered that?" she said. "No, of course you haven't. Because you think the whole world revolves around him, just like he does."

"Okay, so what is your perspective? Tell me."

"I'm a cop. This is who I am and what I do. I don't appreciate some mentally ill guy and his enabler showing up at my crime scenes before I've even had a chance to start working them myself."

"What pisses you off is that Mr. Monk can solve the case before you even get your notebook out."

"Damn right," she said. "I'd like the opportunity to actually do my job. It might take me a little longer than thirty seconds to close a case, but I will do it."

"So you're jealous," I said.

"No, I'm not. There are a lot of cops who are better at this than I am. I have no problem with that. The difference is that they don't stick their noses in my cases unless I ask them to."

She pushed past me and went down the stairs. I followed her.

"So what do you want from him?" I said, my loud

voice reverberating up and down the empty stairwell. "Do you want him to act stupid? To hold on to his deductions until you catch up? Or maybe you'd just like him to quit consulting for the police? I can tell you that none of those things are going to happen."

Devlin stopped at the landing and looked up at me. "Here's what else is not going to happen: I won't change who I am, the way I work, or how I look at the world just so Monk can feel comfortable and believe that he isn't a total nut job, which, in case you haven't noticed, he is."

"He's eccentric," I said. "And sometimes his words and deeds can be unintentionally offensive. Part of my job is to minimize that, but I can do only so much. I have to count on the fact that most people are decent and kind and will give him the benefit of the doubt. I don't think it's asking too much for you to do the same." I walked down a few steps so that we were eye to eye and only inches apart. "In other words, do us all a favor and stop being a total bitch."

She gave me a death stare that I'm sure had caused others to lose control of their sphincters and crumble. There was no question that, in terms of hand-to-hand combat, she could take me. But when it came to strength of conviction, determination, and sheer stubbornness, we were evenly matched. So my stare didn't waver.

*Go ahead, lady, bring it on.*

We might have stood there glaring at each other all day if the door behind her hadn't opened up and two cops hadn't rushed in, barreling past us on their way to homicide upstairs. They broke our childish staring contest without either one of us having to back down.

Devlin grabbed the door before it closed, turned her back on me, and headed for the property room. I caught up to her at the clerk's cage, which was essentially a counter and screen set into a double-wide doorway. Behind the obese clerk was row after row of iron shelving. The upper shelves were lined with identical file boxes, while tagged, oversize items, like bicycles and suitcases, occupied the lower ones.

She told the clerk what I wanted and signed the necessary papers while he went off and got the stuff. He came back with the suitcase and file box. I took the box and Devlin carried the suitcase.

We walked back upstairs in silence. When we pushed open the doors to the homicide department, the first thing we both noticed was that the stacks of file folders were no longer on her desk. Her trash was gone, her computer monitor gleamed, and her pencils had been sharpened so that they were all exactly the same length.

Monk stood beside her desk, his hands in rubber gloves, presenting the scene as if it were the showcase on *The Price Is Right*.

Devlin dropped the suitcase and gave Monk a death stare that made the one she gave me seem warm and affectionate by comparison.

"I told you not to touch my desk," she said, advancing on him.

"A sensible warning, given the amount of filth," Monk said. "Which is why I wore gloves."

"You know what I meant," she said, almost nose to nose with him.

Monk held his ground, though he did tip his head way back. "Of course I did. Someone less savvy than me might have misinterpreted your comment about breaking my arms as a threat, but I knew you were saying that you wouldn't let me risk infection."

Devlin turned around and looked at me. "Is he for real or is he dissing me?"

"That's the real Adrian Monk," I said.

"You'll thank me later," he said.

"Or I'll shoot you," she said.

That's when Stottlemeyer came into the room behind me, a newspaper under his arm, and spotted the clean desk.

"Uh-oh," he said.

"You know better than to leave Mr. Monk alone with a mess," I said. "Where were you?"

"Answering the call of nature," he said. "Though in this case, it was more like a scream."

That was more than I needed to know. "We were just leaving, weren't we, Mr. Monk?"

"Yes," he said, as he sidestepped Devlin and made a beeline to me.

I handed him the box, I picked up the suitcase, and we walked out.

"Do you think she'd really shoot me?" Monk asked.

"Definitely," I said. "She's very irritated."

"That's what happens when you don't floss," Monk said. "If I had those gums, I'd shoot myself rather than waste the bullet on somebody else."

I drove back to the Excelsior Hotel with Monk. I wanted another look at the room where Jack Griffin died. I was hoping that maybe I'd see something that I'd missed the first time around or intuitively glean some new understanding just by being in the room again.

Detectives on TV do that all the time. They go back to the crime scene, stare intensely at this and that, and then have incredibly stylized and revealing visions of what the victim was doing before he died.

I figured there was no reason that couldn't work for me, too.

On the way there, I expected Monk to start com-

plaining, to remind me that I worked for him, not the other way around, and that I was wasting valuable time that he could be spending on something important, like vacuuming his ceiling.

But he remained silent.

I found his silence more aggravating than his complaining. I wanted him to ask me questions, to make me justify my actions, because I wanted to hear the answers myself. Maybe then I'd understand what I was doing and why I was doing it, beyond hoping I'd be blessed with some cool, TV-detective flashbacks of my own.

The same group of vagrants that was hanging out in the Excelsior lobby on Sunday was still there, making me wonder if they'd ever left. The same clerk was on duty, too, eating a Hot Pocket and surfing the Internet on a laptop that was covered with stickers from various bands.

We approached the cage. "I'd like the key to room 214."

The clerk looked over at Monk, then back at me. "You want it for an hour or for the day?"

"I'm working with the police and I want it for the week," I said. "The week that Jack Griffin paid for and still has left."

"He's dead," the clerk said.

"He paid for it," I said. "He gets it. Or would you prefer to refund us what he paid for the remaining week and I'll pass it on to his next of kin?"

The clerk scowled. "Fine. You can have the room. But I don't have the key. I gave it to the cleaning crew."

That got Monk's attention. "Is it being cleaned right now?"

"Yeah," the clerk said.

Monk tugged on my sleeve. "Let's go see."

The only thing Monk liked more than cleaning something himself was telling others how to do it. I wanted to go up, too, but for a different reason—I was afraid that the maid might dispose of any potential evidence.

Evidence of what, though, I wasn't sure.

So we hurried up the stairs to the second floor, where there was an enormous red drum marked "bio-hazardous waste" on a cart equipped with a wet vac-uum, humidifiers, and assorted cleaning equipment and supplies parked outside of the open doorway to room 214.

Two men wearing white, hooded Tyvek coveralls, filtered respirator masks, goggles, and matching yellow rubber gloves and boots emerged from the room carrying a soiled mattress that was wrapped tightly in transparent plastic sheeting and sealed with duct tape.

The two men leaned the mattress against a wall and paused to take a break.

Monk broke into an enormous smile. "This is the finest hotel in San Francisco."

# 6

## Mr. Monk Meets a Fan

One of the guys in the Tyvek suits turned to us, seemed to freeze for a moment, then quickly took off his mask and goggles and peeled back his hood to reveal a youthful, freckled redhead with an electrifying smile.

"Oh my God," he said. "You're Adrian Monk."

He came toward us, taking off his gloves and holding out his right hand to Monk.

"I'm Jerry Yermo," he said, shaking Monk's hand.

"My pleasure." Monk glanced at me, which was my signal to get him a wipe.

"No, no, allow me," Jerry said, snapping his fingers at the other man. "Gene, bring Mr. Monk some wipes. This is such an incredible honor. I have been following your work for years."

Gene was a stocky guy who didn't bother to remove his mask and goggles. He brought over a huge canister of disinfectant wipes and offered it to Monk, who tugged a wet tissue out and cleaned his hands.

"The honor is mine, Mr. Yermo," Monk said. "This is the first time I have ever seen a hotel room cleaned properly."

Monk finished with the wipe. I reached into my purse for a baggie, but before I could take it out, Jerry whipped out a red plastic bag with a big biohazard emblem on it and offered it to Monk instead.

"Call me Jerry, Mr. Monk."

"It's Adrian to my friends." Monk smiled as he dropped his wipe into the bag.

Jerry sealed the bag and handed it to Gene, who deposited it in the biohazard container on the cart, then grabbed a paint scraper off the cart and went back to work in the hotel room.

"When I said that I've followed your work, Adrian, I meant it literally," Jerry said. "I'm a crime scene cleaner. I've been to the scene of just about every murder in San Francisco that you've investigated but, sadly, long after you've gone. I've always hoped that one day I'd get the opportunity to meet the great man himself."

"Excuse me, Jerry," I said. "But I don't understand why you're here. This isn't a crime scene."

"After a murder, suicide, violent crime, or any serious accident where bodily fluids have been spilled, a licensed and certified cleaner has to be called in to properly remove, package, and dispose of all contaminated material—furniture, carpeting, drywall, equipment, you name it—in strict accordance with all applicable OSHA, federal, state, and local health regulations. Then we disinfect, deodorize, and decontaminate the scene before restoring it to its original state."

Monk was visibly moved. "You're a true American hero. I wish the law required licensed professionals like you to clean up wherever people have been. This city is awash in bodily fluids."

"I don't know that I'd go that far, Adrian. But I agree that bodily fluids and other contaminants from injury, death, decomposition, not to mention the regular excretions, expulsions, and ejaculations of the living, certainly spread farther, soak deeper, and are more dangerous to public health and safety than the general population realizes."

"Amen, brother," Monk said. "It's a disgusting world that we live in."

"Tell me about it," Jerry agreed. "In some cases, our work requires us to strip a place down to the studs and replace everything. But this time, since we're only dealing with the postmortem evacuation of bladder and bowels and initial decomp, and no blood spatter or brain matter, we've only had to remove the bedding, mattress, and the carpeting for incineration and simply disinfect everything else."

"You should be taking notes, Natalie," Monk said. "This is what you should be doing in your house every week."

"Including the removal and incineration of my linens, mattress, and carpets?" I asked.

"Don't be ridiculous," Monk said. "You can do that monthly."

"No one has died in my bed, Mr. Monk."

"Yet," he said. "It's only a matter of time until someone does if you don't do something about your slovenly habits."

I looked at Jerry. "He's exaggerating."

"I'm sure your bedroom is very clean and lively," Jerry said, then winced. "Forgive me, that didn't come out at all the way I intended."

I couldn't help smiling at his discomfort. "It's okay, Jerry, I understood what you meant. Did you find anything when you cleaned the hotel room?"

"We find strange stuff all the time," Jerry said, eager to change the subject from his faux pas. "We were cleaning up after a guy who blew off his head with a shotgun, and when we ripped out the blood-and-brain-matter-stained drywall behind him, we found a wedding dress sealed in plastic underneath the insulation. Another time, when we were mopping up after the decomposing corpse from an old lady's unattended death, we found twenty-five thousand dollars in cash and bonds that she'd saved under the floorboards."

"Did you find anything even remotely that interesting this time?"

"I can tell you exactly what we found. We take notes in case the police come back to us." He took a notebook out of his back pocket and flipped it open. "Forty-seven cents, a gum wrapper, a used condom, a bottle cap, three pens, assorted unidentified pills, six paper clips, a safety pin, a Tic Tac, a 7-Eleven receipt, and toenail clippings." He closed his notebook and stuck it back in his pocket. "It was normal detritus, most of it under furniture, slightly less than the usual accumulation for a hotel room with a lot of occupants."

"So are you done here?" I asked.

"We've still got to disinfect, deodorize, lay some new carpet, and replace the mattress."

"May I observe you in action?" Monk asked.

"I'd be honored, Adrian, but I knew it was going to be just a simple, two-man job, so I didn't bring any extra protective gear with me today."

"That's okay, Jerry. Natalie can run back to my apartment and get mine."

"You have Tyvek coveralls, a respirator mask, and goggles?" Jerry asked.

"Who doesn't?" Monk said, then glanced reproachfully at me. "That is, if you're a civilized person."

"This isn't much of a job, and we're almost done. I have a better idea," Jerry said. "The next time you're at a murder, stick around until we get there and you can join the crew for the cleanup."

"That would be amazing," Monk said. "If we're lucky, someone will get killed today."

"You're a real humanitarian, Mr. Monk," I said.

"No, I'm not," Monk said and pointed at Jerry. "But he is. You're doing God's work."

"Thank you," Jerry said. "Speaking of which . . ."

He reached for his hood, pulled it over his head, and gave us a little salute before putting on his mask and goggles and going back into the room.

It looked like I'd have to come back later for my stylized TV-detective flashbacks of Jack Griffin's last days.

Monk watched Jerry Yermo go and then looked at me. "That's a hell of a man."

"You don't know anything about him," I said.

"I know he's single," Monk said, then stood there with one eye closed for a long moment before opening it again.

"Was that supposed to be a wink?"

"You've never seen a wink before?"

"Winks are quick," I said. "That was more like a nap with one eye closed."

We went back downstairs. I stopped by the front desk, told the clerk to hold the room key for 214 under my name, and crossed the lobby toward the front entrance.

"You didn't respond to my subtle suggestion," Monk said. "Was it too subtle?"

"Jerry isn't my type," I said.

"Why not?"

"He spends his day scrubbing up gore."

"So you have a problem with clean, decent, upstanding men who do God's work," Monk said, then gestured to the men in the lobby. "I suppose you'd prefer one of them."

"Those men are indigent, drugged out, mentally ill, and elderly."

"Well, that's the alternative."

"No, it's not. There's a wide variety of men in the world besides Jerry Yermo and them."

"That explains why you're alone," Monk said. "You live in fantasyland."

"Then that makes us neighbors," I said and walked outside to the street.

I dropped Monk off for his weekly appointment with Dr. Neven Bell, his psychiatrist, and took the box of Griffin's possessions with me into McDonald's, where I bought a cup of their cheap coffee and pretended I was in Starbucks.

I went to a table and started sorting through Griffin's meager possessions, making an inventory in my notebook, along with my observations and any questions that occurred to me.

His wallet was in an evidence baggie and contained a few crisp twenties, his fake California driver's license, and a faded slip from a fortune cookie that read, "You will lead many lives." I sniffed the wallet. It smelled of leather, varnish, and fish.

The crisp twenties suggested to me that he'd exchanged his pesos for American dollars somewhere. The smell of varnish and fish on his wallet backed up Monk's deductions that Griffin led a seafaring life. Which raised the first question that I jotted down on my list:

*Did he smuggle himself into the U.S. on a boat?*

If so, perhaps it was with somebody that he'd

crewed for in the past, maybe even an American. If I could find that boat, and that person, that could be a significant lead. But there were marinas and ports all along the Southern California coast and tens of thousands of boats.

*How could I find the boat that Griffin was smuggled in on?*

I set that baggie aside and pulled out another one, which contained a gray ID card with a passport-type photo of Griffin on it. He had a fuller face and a scraggly mustache and short beard.

The card was written in Spanish on one side and English on the other and identified Griffin as a temporary resident and listed his date of birth as October 19, 1955. I assumed the document was a forgery and the birth date was probably a lie.

*Who or what was Griffin hiding from?*

Next I pulled out the old leather binocular case with a thin shoulder strap. It reminded me of Mr. Spock's tricorder.

I pulled out the binoculars, which were heavy and black and in mint condition. I made note of the brand and model—a Jackson/Elite Clipper Model 188—and two serial numbers I found on the front bridge. I knew nothing about binoculars, but based on their bulkiness, the styling, and the materials, as well as the total lack of any integrated electronics, that they were at least thirty years old.

*Why would he buy old binoculars instead of a smaller, more powerful, and lighter-weight model?*

Perhaps it was all he could afford.

*Did he buy them in a secondhand shop here? If so, where? And what did he need them for? What did he want to look at?*

On the other hand, perhaps he'd owned that particular pair of binoculars for years. If so, the fact that he'd taken such great care of them, and brought them with him from Mexico, suggested they held some emotional significance for him.

*What did the binoculars mean to him? Why bring them to San Francisco?*

I rummaged through his shaving kit. All the toiletries were typical brand-name items, the kind that could be found at any local supermarket or drugstore.

I moved on to his collection of a dozen paperback Westerns, all of which were new, English-language titles published in the last few months. I figured he'd probably picked them up off the rack wherever he'd bought his toiletries.

He must have loved Westerns. Of all the things he could have done in his final days, he chose to hole up in a dive hotel room in San Francisco, reading them.

Maybe Western novels were hard to come by in Mexico and represented a pleasure that he'd been denied. Or maybe they, like the binoculars, represented something else to him.

There was one more item in the box, and it was in an evidence baggie for protection—it was the snapshot that Griffin was holding in his hand when he died.

I studied it again and made a list of everything I could see in the picture and what information I might glean from each item.

There was the nurse. *Try to date and trace her uniform? Her shoes? The watch on her wrist?*

There was the little girl. *Try to date the bike? Her clothes? Her shoes?*

There was the house, which appeared to have been recently built at the time the photo was taken. The black address numbers 9-2-8 were glued on a white plastic light that was mounted on the brick trim beside the garage. That design detail, and the style of the house, screamed 1970s to me. *If it's a tract home, can I trace the style to a particular developer and then, perhaps, to a place and a date?*

There were potted plants out front, waiting to be put into the fresh dirt. *Could the plants tell me where the house is?*

There was the car in the driveway. The license plate wasn't photographed, but I could tell the car was a Ford Country Squire, metallic blue with faux wood paneling on the exterior.

*What year was the car? Was the metallic blue color a special-order option? Could that help me track the owner?*

I looked at my list and frowned. I was going to need help with the research.

*But where was I going to get it?*

I wrote that question down, too, as if that would help me find the answer.

Monk never had to make up lists. He absorbed the details that he saw and heard and then noticed the one thing that was missing, was out of place, or didn't fit where it was supposed to. And that's how he solved his cases.

But I wasn't Monk. I'd have to develop my own detecting technique. I just wished that I knew what it was. And that thought gave me the last question for my list.

*What is my technique?*

**7**

# Mr. Monk and the Knee-slapper

Dr. Neven Bell's office in North Beach, with its wood paneling and leather furniture, was so aggressively masculine, I half expected the balding shrink to emerge from his office in a silk bathrobe, a cigar in his mouth, and his arms around two Playboy bunnies.

But Dr. Bell was no Hef. His standard attire leaned more toward cable-knit sweaters and corduroy pants. He greeted me in the waiting room, where Monk was busy organizing the magazines on the coffee table by name and publication date.

"What kind of person leaves a mess like this?" Monk said. "Your patients need serious psychiatric help."

Dr. Bell ignored Monk and smiled at me. "Adrian tells me you're taking on a case."

I glanced over at Monk. "I didn't think he noticed."

"I notice everything," Monk said.

"But you haven't shown much interest in it," I said.

"That's because I have none," he said.

I handed Dr. Bell the snapshot of the nurse and the little girl. "What do you make of this?"

Dr. Bell glanced at the photo, then looked up at me. "What do you make of it?"

"Please don't psychoanalyze me," I said. "Analyze the picture."

"I can't," Dr. Bell said. "The meaning of the picture depends entirely on the interpretation of the person who is looking at it. What I see is irrelevant. Each of us is going to see something different."

"It's not an abstract painting," I said. "It's a straightforward photograph. What's there is there. We all see the same thing."

"Really?" Dr. Bell turned to Monk and held up the picture. "Adrian, what's the first thing you notice when you look at this?"

Monk glanced quickly at the picture, then returned to his magazine sorting. "The house isn't symmetrical."

Dr. Bell turned to me. "Did you see that?"

"No," I said.

"I rest my case," Dr. Bell said. "What do you see in the picture?"

"I made a list," I said, reaching into my purse for the notebook.

"That's not what I meant," Dr. Bell said, then held up the picture in front of my face. "What do you see? Don't think about it. Tell me the first thing that pops into your mind."

"I see a nameless man desperately holding on to a faded memory as he dies alone in a dark hotel room."

Dr. Bell handed the photo back to me. "That's not in the picture."

"But that's what I see," I said.

"Then that's where you have to start."

"What does *that* mean?"

Monk joined me. "Now you know how I feel after every session. One of these days, Dr. Bell might actually offer a solution instead of spewing enigmatic pop-pycock."

"If you believe our sessions aren't helpful to you, Adrian, why do you keep coming back?"

Monk rolled his shoulders and shifted his weight. "Sometimes I just need to hear myself think."

"You don't need me for that," Dr. Bell said. "You could talk to your brother, Ambrose, for instance."

"I can't talk to him," Monk said.

"Why not?" Dr. Bell asked.

"He's crazy," Monk said.

"He's agoraphobic," Dr. Bell said.

"Which is another word for crazy," Monk said. "How else would you describe someone who is afraid to leave the house we grew up in?"

"Agoraphobic," Dr. Bell said. "But I thought you told me that he went on a road trip in a rented motor home with you and Natalie not so long ago."

"Yes, but we had to knock him out with drugs and abduct him first," Monk said.

Dr. Bell looked at him incredulously. "You took him against his will?"

"Of course we did. He wouldn't leave the house otherwise," Monk said. "Because he's crazy."

"You didn't mention that." Dr. Bell crossed his arms under his chest and took a decidedly disapproving posture.

"I told you he was crazy two minutes ago. Don't you listen to anything I say?"

"I'm talking about the kidnapping, Adrian."

I cleared my throat. "Mr. Monk is covered by doctor-patient privilege, am I right?"

Dr. Bell turned to me. "You helped him do this?"

"Nobody is pressing charges," I said.

"Ambrose thanked us later," Monk said.

"Really?" Dr. Bell said, clearly dubious.

"He enjoyed the trip so much that he bought the motor home we had rented," I said. "He likes the idea of leaving home without leaving a home, so to speak."

"He'll probably still have to be drugged to get from his house to his motor home," Monk said. "But he's got an assistant to help him with that now."

Dr. Bell looked at me sternly. "You're dispensing narcotics now?"

"Oh no, not me," I said. "One Monk is more than I can handle. Ambrose has hired a young woman we met on our road trip. She was a researcher for an investigative reporter named Dub Clemens, who passed away. She's also going to help Ambrose with his work. Ambrose writes owner's manuals and technical guides. Up until now, he mostly interacted with the outside world through—"

I had a sudden realization and stopped myself short. I knew where to go to decipher the mysteries of the snapshot, and maybe a few other things, too.

"Thank you, Dr. Bell," I said. "I think we've had a major breakthrough."

Dr. Bell smiled. "Great. I'll send you my bill."

"I hope you're not referring to his poppycock about 'starting with what you feel,'" Monk said. "Because what you feel is probably indigestion."

"I'm visiting your brother," I said. "Care to join me?"

Ambrose Monk lived in Tewksbury, a Marin County community that was across the bay from San Francisco and was so liberal, so thoroughly mired in the 1970s, I felt like I should remove my bra and light a joint as soon as I crossed the city limits.

The Monk family home, a well-preserved Victorian, was perhaps the only property in town that didn't have an outdoor hot tub, and I'm including city hall, the library, and the churches in that statement.

We hadn't been back to see Ambrose since we'd returned from our road trip. The restored motor home, fixed up after our little adventure, was parked in his driveway, and it gleamed. It was a class C, one of those strange vehicles that looked like a Ford truck that backed into a camper and then got stuck. There was a Harley-Davidson motorcycle beside it.

Monk scowled at the motorcycle as we walked up to the front door. "Our front yard looks like the parking lot of a biker bar."

"Have you been to many biker bars with just one motorcycle and one RV parked out front?"

"This is how it starts," Monk said. "Before you know it, the Hells Angels will be camping here for the winter."

He knocked on the door.

"Listening to rock-and-roll music way too loud," he added.

He knocked again.

"Smoking marijuana joint cigarettes," he added.

He knocked again.

"And applying scary skull tattoos on each other that don't wash off," he added. "*Ever.*"

He knocked again.

"Where is he?" Monk asked.

"Maybe he stepped out."

"He's afraid to step out," Monk said. "He's in the house all the time."

"I know," I said. "I was joking."

He turned to face me. "What's humorous about saying he stepped out when we both know that he would never step out?"

"It's the contradiction that creates the humor."

"That's not humor. This is humor: A Japanese woman

experiences discomfort in her eye, so she goes to see a qualified ophthalmologist. After a thorough examination, the doctor tells the Japanese woman that she has a cataract. She says, 'No, I don't. I have a Lincoln Continental.'"

I stared at him. "That's not funny."

"Yes, it is. Here's why: Some Japanese immigrants have trouble speaking English or do so with a heavy accent. She confuses a Cadillac with a cataract. She believes he is talking about American luxury automobiles when, in fact, he is telling her that she has an opacity on the lens of her eye that's inhibiting the passage of light, causing a loss of visual acuity. It's the miscommunication that creates the hilarity."

"Natalie is right," a woman said. "It's not funny."

We turned just as Yuki Nakamura, Ambrose's assistant, opened the front door. She was barefoot, wet, and wearing a bathrobe.

She was in her twenties, with long black hair that went midway down her back, where I knew, and Monk didn't, that she had a snake tattoo coiled around her spine.

"The joke is racially insensitive and perpetuates a nasty and ugly stereotype," Yuki said. "Besides, it's dated. They haven't made Lincoln Continentals in years. When did you hear that joke? In 1975?"

"Actually, it was April 27, 1972, at 3:14 p.m.," said Ambrose, stepping up behind Yuki. "Dad told it to us as an example of a joke."

"A knee-slapper, to be specific," Monk said. "Which means it was a very good one."

They kept talking, but I have no idea what they said because I'd stopped paying attention. I was too distracted by the fact that Yuki and Ambrose were both wearing bathrobes and nothing else. And they were both dripping wet.

# 8

# Mr. Monk and the Girl
# with the Snake Tattoo

Monk noticed how they were dressed, or rather undressed, and drew his own conclusions. "You didn't answer the door right away because you were both showering at the same time."

"That's correct," Ambrose said.

"That wasn't very wise," Monk said. "You know what happens when you run two showers at once in this house. It causes a significant drop in water pressure and rapid depletion of the hot water."

"That wasn't an issue," Yuki said.

Monk cocked his head and looked at Ambrose. "Have you upgraded the pipes and improved the pressure?"

"His piping and pressure are terrific," she said with a sly grin.

Ambrose blushed and spoke up quickly. "What brings you here, Adrian?"

"It was my idea," I said. "I wanted to ask for your

help with something, but I really should have called first."

"Why?" Monk asked me. "He's always here."

"Because he has a life," I said.

"No, he doesn't," Monk said.

"Yes, he does. I'm sorry for intruding on you, Ambrose. We'll come back another time." I grabbed Monk by the arm and started to lead him away. "Let's go."

"Don't be ridiculous," Ambrose said. "Please, come in."

Yuki stepped aside and ushered us in. We walked past her into the entry hall and she closed the door behind us.

I looked around. The living room was still lined with stacks of newspapers going back decades and rows of file cabinets containing every piece of mail that had ever come to the house. The décor everywhere else was the same as it had always been. It looked as if nothing had changed in the house since our last visit several weeks earlier. But I knew that wasn't true. The evidence was standing in front of me in bathrobes.

"Can I offer you some Fiji water? Marshmallows? Perhaps some cinnamon Pop-Tarts?" Ambrose asked, leading us into the dining room.

"No, thank you," Monk said. "Here's something I bet you didn't know, Ambrose. Natalie has worked as my assistant for years and not once has she taken a shower at my house."

"That's a shame," Yuki said.

"She arrives for work already bathed and clean," Monk said. "You should arrive that way, too."

"I don't have to arrive," Yuki said. "I live here."

Monk went wide-eyed and turned to Ambrose. "She's a full-time, live-in assistant?"

I knew the idea was a dream come true for Monk. It

was a nightmare scenario for me. And that wasn't even factoring in the aspects of the situation that Monk still hadn't grasped.

"It's been very advantageous," Ambrose said.

"I hope she's not staying in my room," Monk said.

"Of course not," Ambrose said.

"That would be sacrilegious," Yuki said. "From what I've been told, that room has been kept in the same state since the day you left for college. There should be a red velvet rope across the doorway."

Monk glowered at her. Ambrose spoke up quickly, directing his remarks to me.

"So, Natalie, what do you need my help with?"

Ambrose sat down at the table and we followed his lead, taking seats as well.

I gave him a quick rundown on the man who died in the hotel room, what Monk had deduced about his life in Mexico, and Stottlemeyer's discovery that his fingerprints weren't in the system and that his identification was fake.

"He had this snapshot in his hand when he died," I said and passed the picture to Ambrose. "I'd like to find out who he was, why he was in San Francisco, and locate any family he might have left behind."

"What name did he leave when he registered at the hotel?" Yuki asked.

"Jack Griffin," I said.

"The Invisible Man," she said.

"He shouldn't be," I said. "All lives mean something. Someone must have cared about him, and whoever it is deserves to know about his fate."

"I'm talking about his name," Yuki said. "Jack Griffin was the name of the Invisible Man, as portrayed by Claude Rains in the 1933 movie adaptation."

"Really?" I said.

"His name was just 'Griffin' in the H. G. Wells novel," she said. "They added the first name 'Jack' for the movie. The name changed many times over the years in subsequent adaptations."

Ambrose beamed with pride. "Isn't she amazing? She's full of facts like that."

"That's handy if you are frequently in need of trivial knowledge," Monk said.

"Knowledge is knowledge, Adrian. The value of it is situational. What might seem trivial one moment could be vital the next," Ambrose said. "This might be one such instance."

"It's not," Monk said.

"He chose that name on purpose," I said. "It's telling."

"I agree," Ambrose said. "It clearly indicates that all of this man's actions were carefully premeditated, that he was very self-aware, and that he didn't want to be seen, even in death."

"Maybe we should honor that," Monk said.

"You make a good point, Mr. Monk. But I just can't do that. Maybe that's selfish of me, and maybe it will turn out to be a mistake, and then you can say 'I told you so.'"

"I will," Monk said. "But I won't be petty and vindictive about it."

"Just smug and superior," I said.

"Thoroughly and justifiably," Monk said.

I turned to Ambrose. "I'll understand if you don't want to help."

"I would be glad to assist you," Ambrose said.

"Me, too," Yuki said. "I know something about how terminal cancer affects a man. As Dub got sicker, nothing else mattered to him except finishing his last story. Maybe, in his own way, Griffin was trying to do the same thing."

Ambrose nodded. "Isn't she incredible?"

Monk groaned.

"Thank you both," I said. "I'm hoping that the photograph and his belongings will give us clues that could explain who he was and why he came to San Francisco to die."

I took out my notebook and shared with them my inventory of items, as well as my observations and questions. While I spoke, Yuki went to the living room, got a notepad and pen, and made some notes of her own.

When I was done, Ambrose picked up the picture again, sat back in his chair, and nodded. "That's an excellent start, Natalie. But I think there's a lot more information we can extract from this photograph."

"Like what?" I asked.

"Well, there's the materials used in the roofing, the setback of the home from the street, the location and type of sewer grate in the curb, the dimensions of the sidewalk, and the shape, height, and position of the streetlamp," Ambrose said. "From all of that, we can make some informed assumptions about the building codes and utility requirements that were in force at the time, which could help us pinpoint where and when this picture was taken. We might also be able to determine the manufacturer of the roofing, the sewer grate, the streetlamp, and so forth."

"Wow," I said. "I never thought of that. I wouldn't know where to begin to find that information."

"Of course you do or you wouldn't be here," Ambrose said. "It's with me. I wrote the book on sewer grates."

Knowing Ambrose, I assumed he meant that literally. He probably wrote the books on roofing materials and streetlamps as well.

"There's also the snapshot itself," Yuki said. "We

might be able to determine the type of photo paper and the process used to develop it, and from that, the type of camera that took the picture. If you let us hold on to the photo, I'll scan it and e-mail you a high-res jpeg so you can examine it in detail."

"Isn't she wonderful?" Ambrose said.

"You're sweet, Ambrose. I'm going to go get dressed." She got up and nodded to Monk and me. "It was nice to see you both again. Don't be strangers."

Monk watched her leave the room, and the instant she was gone, he turned to Ambrose.

"Are you out of your mind?"

"Why do you say that, Adrian?"

"You don't even know that woman," he said.

"I know more about her than you knew about Natalie before you hired her," Ambrose said. "And I know how I feel."

"You've lived in this house for decades," Monk said. "Frankly, you are naive in the ways of the world and how predatory and dangerous it is out there."

"Why do you think that I've stayed inside all of these years?" Ambrose asked.

"Well, now you've opened the door and let that outside world right in," Monk said.

"I would have done it sooner if I'd known it would be Yuki. She's changed my life," Ambrose said. "And I have the two of you to thank for it. If you hadn't taken me on that road trip for my birthday, I never would have met Yuki. I feel reborn. That road trip was the greatest present anyone has ever given me."

I smiled and squeezed Ambrose's hand. "I am so happy for you, Ambrose."

"Oh for God's sake, wake up. What do we know about this woman?" Monk asked. "She could be an ex-con."

"She is," Ambrose said.

"She could have killed someone," Monk said.

"She has," Ambrose said.

Monk slapped his hands on the table in frustration. "And you let her into your home? You're insane. You've become a danger to yourself."

"Then so are you, Mr. Monk," I said.

"How can you say that? You know me. I would never act as impulsively, as irresponsibly, and as self-destructively as he has."

"Yes, you would," I said. "You already have."

"What are you talking about?" Monk asked.

"I'm an ex-con," I said.

"You were arrested for a minor offense in college," Monk said. "It's not the same."

"I've killed someone," I said.

"That was in self-defense," Monk said.

"Even so, all those things didn't stop you from letting me into your home."

"But not in my shower," Monk said.

"Is that what's bothering you, Adrian?" Ambrose asked. "That Yuki and I are together?"

Monk stared at him. "You're *together* together?"

"How could you not know that? How could you not see the greatest thing that's ever happened to me?" Ambrose said. "Why does everyone think you're this astoundingly observant detective when you are totally blind?"

"Oh my God," Monk said, lowering his head and covering his face with his hands. "This just keeps getting worse."

He was right. I had to save Monk from himself. I got up from my seat. "I think it's time for Mr. Monk and me to go."

"I'll call you when we have some information for you," Ambrose said.

Monk got up and pointed a finger at Ambrose. "Don't come crying to me when Yuki strips this house of valuables and runs off with her Hells Angels friends to get tattooed."

"She's already tattooed," Ambrose said. "She has a snake on her back. I think it's beautiful."

"The apocalypse is nigh," Monk said. "And the first horseman just rode in on a Harley."

And with that, Monk marched out of the house, slamming the door behind him. I was about to say something when Monk came back in, went straight over to one of the stacks of newspapers in the living room, straightened the issue on top, then stormed out again.

"Please forgive him, Ambrose," I said. "He doesn't handle change well."

"I didn't like change, either, until the change was Yuki. Does that make sense?"

I gave him a kiss on the cheek. "Perfect sense."

# 9

## Mr. Monk Hits the Bottle

The drive back into San Francisco across the Golden Gate Bridge was an ordeal, as I knew it would be.

"Can you believe what Ambrose has done?" Monk lamented.

"I'm very happy for him."

"Then you care nothing for his well-being."

I'd had it with him by that point and couldn't hold back any longer.

"As I recall, Mr. Monk, the whole point of taking your brother out on that road trip was because you'd achieved a balance in your life that you felt he'd been denied. One of the things that saddened you was that he hadn't found someone to love. Well, now he has. So what are you complaining about? Isn't this what you wanted?"

"Not with some biker chick that he picked up on the side of the road."

"Who cares where you find love as long as you find it?" I said. "Or it finds you?"

Monk looked at me gravely. "I think they're forni-cating."

I wanted to slam my head against the steering wheel. "You're missing the whole point."

"Take me to Dr. Bell's office right away."

"You were just there this morning," I said.

"This is a crisis," he said. "A psychiatric emergency."

"Are you having a mental breakdown?"

"No, I'm fine," Monk said. "I'm the epitome of clear thinking and rationality."

"So what's the emergency?"

"Do you have amnesia? My brother is fornicating with a homicidal tattooed motorcycle mama! Dr. Bell might be the only one who can save him."

"How do you expect Dr. Bell to do that?"

"By committing Ambrose to a mental institution."

"On what grounds?"

"Insanity, of course. If what Ambrose is doing isn't insanity, nothing is."

"By that, you mean having sex."

Monk gave me a stern look. "Do you realize what that actually involves?"

"I have a distant memory," I said.

"At least he had the good sense to do it in a shower," Monk said, "where there's plenty of soap, cleanser, disinfectant, rubber gloves, and scrubbing brushes."

I didn't bother arguing any more with Monk. It was pointless when he was that distraught. Instead, I did as he asked and took him to Dr. Bell's office. I didn't think Dr. Bell would do anything about Ambrose, but I hoped that he could do something for Monk.

I dropped him off in front of Dr. Bell's office and sped away. I didn't want to be around when the disinfectant wipes hit the fan.

I found a parking spot a few blocks away off Columbus Avenue and walked down to Washington Square. It was a nice day, and I was happy to just sit there and watch the children play, and the couples make out, and the dogs chase balls, as if all of them were actors on a stage, performing for an audience of one.

But after about an hour, my cell phone rang and a very irritated Dr. Bell insisted that I come get Monk immediately. I didn't ask Dr. Bell how the session went and he wouldn't have told me if I had.

When I drove up to Dr. Bell's office, Monk was already waiting for me, pacing on the sidewalk out front. He got in the car and slammed the door.

"The planet has slipped off its axis and is rolling into the abyss," he said.

The fact that Monk was using a belabored metaphor like that could only mean that things didn't go well.

"I take it Dr. Bell declined to institutionalize your brother for falling in love."

Monk shook his head. "He wasn't paying attention to what I was saying. He was too busy listening to the fatties in his compulsive overeaters group."

"You crashed their session, Mr. Monk."

"Oh come on. What do they have to talk about? So I told them: 'Stop eating so much, you're all fat enough as it is. If you can't do that, simply wire your jaws shut until the tonnage is gone.' There. Done. Problem solved. I assumed we were ready to move on to a real psychiatric emergency, like my crazy brother taking showers with a sociopath. But things inexplicably got ugly."

"I can imagine," I said.

"No, you can't. They became an angry mob. They charged me like rampaging elephants. I wasn't sure whether they were going to crush me, or eat me, or both. Those people desperately need help."

"Which is what they were trying to get from Dr. Bell when you intruded on their therapy session and ridiculed their problems."

"Ambrose is on his own," Monk said. "There's nothing I can do for him."

"He'll appreciate that," I said.

"You say that now," Monk said. "But wait until his heart is broken."

"It's better to have loved and lost than never to have loved at all."

"This isn't love. It's lunacy."

"Love is a kind of lunacy."

"I'm glad you're finally seeing reason," Monk said.

We went back to Monk's place, where he went straight to the refrigerator, took a drink of Fiji water right out of the bottle, and then wiped his mouth with the back of his hand. He looked me in the eye defiantly, as if I represented the conventions he was breaking. Maybe that's because I was the only one around. It actually would have made much more sense for him to look defiantly into a mirror. I had no problem drinking out of the bottle or using the back of my hand as a napkin.

"Am I shocking you?" he asked, then took another sip from the bottle.

"Not really," I said.

"I guess there are no boundaries of human behavior left to cross after what we've seen today."

"You're probably right," I said. "I think I'll go home and try to cope."

He opened the refrigerator again and tossed me a bottle of Fiji water.

"Drink responsibly," Monk said. "Don't open that until you get home."

"Will do," I said. "Are you going to be okay?"

"Nope," he said, took another swig, and wiped his mouth again with the back of his hand.

It was shortly after eight the next morning when my phone rang. As soon as I heard it, I knew for certain that it was Captain Stottlemeyer and that someone was dead. I was right. Sunrise in San Francisco almost always casts light on a corpse.

I called Monk with the news and it immediately put him in a good mood. There was nothing like the violent, tragic end of another human being's life to brighten his day.

I really shouldn't say that. It's not fair to Monk.

The truth is, it wasn't the murder itself that made Monk happy—it was the challenge of solving a puzzle, the opportunity to set things right, and the chance to feel needed. It was just a shame that someone had to die for him to feel those things.

And I knew that this time it wasn't the mystery he was looking forward to as much as the opportunity to clean it up, literally instead of just figuratively.

Although it didn't lift my spirits that someone had been murdered, I did feel that shot of adrenaline, and that flutter of excitement in my chest, that came with the knowledge that I'd soon be caught up in another investigation. I discovered that the death of the Invisible Man wasn't enough to sate my eagerness to prove myself.

Monk was waiting for me on the street outside of his apartment building when I drove up. He was holding the box that contained a set of disposable full-body coveralls, rubber gloves, filtered respirator mask, goggles, and rubber boots. He put the box in the backseat and then got into the car beside me.

I glanced at him. He had dark circles under his eyes,

his hair was slightly askew, and I saw a wrinkle on his sleeve.

"Rough night?" I asked.

He nodded. "I hit the bottle pretty hard and then I went to bed without bathing or brushing my teeth."

"You're lucky to be alive," I said as I steered the car away from the curb and headed for the crime scene, which was down in the Mission District.

"This situation with Ambrose has me reeling."

"He's happy, Mr. Monk. There's no reason to reel."

"Happiness is an illusion, Natalie. It doesn't actually exist."

"Of course it does," I said. "It's what you feel when you're not sad."

"That's unconsciousness. And I'm pretty sure that I'm miserable when I am unconscious, too."

I gave up, as I usually do, in any discussion where I try to change Monk's mind about something. He'd have to make his own peace with Ambrose's relationship.

The crime scene was the Bargain Thrift Store on Mission between Seventeenth and Eighteenth streets. It was a largely Latino neighborhood, and on that block alone there were two taquerias, three nail salons, a check-cashing center, a used-book store, two pawnshops, a beauty salon, a bakery, two corner produce markets, one fortune-teller, and three storefront *iglesias pentecostales*.

The street in front of the Bargain Thrift Store was clogged with official police vehicles, so we had to park a few doors down in front of the Adult Supercenter, a banner above the blacked-out windows reading "Hundreds of New Toys Just In."

"That's disgusting," Monk said as we got out of the car. "They're trying to lure in children."

"No one under the age of twenty-one is allowed inside. The advertising is aimed at adults."

"Adults don't play with toys, kids do. And no parent in their right mind would buy toys for their kids in there."

"I don't think those are the kind of toys that they are selling."

"What other kind of toys are there?" Monk looked back at the store. "Look at the sign on their window: 'We have lifelike dolls of all shapes, sizes, and colors. Come in and play.'"

I thought about what would be involved in explaining why he was wrong, and the examples that I would have to give, and I made a decision.

"You're right, Mr. Monk. My mistake. I don't know what I was thinking."

As we crossed the street, Monk stopped a uniformed officer and pointed to the adult store. "You need to go into that store and tell them that they shouldn't be selling toys in there. What if children wander in, looking for Hot Wheels or Barbies to play with?"

I stood behind Monk and nodded vigorously at the cop, hoping he'd get the message.

"I'll get right on it, Mr. Monk," the cop said and headed for the store.

Monk smiled and we continued on toward the crime scene. "There's an officer who is going to rise quickly through the ranks."

I looked over my shoulder in time to see the officer double back and shoot me a thumbs-up. Monk was right—he would go far.

# 10

## Mr. Monk and the Thrift Shop

Stottlemeyer and Devlin met us outside the door of the thrift store. Monk peered past them through the open doorway at the sales floor, which was scattered with secondhand furniture, racks of old clothes, and shelves overflowing with dishware, linens, hats, lamps, countertop appliances, outdated electronics, and a thousand other discarded items.

"What is this awful place?" Monk asked.

"The thrift shop for the Bay Cities food bank," Devlin said. Monk stared back at her with a blank look on his face. "People donate their used clothing, appliances, dishes, and furniture, which the shop then sells to benefit the charity."

"The charitable thing to do would be to burn it all," Monk said. "What kind of person would eat off dishes and stick silverware in their mouths that other people have used?"

"Oh, just about anyone who has ever been in a restaurant or had a meal in someone's home," Stottlemeyer said. "In other words, everyone on earth but you."

"In those cases, you know where the dishes have been and that they've likely been thoroughly cleaned a thousand times," Monk said. "Who knows where these have been or what has been served on them? Maybe they were used to serve slop to pets or barnyard animals."

"Have you seen a lot of farms here in San Francisco?" Devlin asked.

Monk ignored her question. "What about all this furniture? Who would sit or sleep on furniture other people have been using for God knows what kind of activities?"

"Anyone who has ever been in a restaurant, hotel, or in someone's home," Devlin said.

"Hotels and restaurants have maid services and are regularly visited by health inspectors. The same can't be said for private homes, where most of this has come from," Monk said. "But what I really can't imagine is what sort of a person would wear clothes other people have worn."

"A person who can't afford new clothes," I said. "Or who finds vintage clothing stylish."

"It's disgusting," Monk said. "Shopping here is no different than rooting around in a trash Dumpster."

Devlin tugged on her leather jacket. "I got this at a thrift store."

"That's different," Monk said. "You were in vice working undercover as a crack whore."

"I never went undercover as a crack whore," Devlin said. "And I am not undercover now."

Monk cleared his throat and shifted his weight. "Oh."

"If you're done buttering up the lieutenant, I'd

really like to go inside and investigate this murder," Stottlemeyer said. "What do you say, Monk?"

"I'll need another minute or two," Monk said. "I have to go back to the car and put on my biohazard suit."

"It's a thrift store," Devlin said. "Not a toxic waste spill."

"I don't see the distinction," he said.

Monk and I went back to my car, where I helped him suit up, using duct tape to tightly seal his coverall sleeves and pant legs to his gloves and boots. He put on his goggles and secured his respirator mask over his nose and mouth, and then we returned to the thrift store.

Devlin shook her head. "Don't you think that's overkill?"

"That place is a pit of pathogens," Monk said, the mask giving his voice a Darth Vader–esque quality. "HIV, hepatitis, herpes, E. coli, and hantavirus—it could all be in there."

He turned to look into the store, so he didn't hear Devlin when she said, "It could all be out here, too. The streets aren't any cleaner."

Stottlemeyer nudged her hard with his elbow and whispered, "Shut up before you set us back years with him."

"What did she say?" Monk asked, turning around again.

"That she'll be very cautious inside the thrift shop and that she greatly appreciates your concern for our health," Stottlemeyer said.

"And what did you say?"

"I thanked her for advising us to exercise extreme caution."

"So why did you whisper?"

"Because I was ashamed to admit that you were right," Stottlemeyer said.

Monk nodded, barely hiding his satisfaction with the answer. "Let's get to it."

The four of us went inside the store, which had the musty, dusty smell of someone's attic, tinged with the coppery scent of spilled blood.

Devlin led the way, weaving through the cluttered aisles toward the windowed office in the back, which looked out on the sales floor. The window was spattered on the inside with blood, which explained why the smell was in the air.

We stepped through the open doorway into the cramped office. It was lined with file cabinets and there was a gunmetal gray desk in the corner, facing the door.

A black man was slumped on the floor in the center of the office, his throat slit, his dead eyes staring up at us, a carving knife in the big puddle of blood that seeped out from under the body.

His cut throat explained the spatter. Arterial blood sprayed, and judging by the dispersal pattern, I could tell that the victim was standing when he was cut and then did a half turn as he fell. His blood sprayed around the room like his neck was a sprinkler. Considering how much blood was around, I began to wish I was wearing a biohazard suit, too.

"The victim is Casey Grover, thirty-three, the manager of the store," Devlin said. "His throat was slit with that carving knife. We're assuming the killer picked up the knife in the store."

"Any signs of a break-in?" Monk asked as he began to drift around the room, bobbing and weaving like he was shadow boxing without throwing punches. That's because it was hard for him to move freely in that bulky suit and his field of vision was limited by the hood and goggles.

"No, there wasn't," Devlin said. "Either the back door was left unlocked last night or the lock was picked."

"What about the alarm system?" I asked. "Wasn't it tripped anyway?"

"The existing alarm system is ancient and was left by the previous tenant," Stottlemeyer said. "The thrift store has never used it."

"They will now," Monk said. "Who found the body?"

"The cashier found him when she arrived for work this morning," Devlin said. "We've got her in the back-seat of a squad car, and an officer is taking her state-ment, in case you want to arrest her for murder."

"She didn't do it," Monk said.

"Do you know who did?" she asked.

"Not yet," he replied.

"I'm shocked," she said. "What's taking you so long?"

"I'll tell you what I do know about the killer," Monk said. "He's an experienced criminal."

"How do you know that?"

"The killer deftly picked the lock without leaving any signs and was confident enough in his lethal skills to select a weapon once he got here, leaving that ele-ment to chance. An amateur wouldn't do that."

"Or it was a crime of opportunity," Devlin said. "The manager or some other employee accidentally left the back door unlocked and some street person snuck in and camped out for the night. The manager walked in this morning, startled the guy, and got his throat cut."

"Or he walked in on a burglary," I said.

"I don't think so," Stottlemeyer said. "No money was taken. The safe is untouched and all the cash that's supposed to be there is accounted for."

"Maybe something was stolen from the sales floor," I said.

"In a thrift store?" Devlin said. "It's worthless hand-me-downs."

"Even if something was taken," Stottlemeyer said, "it won't be easy for us to figure it out. They don't keep a close eye on their inventory."

"Maybe somebody came back to retrieve a donation," I said. "That ugly painting that old Aunt Edna had in her attic for sixty years that nobody realized was a Rembrandt until she died and after her dumbass grandson gave away all her junk."

"You've watched too many episodes of *Antiques Roadshow*," Stottlemeyer said.

"Maybe the killer was a disgruntled employee," Devlin said. "Or an angry ex-lover."

"Whatever the killer was after was in here." Monk gestured to a blood-spattered file cabinet, the top drawer of which was slightly ajar.

"How do you know?" Stottlemeyer asked.

"There's blood spatter on the front of the cabinet but not on these exposed folders. The drawer was opened after the killing," Monk said. "Here's what happened. When Grover came into the office, the killer approached him from behind and held the knife to his throat. He asked Grover where to find the item he wanted, then slit his throat and went to the file cabinet."

"The killer was a cold bastard," Devlin said. "He could have knocked Grover out and gone about his business. He didn't have to kill him."

"As I said, he's experienced and ruthless." Monk carefully slid open the file drawer. "Killing means nothing to him."

"What would a pro want in a thrift shop?" Devlin asked, rhetorically more than anything else. But I said the first thing that occurred to me.

"Maybe it was a contract hit," I said. "Grover witnessed something or knew something that the mob couldn't let him sing about to the DA."

Stottlemeyer looked at me, an amused expression on his face. "The mob took out a contract on him so he wouldn't sing."

I winced with embarrassment. "Sorry. I've been watching too much old TV."

"No, you spent too much time hanging around with Randy," Stottlemeyer said.

"There's blood on the top of these files in the back," Monk said. "The killer must have flipped through them with his gloved, bloody fingertips."

"Can you tell what's in the files?" Stottlemeyer asked.

"It appears to be time sheets, donation logs, and accounting records."

"Maybe the killer was trying to cover up evidence of embezzlement," Devlin said.

"I don't think this place generates enough cash to make it attractive for skimming," the captain said. "But I'll have our forensic accountants go through the books anyway."

Monk gestured to the computer on Grover's desk. "There's also blood on the computer's point-and-click device."

"It's called a mouse," Devlin said.

"And there's blood on the keyboard," Monk continued, ignoring Devlin's comment. "Not from the spatter, but from sticky fingers on the keys. The killer looked for something."

"Or he decided to check his e-mail and update his Facebook status before he left," Devlin said with a grin.

"I'll ask the computer forensics group to check it

out," the captain said. "Maybe he left some digital footprints they can follow."

Devlin turned to Monk. "Why won't you call a mouse a mouse?"

"Because I refuse to use gutter colloquialisms to refer to common things."

"*Mouse* isn't a profanity," Devlin said.

"But the creature is. They are no different than rats. And I will not dignify them by memorializing their existence with one of man's technological achievements."

"You're leading a one-man crusade," Devlin said.

"I'm used to it." Monk clapped his gloved hands together, as if to shake dust from them. "We're done here. Let's clear the room so the ME can take the body and forensics can finish up their work."

"Does this mean you haven't figured out who killed Grover?" Devlin asked.

"It does," Monk said.

"Hallelujah," Devlin said. "I actually get to do my job."

We all filed out of the room and back onto the street. As soon as we were outside, Monk took his mask and goggles off and lingered on the sidewalk.

Devlin and some officers went off to question nearby merchants and residents just in case anybody had seen suspicious activity the previous night or that morning.

Stottlemeyer spoke to the forensics team, gave instructions to some uniformed officers, and sent the morgue guys into the store for the body. Then he noticed that we hadn't left.

"Something wrong?" Stottlemeyer asked.

"Nope," Monk said.

"Then why are you still here in that getup?"

"I'm staying to help the crime scene cleaners," Monk said.

Stottlemeyer looked incredulously at Monk. "Why would you want to do that?"

"Sometimes you just have to kick back, let loose, and relieve the stress of the day."

"By cleaning up blood spatter and bodily waste?"

Monk nodded. "It's my lucky day."

# 11

## Mr. Monk Meets the Crew

The cleanup of crime scenes is the responsibility of the property owners, who, not surprisingly, often defer to their insurance companies to handle the matter. The police are not allowed to steer the owners or their agents to any particular crime scene cleaning service. But there was no law preventing Monk from recommending someone, and he did so as soon as the representative from the Bay Cities food bank showed up.

She was a very distressed woman and kept breaking into sobs. She told us that Grover was a former homeless man who'd turned his life around, rising from a food bank patron to become the manager of one of the three San Francisco–area thrift stores that supported it.

She took Monk's advice and called Jerry Yermo's company as soon as the police released the crime scene, which was about three hours after we'd arrived.

Thirty minutes after the last police officer left the scene, Jerry and his crew pulled up in two unmarked white vans. I supposed they were unmarked because nobody wants a vehicle labeled "Biohazard Cleanup" or "Crime and Trauma Scene Decontamination" parked outside of their home, business, park, or school—it would be like signs reading "Truckload of Toxic Human Waste Parked Here." It's bad PR all around, especially in a society that already goes out of its way to shield itself from death. Most people can go through life without ever seeing a corpse, much less the waste left by one.

Jerry and three other crime scene cleaners emerged from the vans in their white coveralls. They hadn't yet donned their hoods, goggles, and respirator masks.

The woman from the food bank intercepted Jerry on the sidewalk, handed him the keys to the store, and practically ran away from the scene.

Monk stood with me outside the door to the shop and was bouncing in place like an excited child, waiting for Jerry to notice him.

Jerry pocketed the keys and pointed out Monk to his team. "You see that fashionably dressed gentleman? That is the legendary Adrian Monk, a consultant to the San Francisco police and probably the best detective in America."

"And France and Germany," Monk said. "Or so they say."

"They do?" I said.

"So I am told," he said.

"That attractive young woman is Natalie Teeger, the Watson to his Holmes," Jerry said. "They will be working with us today."

"I am so excited," Monk said.

"Actually, I'm not going to be staying," I said.

"You really should," Monk said. "You could learn a few things that you desperately need to know."

"We have an extra Tyvek suit with your name on it," Jerry said.

"It's tempting," I said. "But I'll pass."

"But your name is on it," Monk said. "How cool is that?"

"I'll still pass," I said.

"Let me introduce you to my crew before you go," Jerry said and turned to a big, stocky man in his forties with a military buzz cut. I recognized the man's build, if not his face, which had been hidden behind a respirator mask when I saw him at the Excelsior. "This is Gene Tiflin. You could call him our construction supervisor. He oversees the demo and handles most of our reconstruction."

"I used to build tract homes, but the company I worked for didn't survive the collapse of the housing market and now nobody is building anything," Gene said. "So here I am."

The petite woman standing next to Gene jumped up, raising her hand as if she were a contestant on a game show. "Can I be next?"

"Sure," Jerry said.

"I'm Corinne Witt from Mendocino, California. I'm a medical student working part-time for Jerry to pay my bills and see the other side of my work."

"The other side?" I asked.

"The death side," she said.

"She's the only one of us who doesn't mind cleaning up after decomposing corpses," Jerry said. "Like that guy in Golden Gate Park who died in his parked car with the windows rolled up."

"It looked like he exploded," Gene said.

"The temperature in a closed vehicle can rise fifty degrees Fahrenheit within an hour, even on a cool day," she said. "But the day he died, and the two days that followed until he was discovered, were scorchers. It was fascinating to see how the intense heat and the confined space impacted his decomposition."

"It was unbelievably disgusting," said the final member of the team, a Chinese man who did a full-body cringe just thinking about it. "I couldn't look at a pizza for a month without gagging."

"That's William Tong," Jerry said. "A former elementary school teacher downsized out of the classroom by the California economy. He's the newbie on my team."

"I can't help noticing everyone seems to be a part-timer or a former something else," I said.

"There's big turnover in this profession," Jerry said. "Nobody wants to get into it, and those who are can't wait to get out."

"It's a calling," Monk said. "Like the priesthood. Not everyone is cut out for it."

"Speaking of which," Jerry said, "why don't we get to work?"

"Shouldn't we wait for the others?"

"What others?" Jerry asked.

"This is a thrift store," Monk said. "You're going to need more men."

"I was told that the murder occurred in the back office," Jerry said, "and that the spill was contained within that limited space."

"Yes, but what about all of that?" Monk waved a hand toward the sales floor.

"What about it?" Gene asked.

"It has to go," Monk said.

"Why?" Corinne asked.

"None of it has been cleaned and disinfected," Monk said. "Every cushion, pillow, and mattress in that place is a sponge soaked with bodily fluids and disease."

"No more so than the furniture in a typical home," William said.

"That's exactly what I mean," Monk said.

Jerry nodded. "I see what you're getting at, Adrian, but I'm afraid the job you're talking about is beyond the scope of our responsibilities. We'll do whatever is necessary to remove any decontamination created by the murder, but we have to draw the line there, otherwise we could find ourselves demolishing the whole building. Where would it end?"

I was impressed. Jerry showed remarkable patience, understanding, and respect in the way he dealt with Monk.

"I understand," Monk said grimly. "You're a stronger man than me to be able to deal with that harsh reality and make those tough choices every day. Shall I show you the scene?"

"That would be an honor," Jerry said, and I think he actually meant it.

I was beginning to really like the guy.

As Monk led Jerry and his team into the store, Corinne lagged behind, pausing for a moment to talk to me.

"How extreme is his obsessive-compulsive disorder?" she asked.

"Off the charts," I said.

She smiled. "At least he hides it well."

My little Victorian row house was less than ten minutes by car from the thrift store. So I told Monk to call me when he was done, and I went home.

By sticking around to clean things up with Jerry, Monk had basically given me the rest of the day off. I intended to make the most of it.

I brought a burrito home for lunch, washed it down

with green tea, and sat down in front of my laptop computer and telephone to tackle the questions that I'd compiled after sorting through Jack Griffin's belongings.

I began by checking my e-mail. Yuki had sent me the jpeg of Griffin's snapshot, so I downloaded it and brought it up on-screen. I don't know if Yuki did some enhancements to the photo, but the image seemed crisper and bolder, and I was able to zoom in and examine more details.

One thing I hadn't picked up before was the name of the girl's bicycle. But now, magnifying the image on my laptop screen, I could make out the words *Dandelion Racer* along the crossbar and even see the white dandelion decals on the fenders.

I searched the Internet for related information, found a Web site and blog devoted to vintage children's bikes, including the Dandelion Racer, and learned it was one of many styles made by Wheeler Wheels in the 1980s.

I cropped the Griffin snapshot in Photoshop so it included just the bike and sent the jpeg to the blogger, along with a plea for any information she might have on the Dandelion Racer.

I also found the Wheeler Wheels Web site, filled out their contact form, and asked for any information they might have on the pink Dandelion Racer with a white basket and white dandelion stickers on the fender.

With that done, I moved on to researching the Jackson/Elite Clipper Model 188 binoculars. I soon discovered that Jackson/Elite was bought out twenty years ago by a larger company, which was bought out by another company, which was bought out by yet another company, which then discontinued the Jackson/Elite brands. I e-mailed the company for information and also left messages on a half dozen binocular-aficionado discussion groups.

It was tedious, time-consuming work—the investigative drudgery that every detective has to slog through, except for Adrian Monk, who somehow managed to solve every case by relying on just his instinct, his powers of observation, and deductive reasoning. I was beginning to appreciate why Lieutenant Devlin resented that so much—and I'd been detecting in earnest for only a couple of hours.

I was about to call it a day and rejuvenate myself with some Oreo cookie ice cream, when an e-mail arrived from the vintage-bike blogger. She told me that the Dandelion Racer was an extremely popular brand and that the color schemes of the bikes were often adapted for the various department store chains that sold them.

So a Dandelion Racer offered by Montgomery Ward, Ardan, or Walmart might have had different colors, decals, tassels, and baskets than the model sold by Woolco, Target, or Sears, Roebuck. Unfortunately, she didn't know anything about the specific Dandelion Racer in my photo or what, if any, department store chain it might have been designed for, but she agreed to ask around the vintage-bike community for me.

I thanked her for her help.

That's when Monk called and asked me to pick him up. I was surprised that he'd called so soon, but then I glanced at the time on my computer and was stunned to discover that I'd been sitting there for six hours.

I knew that I'd been working for a while, but I wasn't aware that I'd actually spent the whole day with my butt in a chair and my eyes on a computer screen.

But I felt all of those hours, and every decade of my

life, when I finally got up, and I resented Monk some more for never feeling the lower back and shoulder pain of detecting, either.

Then again, he'd never been able to experience so much of the pleasure and enjoyment in life that I have because of his OCD, which, in a cruel joke of nature, was the root of his detecting genius.

When I looked at it that way, I decided I'd rather live with the drudgery and back pain of an ordinary detective. And once I came to that conclusion, my resentment toward Monk—at least that particular resentment—disappeared.

# 12

## Mr. Monk, Matchmaker

As I pulled up in front of the thrift store, Jerry and his team were just leaving in their vans. Monk waved good-bye to them, a wistful look on his face. He stood there in his shirt and slacks and yellow boots, holding his mask in his hand, and continued to wave until the vans disappeared around the corner.

I assumed that Jerry had disposed of Monk's biohazard outfit. It wasn't a loss. Monk had plenty more of the Tyvek coveralls. They were hanging in his closet to keep them from getting wrinkled.

Monk climbed into the car and sighed.

"Why are you so sad?" I asked.

"Because it's over," he said. "Don't worry, my boots have been decontaminated and disinfected."

"I wasn't worried," I said as I pulled away from the curb.

"You should have been. I hope you don't make a habit of letting people in your car with suspect boots."

"How did the cleaning go?"

"It was great. The blood was everywhere, it dripped and splattered in places you wouldn't believe, and we had to get it all. Jerry is relentless when it comes to finding every speck."

"Wow," I said, trying to sound impressed.

"He removes every piece of furniture, opens every drawer, and examines every item. That attention to detail extends to the entire room," Monk said. "He has this incredible spray, a mix of enzymes and surfactants, that liquefies the dried blood so it can be scrubbed off with industrial tissues, stiff brushes, and putty scrapers. It's hard work."

"But you liked it," I said.

"I loved it. There are no half measures with Jerry. The linoleum was covered with blood. Some less dedicated people might have just mopped it up, scrubbed the floor, and moved on. But he could see some tendrils of blood had reached the wall's edge. So he insisted that we remove the baseboards and lift up the linoleum. Sure enough, the wood underneath the linoleum was soaked. The linoleum had to go. Then we all got on our hands and knees, scrubbed the wood with that miracle spray, and then coated it with sealant so no moisture could get in or out again. I want to do that when I get home."

"You want to rip up your floor?"

"I bet the wood underneath has never been thoroughly cleaned and sealed."

"That's because it's always been covered with a floor," I said. "No one has died on your kitchen floor. I don't think your landlord would appreciate you tearing it up so you can scrub the wood."

"He'll thank me later," he said.

"No, he won't. He'll kill you, and then there will be a reason to clean up your kitchen, only you won't be around to do it," I said. "How did Jerry and his crew treat you?"

"They're my new posse," he said. "They are such a wacky, zany gang. Gene, he's the jokester. He says the funniest things."

"Like what?"

"He said that I was a lunatic at best, a pervert at worst, because I enjoy crime scene cleaning."

"That's not funny," I said. "It's an insult."

"No, you don't get it. What he said is the opposite of what everyone knows to be true, which makes it a comical absurdity. You'd be crazy *not* to enjoy cleaning, but he said I was crazy because I *do*. Get it? Hilarity ensued."

"Uh-huh. What about the others?"

"William is the newbie, so he's the brunt of lots of good-natured ribbing, too. Gene would recount particularly gruesome cleaning assignments from the past in an effort to make William gag."

"Gene sounds like a lovable guy."

"He's the class clown," Monk said.

"What about Corinne?"

"She's the Hermione Granger," Monk said. "That's the studious witch in the Harry Potter books and motion pictures."

"Yes, I know. But I am wondering how you do, since your knowledge of popular culture is virtually nonexistent."

"Jerry calls her Hermione, so I asked him to explain it to me, and once he did, I concurred that the comparison was appropriate, although she has no magical powers. But she is very conscientious and thorough."

"Like me," I said.

"Yes, just like you, except that she's younger, cleaner, better educated, and conscientious and thorough. For example, on her own initiative, she used luminol to find any blood that might have been tracked out of the room by the police officers and forensic techs, then got on her hands and knees to clean off every speck that she found. That's dedication."

"It's a good thing she wants to be a doctor and not a detective's assistant."

"I bet she uses luminol at home when she cleans."

"You sound like you really like her."

"What's not to like?"

"You should ask her out, Mr. Monk. You could invite her over to help you clean your house."

"Get real, Natalie. She's twenty-three. And do you really think that someone so clean, conscientious, and thorough would still be unattached? She's got a boyfriend and a line of willing suitors waiting in the wings," Monk said. "Oh, that reminds me. You have to get cleaned up."

"So you keep telling me."

"No, I mean immediately, right after you drop me off. You don't have much time before Jerry picks you up."

"For what?"

"Your date, of course."

I jammed on the brakes and nearly got us rearended. "We don't have one."

"Yes, you do," Monk said. "Tonight at eight. I told him how much you liked him, that you never go out anymore, and that you're steadily gaining weight."

"I never said I liked him. In fact, I told you emphatically that he wasn't my type."

"But you were wrong," Monk said. "You'll thank me later."

Cars started honking, so I drove on. "Has anyone ever thanked you later?"

"I can wait," he said.

\* \* \*

I wasn't going to admit it to Monk, but my opinion of Jerry had changed. I was excited about the date, though I wasn't thrilled that Monk had portrayed me as this plump, slovenly, desperate spinster living in squalor. The fact that Jerry was interested in me anyway was another point in his favor.

I showered, changed into a simple black dress, and scrambled to straighten up the house, though considering Jerry's line of work, any mess I had would look inconsequential compared to what he usually saw.

Jerry rang my doorbell promptly at eight. He was dressed stylishly casual in a short-sleeve blue silk shirt, khaki slacks, and loafers. The colorful ensemble seemed to make his red hair and megawatt smile even brighter.

"I hope you can forgive me for asking you out without actually asking you out," he said. "But when Adrian told me that you were single, and that you'd been looking for a guy like me, I was afraid that you'd find him, and that it would be tonight, and that it wouldn't be me. I've been thinking about you since we met at the hotel, and I was gathering my courage to ask you out this morning, but I lost my nerve when I saw you."

"Why? After the horrible picture Mr. Monk painted of me, how could I possibly have seemed intimidating?"

"You're smart and attractive, which means you wouldn't want to be around a guy who spends his days and nights cleaning up gore."

"That never crossed my mind," I said. It was a lie, of course, and ordinarily that's not the best way to start off a relationship with someone, but I had no choice. I vowed to myself that I would be honest with him from that point forward. More or less.

His megawatt smile went supernova. I almost reached for a pair of sunglasses.

"Do you like Italian food?" he asked.

"I like anything that I don't have to take out of the freezer and put in my microwave."

"I can see this is going to be difficult," he said.

He led me out to his car, which was a Porsche.

"You seem surprised," he said. "You didn't think I'd take you out in one of the vans, did you?"

"Of course not," I said. "I just didn't know your profession was so lucrative."

"We aren't Merry Maids," he said.

He opened the passenger door for me, an act of gallantry rarely performed by men these days.

I sat down on the leather seat and he closed the door gently. The car was immaculate inside. I took a deep breath, drawing in the scent of leather and that oh-so-fleeting but luscious new-car smell.

"Did you buy this car on your way here?" I asked Jerry as he got in and buckled up.

"I've had this clunker for six years," he said.

"You have? So what's the secret to keeping the new-car smell?"

He shrugged. "I don't smell it. My work requires me to concentrate so hard on detecting the slightest whiff of decay or rot that I don't notice the nice smells anymore."

"What a waste," I said.

"But on the other hand, I appreciate beauty even more because of what I have to see every day," he said and smiled at me. "I could look at you all night."

It was a cheesy line that he'd probably used on a hundred women, and I'm ashamed to admit that it worked on me anyway. I felt a hot flush rising on my skin. Or maybe it was menopause arriving early. That would be just my luck.

# 13

## Mr. Monk and the Date

Jerry took me up to Columbus Avenue in North Beach, the same neighborhood where Dr. Bell's office was located. The street was lined on both sides with Italian restaurants, and I always found the selection overwhelming. There were just too many restaurants to choose from.

What made it worse was that they all had somebody standing outside their door like carnival barkers, doing everything short of clubbing you over the head and dragging you inside their restaurant. Their desperation for my dining dollar was too much. I'd rather have a Big Mac than deal with it.

But Jerry had a cozy little bistro already picked out, and a candlelit table was waiting for us by a bay window. There was something very homey about the place, despite the usual Tuscan architectural flourishes, the red-checkered tablecloths, the salami hanging behind the counter, and the bad paintings of gondoliers and Italian landmarks on the walls.

The candlesticks on the tables were caked in layers of wax, the seats were wooden benches littered with hand-sewn pillows of all sizes, and the silverware was a hodgepodge of unmatched pieces.

Over a very basic but delicious dinner of spaghetti and meatballs, salad, garlic bread, and wine, we did the usual first-date interviews, asking each other to summarize our lives in three thousand words or less. I went first, telling him the broad strokes of my story, and then I asked him how he became a crime scene cleaner.

"It wasn't exactly my lifelong dream," he said.

"What was your dream?"

"To be a private eye, a rock star, or an astronaut. So, naturally, I became a real estate agent."

"Makes perfect sense," I said.

"I went to Diablo Valley College and bounced around all kinds of different jobs, and I was getting ready to bounce out of real estate, too, when I got a listing for a house in Concord that had belonged to this old grandmother. She tripped and died. Her body wasn't discovered for a couple of weeks. Are you sure you want to talk about this now?"

He gestured to my plate of spaghetti, which I was in the midst of devouring in a very unladylike fashion.

"You're forgetting my line of work," I said, wiping the spaghetti sauce off my face with my napkin. "It's going to take more than some talk about decomposing corpses to kill my appetite."

"Is it too soon for me to fall in love with you?"

"Yes," I said. "Go on with your story."

"The granddaughter was willed everything and hadn't set foot in the house since her grandmother was found. She associated the house with the smell of Nana's fresh-baked pies. She didn't want that memory ruined by the smell of fresh-baked Nana. Part of my job was getting the place cleaned up so it could be sold. I had to get rid of the stench, the stains, and the insects or I'd never unload the house and get my commission. That's when I discovered the world of crime scene cleaning."

"You saw how you could help people avoid the pain and ugliness of death."

"I'm ashamed to say that what I saw were dollar signs. It was a guaranteed revenue stream, a profession that was totally immune to market forces, to the ups and downs of the economy, or even seismic cultural and political shifts in our country. Everybody dies and nobody wants to deal with the mess, except maybe Adrian. I didn't want to, either, but money is a strong motivator."

I appreciated his honesty, probably because I knew from personal experience what he was talking about.

"You don't have to be ashamed of wanting to make a buck, Jerry. Assisting Mr. Monk and investigating homicides wasn't something I set out to do, either. I stumbled into it, just like you did with crime scene cleaning. I stuck with it, despite my discomfort around dead bodies, because I needed a good job. I wanted a steady income to support myself and my daughter. And you're right. Death is one thing you can always depend on."

"Looks like we have a lot in common," he said.

"We're both in an ugly business," I said. "You impressed Mr. Monk with your attention to detail and your dedication to your work. I don't think it's just about money for you anymore."

"I don't think I could still be doing such a gruesome job if it was. Once I really got into it, once I started dealing with all those bereaved people, it became about much more than the money. I realized that my job wasn't just about cleaning up messes. It was about sparing people from as much pain and misery as possible," he said. "It's bad enough losing a loved one without having to clean up after it. My nightmare is that I will miss something while I'm cleaning, and six months later, someone will move a piece of furniture and find a tooth, or a bone fragment, or a glob of brain from their dead kid or spouse. Can you imagine how horrifying that would be for them?"

"You're a knight in shining Tyvek," I said.

"Finally, someone who sees me as I really am," he said. "So what about you?"

"What do you mean?"

"When did helping Adrian become more than just a job for you? And when did homicide investigation become not just what he does, but something that you love, too?"

"Am I that transparent?"

"Maybe I'm just incredibly observant."

I finished my glass of wine and he quickly refilled it. That's when I realized we were already on our second bottle. I'd have to slow down or he'd be carrying me home, which, I have to admit, was beginning to have some appeal.

"I can't tell you exactly when Mr. Monk became family to me. It was a gradual thing. But you're right— whether I continue working with him or not, he'll always be in my life."

"So if you're that close, why do you call him Mr. Monk instead of Adrian?"

"Because he's my boss," I said.

"What if you stop working for him someday?"

"He'll always be Mr. Monk to me," I said. "Besides, he hates change."

"Maybe you're not so fond of it, either."

"You think Mr. Monk is influencing me?"

"I know he is," Jerry said. "Isn't that why you're interested in being a detective now, too?"

I shrugged. "Or maybe it's like you and crime scene cleaning. It was survival instinct. If I didn't find a way to invest myself emotionally and intellectually in my work, I wouldn't have been able to deal with the violent death I see day after day."

"Or maybe I was always meant to clean up awful messes and you were always meant to be a detective. We just didn't know it."

"You think it's our destiny," I said.

He shook his head. "I believe there are people who are great garage door installers, or bus drivers, or insurance salesmen, or whatever, and I'll bet you that ninety-five percent of them never intended to be in those jobs but love what they do and can't imagine doing anything else."

"So if it's not fate, then you're saying we just naturally drift into what we're best at," I said. "And then find a reason to invest ourselves in it so we can keep on doing it."

"We find our place in life and then, if we are very lucky, we find a way to love it."

"That sounds a lot like self-delusion to me."

"Isn't that what happiness is?"

"That's a cynical way of looking at it," I said.

"What did you expect from a guy who cleans up after murders, suicides, and natural deaths every day?"

I smiled. "Everything you've turned out not to be."

"I'll take that as a compliment," he said.

It was.

We chatted about this and that and flirted some more, and then he took me back home. It was nearly midnight when he walked me to my door. I thanked him for a wonderful evening.

"Does that mean you'd be open to doing it again sometime?" he asked.

"Very open," I replied with a smile.

"How does Friday night work for you? Or would that be moving too fast?"

"Friday it is," I said, gave him a kiss on the cheek, and went inside.

I felt ridiculously, childishly giddy about our first date. I really liked Jerry. I didn't know where things would go, but I liked how things were starting out.

I was heading to bed when I noticed that I'd left my laptop computer on. I went over to the table to turn it off and saw that I had a few new e-mails waiting for me. One of the e-mails was from the bike blogger. She'd heard from a Wheeler Wheels expert who'd identified the Dandelion Racer in my picture. It was made for Cantwells, a local, Northern California department store chain that went out of business in 1989.

I Googled Cantwells and discovered that, in their heyday in the 1970s, their southernmost store was in San Jose, their northernmost store was in Redding, and most of their stores were clustered in the Bay Area and the Sacramento area.

That would certainly help us narrow down where the photo was taken, unless, of course, they'd moved away from Northern California and had taken the bike with them.

Even so, I was pleased to have made a small step forward in my investigation. The day had ended up being a good one all around for me. I e-mailed the information to Ambrose and Yuki and went to bed.

# 14

# Mr. Monk Has a Chat

I was having my morning coffee and perusing the newspaper when I heard the sound of a motorcycle pulling into my driveway. I peeked out of my kitchen window and saw Yuki getting off her Harley.

I opened the front door and waited there for her as she came up the front walk, her helmet under one arm, a messenger sack slung over the other.

"What brings you out here?" I asked.

"I was coming into the city for our midweek shopping run anyway, so Ambrose thought it would be a good idea if I briefed you personally on what we've learned."

"Come on in," I said. "Would you like a cup of coffee?"

She walked past me into the living room. "That depends. Is it fresh ground or instant?"

"Instant," I said.

"Perfect," she said.

"You prefer instant over fresh ground?"

"I also prefer orange juice made from concentrate over fresh squeezed," she said. "Does that make me a freak?"

"It makes you far more likely to be satisfied with what I've got to offer guests. How do you like your coffee?"

"Black," she said. "I never sweeten anything."

She sat down at the kitchen table and set her pack and helmet on the seat beside her. I poured her a cup of coffee, refreshed my own, and sat down across the table from her.

"Because you don't like sugar?" I asked.

"Because I don't want to miss it if I can't have it," Yuki replied. "Besides, I think it's a good idea to take things as they are and not try to cut the bitterness with something else. I take the bitter as it comes."

"You're the first person I've ever met who takes a philosophical stand on coffee."

She sipped her coffee. "The truth is, I would have stopped by to see you anyway. I thought we should talk. Are you and I going to have any problems?"

Yuki posed the question casually, without the slightest trace of confrontation.

"Over what?" I asked, genuinely mystified.

"Ambrose."

"Not as long as you don't hurt him."

She smiled with relief. "I was afraid that maybe you disapproved of our relationship. Monk obviously does."

"Mr. Monk and I often have differing views about things," I said. "He'll come around eventually."

"Ambrose was more worried about you. He thought that maybe he'd broken your heart by hooking up with me."

"I adore Ambrose," I said, "but not romantically."

"You don't know what you're missing," she said. "But I'm glad you left the door open for me."

"Speaking of open doors, isn't it hard being involved with someone who won't step out of the house?"

"Since I've met Ambrose, I haven't wanted to leave the house, either." Yuki smiled coyly at me over the rim of her coffee cup. "Or the bed. He's the most amazing lover I've ever had."

It was hard for me to believe that someone who was so awkward around people, and who had very little social contact with anyone, much less women, could be a great lover. Perhaps my skepticism showed on my face, because Yuki spoke up again.

"Ambrose is attentive, sensitive, and he wrote the book on the female body," she said. "Literally."

"He wrote a sex book?"

"He wrote an anatomy book, sort of an owner's manual for women," she said. "I'm surprised you haven't read it."

"He only gave me his manuals for DVD players, hair dryers, and toasters."

"That's probably because he was afraid that you'd take it the wrong way."

"How did you take it?"

"We're going through it together, page by page," she said. "I'm making him show me how my body works."

That was more than I wanted to know. Far more. "If I were you, I wouldn't mention any of this to Mr. Monk."

"Is he a prude?"

"That's an understatement," I said. Then again, until that moment, I would have said the same thing about Ambrose.

Yuki reached into her messenger bag and pulled out an ultrathin laptop, which she set on the table and powered up.

"We found out a lot about that photo. Your lead about the bike was one more piece that makes us believe that the picture was taken in the Bay Area, Contra Costa County to be exact, sometime in the late 1970s or early 1980s."

"How did you zero in so fast on one particular county in the United States?"

She brought the photo up on-screen. "Well, for one thing, you told us that the bike was sold by Cantwells, which had stores in Contra Costa County. That's also where this house was built. Ambrose was able to determine this based on building codes, setbacks, sewergrate placement, etcetera."

"That's amazing," I said.

"Save your amazement, I'm just getting started. The house was constructed by Dalander Homes, a tract-home developer that went under in the 1990s. The house is a modified version of their standard Inglenook model and was featured in tracts that they built in the late 1970s all over the western United States, including a dozen in Contra Costa County. This could be a corner house in any of those tracts." Yuki took a folder out of her messenger bag and passed it across the table. "Here's a list of all of the Dalander developments in the Bay Area. The nurse's uniform was designed by Pablo Gallastegui in 1979 exclusively for Flax Uniforms of Cincinnati, Ohio. Hospitals all over the country used them, including four in the San Francisco Bay Area, two of which were in—"

She held back on the rest to give me a chance to pipe in.

"Contra Costa County," I said.

"Are you beginning to see a pattern here? Those hospitals are listed in the file, too."

"I can't thank you and Ambrose enough for doing all of this work for me," I said. "You've given me a lot to go on."

"It was fun," Yuki said. "Ambrose and I really enjoy this kind of research. So consider us your legmen and keep it coming."

"I will," I said.

Yuki stuffed the laptop back into her messenger bag and grabbed her helmet. "I've got to run. I have a million errands to do."

"Stop by anytime," I said.

I walked her to the door and watched her speed off on her Harley before I realized I was going to be late getting to Monk's. I stuffed her file into my bag, grabbed my car keys, and drove over to Monk's place.

I expected him to be waiting in the entry hall so he could confront me about my tardiness the instant I walked through the door, but he was in the kitchen when I arrived, blissfully cleaning the countertops. There were two plates with eight Wheat Thins arrayed around the edges, two bottles of Fiji water, and two glasses set out on the center island.

"Sorry I'm late," I said.

"It's okay. You had a long night." Monk attempted to wink, an action that anyone else but me would have mistaken for a facial tic or perhaps a stroke.

I gestured to the spread. "What's the special occasion?"

"It's been a while since we just sat and had a nice chat."

"What do you want to chat about?"

"Oh, I don't know. How about your date with Jerry, for instance?"

"It was nice," I said, and ate a Wheat Thin, just to be sociable.

"So, in other words, I was right," he said. "This is where you're supposed to thank me."

"Thank you, Mr. Monk," I said. "Satisfied? Now you can finally say that someone actually thanked you later."

"I want all the details."

"There's not much to tell," I said. "We had dinner. We talked. He took me home. End of story."

Monk opened a drawer, took out a legal pad and pen, and set them down in front of me.

"I want a full statement. Don't leave anything out. Penmanship counts."

He poured himself a glass of Fiji water, smelled the aroma, and then sipped it as if it were fine wine.

"I'm not giving you a statement, Mr. Monk. What I do on my dates is personal."

"Did you throw yourself at him?"

"No, of course not."

"Big mistake. You should have. He's a catch and you aren't getting any younger." He helped himself to a Wheat Thin, which seemed to spark a thought. "Or thinner."

"Thank you."

"You should get rid of all the unhealthy food in your house and start exercising. House cleaning is good exercise and, as a bonus, it also cleanses the mind and spirit. When are you seeing him again?"

"Friday night," I said.

He narrowed his eyes at me. "Why in God's name are you putting him off for so long?"

"It's the day after tomorrow."

Monk shook his head, dismayed. "Your cavalier attitude could cost you the best man to walk into your life since I've known you. Hopefully someone will die a messy death before Friday and I'll have the opportunity to talk you up to him. Otherwise, he might lose interest and get lured away by the first young vixen that walks by."

"You're going to clean with him again? I thought it was just a onetime thing."

"I liked it," Monk said. "It was very relaxing."

"You can't investigate murders and clean them up, too."

"Why not? It's all the same thing as far as I'm concerned."

"Because time spent cleaning up the crime scene is time not spent investigating the homicide. And if you do both, you will exhaust yourself," I said. "Besides, Captain Stottlemeyer is paying you and Jerry isn't."

"I could ask Jerry to pay me, but I'm afraid if I do, he might refuse, and then it would be awkward if I showed up to clean anyway. I suppose if that happened, I could always pay him."

I stared at Monk, hoping he'd sense my incredulity and disapproval, but as attuned as he was to the minute details of his environment, he was blind when it came to human expression.

"Why would you pay him so you can do the work that someone else is already paying him to do?" I asked.

"So he won't feel that he's taking advantage of me by not paying me."

I shook my head, twisted the cap off the Fiji water, and drank out of the bottle. I was beginning to wish I had an Advil to wash down with it.

"So you think it makes more sense for him to exploit you if you pay him to do it."

"Exactly," Monk said.

"No wonder you think I should be working for you for free," I said.

"Will you?"

"No," I said. "So what's on our investigative schedule for today? Do you have any leads to pursue on the thrift store killing?"

"Not yet," he said, savoring another cracker.

"Well, they won't come to you sitting here."

"I'm waiting for something to break. The manager, Casey Grover, was killed by a professional. This is one instance where the police are better able to flush out possible suspects and motives than I am. Once they do, I can come in, spot the inconsistencies in the suspects' stories, and reveal who the killer is."

I studied him, sitting there eating his crackers and sipping his water. He seemed pretty smug and pleased with himself to me.

"So what you're saying is that you'll let the police do all the scut work and then you'll stroll in and take the glory."

"Sounds like a good plan to me," Monk said.

"I can see why Lieutenant Devlin resents you."

"How's your little mystery going?"

"Do you have to be so condescending?"

"I don't know what you're talking about," he said.

"You called it a little mystery," I said.

"Because it is. The man died of natural causes. All you want to know is why he died here in San Francisco instead of Mexico. So how's that coming along?"

"I'm not telling you."

"Why not?"

"Because you'll probably solve it. This one is mine."

"That didn't stop you from sharing the details with Ambrose and his homicidal biker chick."

"Because I know they won't solve it."

"What makes you so sure?"

I wanted to say because I had a hunch that solving this mystery would require an understanding of human nature, something that Ambrose didn't have. But after what I'd learned from Yuki that morning, I was beginning rethink all of my long-held assumptions about him.

"Call it instinct," I said.

My cell phone rang and my instincts told me something else. Somebody in San Francisco had met a violent end.

# 15

## Mr. Monk and the Couch

The crime scene was a narrow, four-story Victorian home, one of six nearly identical houses that were crammed side by side and staggered in height along the steep, southwestern side of Castro Street.

It was only a few blocks away from the Noe Valley neighborhood where I lived, so I'd driven by and admired those homes a thousand times before, but I'd never imagined that someday I'd visit one of them to look at a corpse.

The victim's house was the same shade of yellow as the crime scene tape that cordoned off the property. The first floor was taken up by the tight, street-level garage and steps that led to the second-floor porch, the front door, and a bay window. The third floor had a matching bay window and a deck, while the fourth floor was essentially a windowed attic under a sharply arched roof. Both the third- and fourth-floor windows had nearly unobstructed views of the hilly neighborhoods to the west. The deck, porch, and cornices were adorned with flamboyant, white-painted fretwork.

I saw Lieutenant Devlin on the street, talking to an attractive young woman sitting in the back of an ambulance, a blanket wrapped around her. The woman had bloodshot eyes, pale skin, and tear-streaked cheeks, and clutched a bottle of Gatorade to her bosom as if it were a lifeline. It wasn't hard to deduce that she'd found the body and was in shock. Getting straight answers out of her wouldn't be easy.

Devlin acknowledged us with a quick glance and kept her attention focused on questioning the woman. We went inside the house. The entry hall was cramped, the ceiling was low, and the place was packed with forensic investigators and photographers. I immediately felt claustrophobic.

The first thing I noticed was that the place had been ransacked. Books, dishes, and artwork were scattered all over the floor. Even the refrigerator had been emptied, the food and drinks thrown everywhere.

Between the mess on the floor, and all the forensic investigators crammed inside the house, it was hard to move without brushing up against someone.

Monk drew himself inward as much as he could and tried to flatten himself against the wall as others passed, but he still couldn't completely escape bodily contact.

Captain Stottlemeyer came down the stairs and immediately noticed Monk's discomfort.

"Can we please clear the house for ten minutes?" he called out, his voice booming in the close quarters. "Everyone out except Monk and Natalie."

We stepped back outside onto the porch while everyone filed out, Monk gasping for breath as if he'd just been saved from drowning.

"Don't breathe so fast, you'll hyperventilate," I said, handing him a half dozen wipes before he could ask for them.

He immediately started swabbing his hands, face, and neck with the wipes. I held out a baggie for him and he dropped the used wipes inside.

Stottlemeyer joined us outside. "Sorry about that, Monk. The victim is upstairs in the second-floor bedroom. We'll go up whenever you are ready."

Monk nodded, still breathing hard. "What do we know about the victim?"

"His name is Mark Costa, he's twenty-nine years old, and he's a real estate appraiser who works out of his home." Stottlemeyer gestured to the woman who Devlin was talking to. "That's Mrs. Rachael Nunn. She had a ten a.m. appointment with Costa."

"The door was unlocked?" I asked.

"It was, but she also had a key. She and Costa were having an affair. She went upstairs to the bedroom expecting to have their usual morning tryst and she discovered his body. Her big concern now is keeping all of this from her husband."

"Maybe he already knows," I said. "Maybe he did the killing."

"It's possible. We're checking into his whereabouts right now," Stottlemeyer said, then glanced at Monk. "You ready?"

Monk nodded. The captain led us inside and up the stairs in silence, giving Monk a chance to detect in peace.

Now that we had the place to ourselves, I noticed the décor, which usually can tell you a lot about a person's life or personality.

The furniture was simple, an eclectic mix of contemporary, vintage, and thrift shop finds. Apparently,

Costa had blown his bank account on the house and didn't have much left over for furnishings. The artwork on the walls consisted of framed prints and the kind of knickknacks you'd find at any weekend sidewalk arts-and-crafts show. This told me that Costa saw his home merely as a shelter, perhaps even temporary. He wasn't someone who was ready to commit to one place or, perhaps, to any one person. I admit, though, that my last deduction may have been more than a little biased by what I'd already learned from Stottlemeyer about the guy.

The bedroom had gleaming hardwood floors, white walls, and a big, four-poster bed, angled to face the window and the terrific view.

Mark Costa was naked on the bed, a pillow over his face and a big kitchen knife deep in his chest. The white sheets were stained with blood, which had also dripped onto the floor and puddled there. It didn't seem possible that so much blood could come from one person.

"The ME puts the time of death around midnight," Stottlemeyer said. "Neighbors didn't hear a thing or notice any unusual activity."

Monk walked around the bed, his hands framing the scene in front of him in his usual fashion, tipping his head from side to side as he studied the gory tableau.

I glanced around the room. The drawers of the dresser had been pulled out and all the clothes thrown out onto the floor. The closet had been emptied, too.

"A jealous husband wouldn't waste time ransacking the house," I said. "Unless he wanted to make it look like a robbery."

"But there's no sign of a break-in and nothing of value appears to have been stolen," Stottlemeyer said. "There's also about a thousand dollars in cash and a lot of expensive gadgets and computer equipment still in the house."

"You said the door was unlocked when Costa's lover arrived," I said. "So that means that the killer may have had a key or was someone that Costa knew. Maybe it was another lover, upset that he was cheating on her with other women."

"That's a good theory," Stottlemeyer said. "It would also explain the mess—it's not a ransacking, it's explosive rage."

"What's upstairs?" I asked.

"More of the same," Stottlemeyer said. "Only without the bloodshed. I'll show you."

He led us up to the fourth floor. It was bright and airy, the front window and the skylights in the pitched ceiling filling the small space with sunshine. The low walls were lined with bookshelves, which gave the office a cozy feel, at least for me. Costa's desk and computer were facing the window, giving him the same great view from his desk that he had from his bed.

The only other piece of furniture in the room, a boxy red couch, had been slashed and gutted, the stuffing and springs scattered all over the floor. The couch seemed to have been designed to be stylish more than comfortable. It had that hard, sculpted, contemporary feel to it that made my shoulders and lower back ache just looking at it.

The couch must have been ripped up by one of Costa's lovers, or an angry husband, or anyone who'd ever tried to read a book or take a nap on it.

Monk cocked his head and headed back downstairs without a word to us. We followed him and were joined by Lieutenant Devlin, who'd just walked in the front door.

"Rachael Nunn is a mess," Devlin said.

"Just like this kitchen," Monk said. "And this entire house."

"She and Costa have been meeting once a week for a year, ever since he appraised her house," Devlin said. "She likes to stop by for a morning pick-me-up on her way to work and claims her husband knows nothing about it. And she wants to keep it that way."

"Where was her husband last night?" Stottlemeyer asked.

"Sleeping right beside her, or so she says. On the other hand, she has bad allergies and takes a couple of Benadryl tablets before she goes to bed at night. That would knock her out cold," Devlin said. "He could have left the house, killed Costa, and slipped right back into bed afterward without her knowing a thing."

"See if that's enough grounds for the DA to get us a search warrant," Stottlemeyer said.

"There goes her happy marriage," Devlin said.

"If it was so happy, she wouldn't have been playing around," Stottlemeyer said. "Does she know if Costa had other lovers?"

"She says he had plenty," Devlin replied. "He was a very popular appraiser."

Stottlemeyer turned back to Monk. "What's your take on all of this?"

"It's going to be a major cleanup job," he said.

"I meant about the murder."

"The blood has seeped onto the floor and probably between the floorboards," Monk said. "The whole floor might have to be pulled up and maybe the ceiling down here."

"You think there might be evidence under the floor?" Stottlemeyer asked.

"I think there might be blood," Monk replied.

"The killer's blood?"

"No," Monk said.

"Then why would we want to pull up the floor?"

"To clean it, of course," he said.

"I don't care about the mess, Monk, I care about catching the killer. What can you tell me about *that*?"

"You mean besides the fact that we're dealing with a serial killer?" Monk said. "Not much."

He made the comment in such a matter-of-fact way that it made his statement far more powerful than it would have been if he'd made a big, dramatic announcement.

"What makes you think that a serial killer did this?" Devlin asked.

"Because whoever did it has killed more than one person."

"Yes, we all know what *serial* means," Devlin said. "What we don't know is who else you think he's killed."

"Isn't it obvious?" Monk said. "The manager of that godforsaken hellhole you call a thrift store."

"That was an entirely different situation," she said.

"On the contrary, all the elements are the same. The killer either entered through a door that was left unlocked or he picked the lock without leaving a trace. Same as the thrift store. He didn't steal anything, at least not as far as we can tell, and didn't bring his own weapon, opting instead to use a knife that he found at the scene. Again, same as the thrift store. And he searched the premises, though this time it feels improvised and fueled by anger, as the level of destruction increased as the killer moved through the house."

Now that he'd laid it all out, the similarities were obvious to me, too, and I felt like a moron for not seeing them before. I'm sure Stottlemeyer and Devlin felt the same way.

At least Stottlemeyer was used to it and had developed protective scar tissue around his ego. But for Devlin, each time it happened was a fresh slap in the face.

Her reaction was anger, probably directed more at herself than at Monk. I figured that after her many years working undercover, each mistake revealed to her a personal weakness that could get her killed.

Stottlemeyer sighed. "So the big questions are is he picking his victims at random or is there a connection between them? And what the hell is he looking for?"

"*If* it is a serial killer," Devlin said, "perhaps what he is searching for is a particular kind of souvenir, something that has no apparent value to any of us but is enormously significant and symbolically meaningful for him."

"You missed the biggest question of all," I said. "Both killings have been in the same general neighborhood—*mine*. What I want to know is if he's going to strike again."

"He will," Devlin said and gestured to the broken dishes, spilled food, and open drawers. "Looking at that, I'd say he's unsatisfied. Whatever he wanted from this killing he didn't get."

"The least he could have done was straighten up before he left," Monk said.

Devlin stared at him. "He smothered a man with a pillow and impaled him to a mattress with a butcher knife. And you're upset that he didn't clean up after himself?"

"Aren't you?" Monk said, then turned to Stottlemeyer. "How soon can you wrap up here so we can start cleaning?"

"We?" Stottlemeyer said.

"I've been helping out the crime scene cleaners," Monk said. "Just for fun."

"We don't pay you to have fun, Monk. We pay you to solve murders. That should be your priority."

"It absolutely is," he said. "So when do you think you'll be releasing the scene?"

"It's a big mess in tight quarters and the forensic team just got started. They probably won't be done until late this afternoon. That gives you most of the day to do some actual work, like, you know, helping us catch a serial killer."

The captain walked out and Devlin followed him. I turned to Monk.

"Told you so," I said.

# 16

## Mr. Monk and the Missing Piece

There wasn't much for Monk to do. As I've said before, performing the backaching, shoe-leather-grinding, butt-in-the-chair basics of investigative work wasn't one of his skills, though it was clear to me that his brother excelled at it.

I was still marveling at all the information Ambrose had managed to glean, and so quickly, from a single photograph of the nurse and the little girl. Genius was a quality that seemed to run in the Monk family, though it was offset by psychological problems of equal scale.

I'd come to the conclusion that Monk's detecting style, his nearly crippling obsessive-compulsive disorder aside, was based on observing people's actions and the placement of things around him. He relied almost entirely on discrepancies in the environment and in an individual's behavior as the basis for his deductions.

That dry, analytical explanation might make what Monk does sound simple and even easy, but as you've probably gathered already, it's not. It's a gift and, as Monk was fond of saying, also a curse.

But at that particular moment, stuck in police head-quarters, we were both cursed.

Ostensibly, Stottlemeyer wanted Monk there to assist in the investigation. But Monk had nothing to contribute at this early stage, and I had even less.

So he began passing the time by sweeping floors, and I read old issues of *American Police Beat* while the detectives dug into the backgrounds of Casey Grover, the thrift store manager, and Mark Costa, the real estate appraiser, to see where their paths may have intersected with each other and with that of a serial killer.

Meanwhile, Devlin went through the motions of checking Costa's many lovers and their spouses and significant others to confirm their whereabouts during the killings, rule them out as suspects, and to see if they might have had a connection with Grover.

Monk and I observed as some of those people were brought in and questioned, we read some of the forensics reports, and we were generally about as useful to the investigation as two potted plants.

But after that brief flurry of detecting excitement, Monk busied himself dusting, emptying trash cans, and organizing the squad room while what he really wanted to do was get over to Costa's house and help Jerry and his team clean up.

I decided to take advantage of the situation. I sat myself at an empty desk in homicide and used the phone to call the hospitals on Yuki's list.

At each hospital, I asked for the personnel director and then asked that person if I could speak to any doctors, nurses, technicians, or custodial staff who'd been working at that facility since the late 1970s or early 1980s.

I contacted those employees, then asked if I could show them the photo of the nurse, either in person or by e-mail, to see if anyone recognized her or the girl on the bike.

Once I got their e-mail addresses, I told them I'd be in touch soon and gave them my cell phone number and the phone number of my temporary desk in police headquarters.

I knew, of course, that by doing so, that I was implying that I was a police officer even though I was careful not to claim that I actually was one. I simply said that I was Natalie Teeger, that I was trying to identify a dead man, and that I was calling from the homicide department of the San Francisco Police Department, all of which was true.

Was it also deceptive?

Yeah, it probably was.

But it was also something that Thomas Magnum or Jim Rockford would have done in my position, so that made it okay.

My cleverness paid off almost immediately. Many of the personnel directors or employees that I contacted called me back within minutes through the SFPD switchboard on the pretense of confirming my e-mail address or some other insignificant detail, when, in fact, they were really just double-checking that I wasn't some scammer.

Which, of course, I was, but kudos to them for making the effort to unmask me.

I was heading toward Stottlemeyer's office, preparing to argue that keeping us there was a waste of our time, when he bolted out, nearly colliding with me.

"There's been another murder," he said.

"Is it connected?" I asked.

Stottlemeyer glanced past me at Monk, who was

making his way over to us. "He can tell me when we get there. All I know is that the victim is a young woman, she was killed in her home, and it's near Twenty-third and Vicksburg."

That was only a few blocks away from the thrift shop, Costa's place, and my house. So I didn't really care whether or not it was the same killer. Three people had been murdered practically right outside my door, and that was too close for comfort. Until this killer was caught, I'd be sleeping with my doors locked and a baseball bat beside my bed.

We weren't usually at police headquarters when a homicide call came in. It was a bit like being at a fire station when the alarm goes off, only there were no poles to slide down and no uniforms to put in a hurry.

And although we were off to see a corpse rather than rescue anyone in immediate danger of becoming one, we still left the police station in a rush, sirens wailing, faces taut with grim determination.

Except for Monk, who seemed preternaturally relaxed, totally distanced from the urgency and seriousness of the situation.

But show the man spilled milk, a crooked picture, or a shelf of unalphabetized books, and he'd jump on those situations as if he were preventing the imminent release of poison gas in a nursery school.

The crime scene was a house on Twenty-third Street, a half block east of Vicksburg at Nellie Street, which was basically a long alley that somebody had actually bothered to name.

When we got there, the paramedics were sitting in their unit out front, waiting to deliver their official report that the woman inside wasn't merely dead, but really most sincerely dead.

There were also two police officers at the scene. One of them stood at the front door while another unfurled crime scene tape around the house, which looked like someone had lopped off the top three floors of Costa's place, dropped them on the corner, stripped off the fretwork, and painted everything powder blue.

Stottlemeyer approached the officer at the door, a woman built like a wrestler. From her physique, I wondered for a moment if *she* might have once been a *he*, which wasn't entirely outside the realm of possibility, especially in San Francisco.

"Howdy, Claire," Stottlemeyer said. "How are your feet?"

"Sore as hell, Captain. Have been since the day I left the academy."

Devlin spoke up before Stottlemeyer could.

"When they stop hurting, that's when you know you're sitting on your ass too much and it's time to retire." Stottlemeyer and Claire both looked at her. Devlin shrugged, almost sheepishly. "I trained under Captain Hudson at the academy, too, right before he traded in his gold shield for a fishing pole."

Claire didn't appreciate the intrusion on her little ritual with the captain. She turned to him and asked him a question that made her feelings very clear.

"Have you heard from Randy lately?"

"You mean the chief," Stottlemeyer said. "That's what he likes to be called now. We spoke a couple of days ago. He's leading a crackdown on scofflaws who chain their bikes to trees on the mean streets of Summit."

"I'd trade those streets for this one any day," she said, tipping her head toward the house. "This is some ugly stuff."

"Tell us about it," Stottlemeyer said and we all gathered closer around the officer.

"The victim is Cheryl Strauss. Twenty-nine years old, single, a sales associate at a clothing store. She lived at this address for only a few months," Claire said. "The mailman was crouching down, trying to shove some big magazines through her mail slot, happened to catch a peek inside and saw it."

"It?" Devlin said.

Claire took out her nightstick and used it to nudge open the front door of the apartment behind her.

The door swung slowly into the living room, almost like a curtain opening on a stage.

And there, draped on her back over the coffee table, her arms and legs bound to it with tie strips, was Cheryl Strauss, covered with cigarette burns and knife slashes, her mouth duct taped shut, a clear plastic bag over her head, her dead eyes staring past us into the abyss.

I didn't have to be a medical examiner to know that she'd been tortured and asphyxiated.

It was a shocking sight that galvanized everyone except Monk, who stepped past all of us and went into the room. He walked right up to her, his head cocked at an angle, his hands out in front of him, framing the gruesome image along with the matched red chairs that were at either end of the table.

And then he lowered his hands, turned around, and faced the three of us. He rolled his shoulders and tugged his sleeves.

"This is a four-piece living room set," Monk said.

Devlin marched angrily into the room, careful not to step on the mail on the floor.

"There's a woman in front of you who suffered an agonizing, horrific death and all you can see is the living room set? What the hell is wrong with you, Monk?"

"It's what I'm not seeing that matters," he said.

"Yes, exactly," Devlin said. "Try to focus on what really means something."

Monk nodded and said, "The matching couch that's missing from the set."

"No, Monk, the life that was taken here. *That's* what matters. What difference does a couch make compared to that?"

"Because it's the couch that she donated to Casey Grover's thrift shop and that Mark Costa bought for his home office," Monk said. "And it's the couch that got them all killed."

# 17

## Mr. Monk Has a Theory

Well, that certainly put things in a new perspective, at least for Captain Stottlemeyer and me. We'd learned a long time ago that whenever Monk made a totally ridiculous assertion, like saying that three people were murdered over a thrift store couch, we had to take it seriously.

Devlin hadn't learned that yet. All she heard was the absurdity of Monk's statement, and she couldn't get past it. I could sympathize with Devlin's difficulties, since I still had to make a conscious effort to look for the sense in Monk's theories.

So while the captain and I mulled what Monk said, she fought him.

"You don't know the couch has anything to do with these killings," Devlin said.

"Yes, I do," Monk said.

"That same living room set could be in a thousand homes," Devlin said. "Just because she and Costa both own a few pieces doesn't mean there's a connection."

"They're both dead and they both lived within a few blocks of each other and the thrift store. That's three more connections."

"And maybe they both have a six-pack of Diet Coke in their refrigerators, or own clothing made by Ralph Lauren, or have Visio flat-screen TVs. And maybe so do a hundred other people within a square mile of here. That doesn't mean they are connected to each other. It means they bought some of the same mass-produced, widely sold products. Let's not jump to conclusions until we have facts."

The captain spoke up. "My gut tells me Monk is right, but you make a valid point, Amy. So after you've processed this crime scene, go back to the office and prove Monk wrong. Look at the records we pulled from the thrift shop and see if Strauss' or Costa's name comes up."

"Where are you going?" she asked.

"Back to Costa's to get that damn couch."

Stottlemeyer headed back to his car. Monk and I went with him.

Devlin called out after us. "Maybe it's made of gold and upholstered in dinosaur hide."

Monk shook his head and whispered to me, "That's just not possible. Dinosaurs have been extinct for millions of years. Nobody has found one of their hides and certainly wouldn't upholster a piece of furniture with it if they did. It would be in a museum. She's being silly."

"Yes, she is," I said. "But at least she's not threatening to shoot you."

"That's true," Monk said. "So this is progress."

We got in the backseat of Stottlemeyer's car and he immediately hit the siren and floored it, pinning us against our seats and burning rubber as he sped from the curb.

I think the captain got a rush out of it and so did I, and not just because I found the speed exhilarating. I wanted to get as far away from that gruesome scene as fast as I could.

But Monk was terrified. He sat with his feet pressed against the back of the seat in front of him, one hand gripping the armrest on the door, the other clutching the strap of his seat belt.

As Stottlemeyer drove, he called the forensics unit and sent them back to Costa's house to confiscate the couch.

"Slow down," Monk said. "There's no hurry."

"I already released Costa's house to the crime scene cleaners," Stottlemeyer said. "We've got to get there before they touch that couch."

Monk turned to me. "Call them. Quickly. Before we're killed in a traffic accident."

I took out my phone and called Jerry. He picked up almost immediately. "Hey, Jerry, it's Natalie."

"It's great to hear your voice," he said. "I was just thinking about you. The truth is, I've been thinking about you all day."

"That's sweet," I said, very much aware that both Stottlemeyer and Monk were eavesdropping. "I'm on my way over to Mark Costa's house with Mr. Monk and Captain Stottlemeyer. We think the couch in Costa's office may be evidence in his murder. You haven't done anything with it yet, have you?"

"No, we haven't," he said. I could hear the disappointment in his voice that I wasn't calling just to be sociable. "It hasn't been touched."

"Great, we'll be right there," I said, and then added,

as quickly and quietly as I could, "I'm looking forward to it."

"Me, too," he said, perking up.

I dropped my phone back in my purse. Monk smiled with approval and Stottlemeyer stole a curious glance at me in the rearview mirror.

I pretended not to notice their interest. "The couch is secure."

"Good," Stottlemeyer said. He slowed down as a courtesy to Monk but kept the siren on so we wouldn't have to creep along in stop-and-go traffic.

Jerry was waiting for us on the curb outside of Costa's place when we arrived. He was in his Tyvek suit, only without the hood, goggles, and mask.

He smiled at me as the three of us got out of the car.

"Hello, Natalie, Adrian." Jerry turned to the captain and offered an ungloved hand. "I'm Jerry Yermo, Captain. I've been following your work for years."

That seemed to be Jerry's stock greeting to detectives, but it was also a statement of fact.

The captain shook hands with Jerry. "Leland Stottlemeyer. Monk speaks very highly of you."

"The feeling is mutual," Jerry said. "If you don't mind me asking, what's so special about that couch?"

"That's what we'd like to know," Stottlemeyer said. "The CSI guys will be down here in a few minutes to take it back to the lab, but I'd like to take another look at it beforehand."

"Be my guest," Jerry said. "Would you like a biohazard suit?"

"No, thanks," Stottlemeyer said.

"I would," Monk said.

Stottlemeyer rolled his eyes. "I'll meet you inside."

"I will, too," I said.

"You both really should wear a suit," Jerry said to

us. "Not just now, but every time you enter a crime scene where bodily fluids have been spilled."

"I'll keep that in mind," Stottlemeyer said in a way that made it clear that what he was *really* saying was "No way in hell."

I knew Jerry was probably right, but I'd survived walking into a hundred crime scenes already without being clad in a bulky and uncomfortable biohazard suit, so I was pretty sure I'd be okay now.

I gave Jerry a smile and walked behind the captain as he went up the steps to the front door.

"Why did you smile at him?" Stottlemeyer asked.

"I'm a polite person," I said.

"You got something going with him?"

"We had dinner last night," I said. "It's not something yet."

"But you're hoping it will be," Stottlemeyer said, pausing at the door.

"I'll see how things go," I said.

"You really want Monk and a crime scene cleaner in your life?" Stottlemeyer asked, heading inside. "You haven't endured enough incessant nagging about dirt and germs for one lifetime already?"

"Jerry isn't as bad about it as Mr. Monk."

"That doesn't make it any less irritating, especially if you're getting it 24/7."

"I already am."

"But not in stereo," he said.

We walked in and I waved at Corinne, who was in her suit and cheerfully picking up rotten food off the floor in the kitchen with her gloved hands. She waved enthusiastically back at me.

"What's her problem?" Stottlemeyer whispered to me.

"She enjoys her work," I said.

"That *is* a problem. She and Monk should date."

"The idea has already been raised."

"By Monk?"

"By me," I said.

"If that happens, and you hit it off with Jerry, your life will be a sanitary, germless, spotless hell."

"I hadn't thought of it that way," I said.

We went on upstairs to the bedroom, where Gene and William, fully clad in their biohazard suits and looking like astronauts, were wrapping the bloody mattress in plastic and sealing it with duct tape. They acknowledged us with a nod and kept working as we continued up to the top floor.

The only change since we'd left was the presence of fingerprint powder everywhere, left over from the forensics team.

The two of us stood in front of the trashed couch and silently regarded the loose stuffing, the exposed springs, and the torn upholstery. I crouched and examined the metal framing. Maybe there was gold underneath the layer of chrome, but I doubted it.

That's when Monk joined us, wearing the full biohazard suit, respirator mask and all.

The captain glanced at him and shook his head, which was his only comment on the suit. He knew as well as I did that there was no point arguing with Monk about it.

"So your theory is that the killer broke into the thrift store to find out who bought Cheryl's couch and tracked it here."

"Yes," Monk said, his voice filtered through his mask.

"Have you got any ideas what makes this couch so special?" Stottlemeyer asked.

"Only that it was part of a matched set. Perhaps it

was Cheryl breaking up the set that made the man snap and go on a killing spree."

"I can't see that," Stottlemeyer said.

"Think about it. Maybe this isn't the first set of something that she's broken."

"I still don't see it."

"What if she gave away half of her bedroom set? Or lost the salt shaker from a matching pair of salt-and-pepper shakers? Or willfully split up a pair of book-ends? Surely you can see how, over time, someone close to her could have been driven insane by that kind of irrational behavior."

"You've certainly made me frustrated enough to want to shoot someone, but that someone has always been you," Stottlemeyer said. "So why did he kill the thrift store manager?"

"Because our mystery man didn't want to get caught breaking and entering," Monk said.

"But he was okay with murder?" I asked.

"He was insane and, as I said before, an experienced criminal," Monk said. "That's a lethal combination."

"Okay," Stottlemeyer said. "So why kill Costa?"

"Maybe when the killer came here to get the couch back, he discovered that Costa had permanently stained it," Monk said. "And that drove him into a murderous rage."

"Over a stain," I said.

"I don't condone his actions, Natalie, but I can certainly understand them."

"I'm sure you can," Stottlemeyer said. "But there's a big hole in your theory, Monk. If you're right, why was Strauss his *last* victim and not his *first*?"

Monk rolled his shoulders and shifted his weight as if he wasn't just mulling the question, but also checking its balance as he carried the thought.

Jerry came in behind Monk. He was in his suit but hadn't bothered to put his hood and mask on. I think that's because I was there and it's hard to flirt with a respirator on your face.

"So this is the couch you're all so interested in. I don't see what the big deal is."

"Neither do we," I said.

"Why did he rip it up if it's so special?" Jerry asked.

Monk cocked his head from side to side and regarded the couch anew. "Because it's not."

"Now you're saying the couch *isn't* the connection?" Stottlemeyer asked.

"It definitely is. But you were right that there was a flaw in my theory. The killer wasn't after the couch itself," Monk said. "He was after what was *in* it."

# 18

## Mr. Monk Closes the Case

"Like what?" Stottlemeyer asked. "Drugs? Jewelry? Cash? Microchips? Bonds?"

"I have no idea," Monk said. "But I believe there was something very valuable hidden in the couch and he wanted it back. He went to Cheryl's to get it but discovered that she'd donated the couch to the thrift shop without knowing it contained his valuable item."

"So he broke into the store to find out who bought the couch and tracked it here," Stottlemeyer said.

Monk nodded. "I think the first thing he did was kill Costa when he came in and then went to the couch to retrieve his object. But it was gone. When he didn't find it in the couch, or elsewhere in the house, he assumed that Cheryl had it all along. So he went back and tortured her into telling him where it was and then killed her."

"It's still speculation," Stottlemeyer said, "but it makes a lot more sense than the stain theory."

"I think they are on equal footing," Monk said.

"Maybe the lab guys will find some trace of the valuable object in the couch or its stuffing," Stottlemeyer said. "Meanwhile, we'll dig into Cheryl's life and see if we can find out the identity of this mystery person who was close enough to her to use her couch as a safe."

"I've heard of stuffing money in your mattress," Jerry said, "but never in your couch."

"Maybe she had a water bed," I said.

Jerry laughed. "I hadn't thought of that."

Stottlemeyer sighed. "Okay, I think we're done here."

"I'd like to stay and help them clean up for a while," Monk said.

"We're in the middle of a murder investigation, Monk."

"Can't I stay for even a little while?"

Jerry sighed. "I appreciate your enthusiasm, Adrian, but actually it's probably better if you go. It looks like we're going to have to pull up the hardwood floor in the bedroom, and that's more of a demolition and construction job than a cleanup anyway. No offense intended, but it's a tight space here as it is, and the fewer people around the better."

"I understand," Monk said, slouching with disappointment. "Could I at least stay and help Corinne clean up the kitchen while the captain drives Natalie back to the station to get her car?"

Jerry nodded. "Of course."

Monk practically ran down the stairs before Jerry could change his mind.

"I've never met anyone who liked cleaning so much," Jerry said.

"Consider yourself lucky," Stottlemeyer said and walked out, leaving Jerry and me alone for a moment.

"You look great," he said.

"So do you," I said. "You wear that biohazard suit like it's a tuxedo."

"That's good to know, because this is what I was planning on wearing Friday night."

"Oddly enough, so was I," I said.

"You'd look good in a burlap sack," he said.

"That was my second choice." I gave him a smile and headed for the stairs before he could start another round of flirtation. I can only take that kind of banter in small doses, mainly because I'm not creative enough to keep up my end.

I went outside and got into the car with Stottlemeyer, and we went back to the station.

I picked up Monk forty-five minutes later outside of Costa's place and dropped him off at his apartment. By then it was early evening, so I called it a day and Monk didn't argue with me about it.

I went home and immediately fired up my laptop and began e-mailing the picture of the nurse and the little girl to the contacts that I'd made at the Bay Area hospitals. With luck, someone would recognize her and I'd have my first real break in my investigation.

I blasted a Lean Cuisine in the microwave and picked at it while watching one mindless situation comedy after another, *mindless* being the key word.

I'd put myself in a primetime TV trance, turning off my mind for a few hours so my brain could work in the background, rendering the horrific images I'd seen that day, stripping them of their emotional impact, and filing them for detached analysis.

After two hours of snappy insults, wacky neighbors, bright lights, and computer-generated laughter, I shuffled off to bed and immediately fell into a deep, dreamless sleep.

*          *          *

Getting up in the morning took a conscious effort. I felt like my entire body was encased in concrete. I took a hot shower that bordered on scalding, drank a gallon of coffee sweetened with a pound of sugar, and avoided the newspaper. I wasn't ready to read about the homicide scene that I'd experienced firsthand, or any number of atrocities worldwide that I was lucky enough to have missed.

Instead I went to my laptop to see if anybody had replied to my e-mail blast. I had one response from Dr. Everett Long, a pediatrician at Alta Bates Hospital in Berkeley, who said that he recognized the nurse and was willing to meet me to discuss it.

I was excited by the news but it pissed me off a little, too. Why couldn't he just tell me who she was? Why did he have to hold back the information until we met? What was there to discuss that he couldn't simply tell me in an e-mail?

I sent him a quick reply, letting him know that I would be in touch soon to set up a time to meet. I was hoping there would be no immediate developments in the couch case, that Monk wouldn't need me, and that I could see Dr. Long that morning, but those hopes were quashed when my cell phone rang.

It was Captain Stottlemeyer, who wanted to see us right away in his office. At least I wouldn't be starting the day off with another corpse.

I picked up Monk and we headed downtown. On the way, I asked him how he'd spent his night. He told me that he'd had a very relaxing evening emptying his kitchen cabinets and cleaning them. I'm sure that he had been just as zoned out cleaning as I'd been while watching those lousy sitcoms, and probably for the same reason. At least he had something to show for it.

We found Stottlemeyer and Devlin in the captain's office. He was leaning back in his desk chair and she was sitting on his beaten-up vinyl couch. They were both wearing the same clothes we'd seen them in yesterday and looked like they hadn't slept at all.

"You two should get some rest," I said.

"After we catch this guy," Stottlemeyer said, rubbing his eyes.

"Are you any closer?"

Stottlemeyer glanced at Devlin, who took that as her cue.

"We know everything except where we can find him," Devlin said. "And I owe you an apology, Monk."

"I knew you'd realize the importance of flossing and good dental hygiene," Monk said.

"I'm talking about the case," she said. "You were right. It's all about the couch. Cheryl Strauss donated the couch to the thrift shop when she moved from a larger place to her smaller, current residence. Mark Costa bought the couch from the thrift store a few weeks later with his credit card, a transaction that was logged in the thrift shop's computer."

"So what was in the couch?" I asked.

"That's where it gets interesting," Stottlemeyer said. "It turns out Cheryl Strauss' ex-boyfriend is Rico Ramirez, a nasty piece of work with a long history of violent assaults, most recently jumping diamond merchants, beating them nearly to death, and taking their stones. He got nabbed and was sent to prison five years ago, but most of the diamonds from his last job were never found, about half a million dollars' worth. Now we know where they were."

"Cheryl Strauss had no idea she was sitting on a fortune in diamonds when she gave away that couch," Devlin said. "But you can imagine how pissed off Rico was when he got out of prison two weeks ago, looked her up, and found out his stash was gone."

"How did Ramirez get out of prison so soon?" Monk asked.

Stottlemeyer sighed and tapped a file on his desk. "He was paroled as part of the settlement in a class action lawsuit leveled by the ACLU against the state over the extreme overcrowding and inhumane conditions in our prisons."

"Apparently, a prison sentence is supposed to be like an extended vacation at Club Med," Devlin said. "The next thing you know, the ACLU is going to say it's a human rights violation if prisoners don't have satellite television, Jacuzzis in their cells, and meals prepared by Gordon Ramsey."

Monk rolled his shoulders. "Why did Ramirez kill Cheryl Strauss?"

"I'm glad you asked," Stottlemeyer said. "We've got a couple of possibilities to run by you. Here's one: she tells Ramirez that she gave the couch away. He goes after it, kills Costa, and rips up the couch. But the diamonds aren't there and then it hits him—he's just killed the one guy who could have told him where they are. That was a dumb move and it really hurt."

"More for Costa than for Ramirez," I said.

"But Ramirez isn't the kind of guy who takes disappointment well or can live with looking like a fool. He'd want to make somebody pay," Stottlemeyer said. "It's too late to do anything more to Costa, so he goes back to see Cheryl and takes his fury out on her. That's scenario number one."

"For scenario number two, we've got to go back to what's going through Ramirez's mind when he's ripping up Costa's couch and doesn't find the diamonds," Devlin said. "He's thinking, yeah, maybe Costa found them and hid them someplace. Or maybe Cheryl lied to him, maybe she found the diamonds years ago and sent him off on a pointless search and is laughing her ass off right now. The more he thinks about it, the more he believes Cheryl has screwed him. So he goes back to her place, tortures her until she reveals where she's hidden the diamonds, and then kills her. Now he's out there someplace with a fortune in diamonds he's got to fence."

Monk nodded. "Both theories make sense. It could be either one."

"Yeah, that's what I figured," Stottlemeyer said. "It doesn't really matter at this point which theory is correct. We know Ramirez is our guy. We just have to find him."

"What can I do to help?" Monk asked.

"You've done your job, Monk. The mystery is solved. We know how and why these three people were killed. All that's left now is for us to chase the guy down."

It sounded easier said than done to me. "How are you going to do that?"

"We've got a list of his known associates and previous haunts," Devlin said. "Plus, if he's got the diamonds and wants to convert them into cash, he's going to have to fence them. We've got our eye on the fences with the connections to pull that off."

"Maybe he's left San Francisco by now," I said.

"That's possible, and we've put the word out to other law enforcement agencies," Stottlemeyer said. "But my guess is that he's going to hunker down on familiar turf."

"It's also mine," Devlin said. "If he's hiding on these streets, I will flush him out and take him down."

I had no doubt that she would. She actually seemed excited about it. No doubt she was happy to finally be working in her comfort zone, one far outside of Monk's.

"We'll let you know how it goes," Stottlemeyer said. That was his polite way of throwing us out of his office so they could get back to work.

I was glad to be done with the case and relieved that there were no other homicides demanding Monk's attention or my own. It meant that I could concentrate on solving the mystery of Jack Griffin.

Monk was already restless by the time we got to the car. "What are we going to do today?"

"We've just come off a couple intense days of investigating three back-to-back murders. I think we can take the day off."

"What would I do with a day off?"

"You could relax," I said.

"What are you going to do?"

"This and that."

"I could do this and that with you."

The last thing I wanted was Monk joining me on my investigation because then it wouldn't be mine anymore. He'd solve it in five minutes.

"I've got a lot of errands to run that I haven't had a chance to do for a while."

"I like errands, especially if there's a list of tasks that must be completed."

"Okay, great. Let's make a list. Our first stop is Macy's. My bras are getting pretty ragged and I need a couple of new ones, maybe some panties, too. Then we can swing by Rite Aid and pick up a new razor for my legs, some skin cream, and I'm running low on tampons—"

Monk covered up his ears. "Never mind. Drop me off. You didn't say it would be those kinds of this and that."

"What do you mean?"

"The activities women are supposed to do on their own, in secret and in silence, preferably in the dead of night."

I'd achieved my goal, but I couldn't resist challenging him, only because it might create suspicion if I didn't.

"I'm not ashamed that I need undergarments and toiletries, Mr. Monk. Would you prefer women went without them?"

"I'd prefer never to hear about it," Monk said.

"Like pregnancy and birth," I said.

Monk shuddered. "It's sickening."

"It's magical," I said.

"As long as you don't have to see it, think about it, or experience it."

"We've all experienced it, Mr. Monk. How do you think you got here?"

"I don't think about it," Monk said. "But I have been trying hard to forget it."

# 19

# Mr. Monk's Assistant Investigates

Dr. Everett Long's office in the pediatric department was barely larger than a closet and was stuffed with files. He sat behind a chipped wooden desk and was wearing a starched white lab coat with his name embroidered on its breast pocket. He had a stethoscope draped around his neck, though it seemed to me that he wore it more like a fashion accessory than as a necessary tool of his trade.

He was an old man, his wrinkled skin making his face look like a melting wax mask that was slowly dripping off his skull. His bifocals were perched on the edge of his bulbous nose as he squinted at the original photograph of the nurse and her daughter, then up at me, sitting across the desk from him.

"What do you want to know about her?" he asked, handing me back the photo.

"Her name, for starters, and anything else you can tell me." The office was so cramped that my knees were pressed against the front of his desk.

"Her name was Stacey O'Quinn and she was a nurse here with me in the pediatric department for two or three years. I think it was around 1980. All the years tend to blur together when you get to be my age."

I wrote her name on my notepad, not because I was afraid that I would forget it, but because I needed to force myself to remain calm and professional. What I really wanted to do was cheer and stomp my feet over my first real bit of progress.

"What can you tell me about Stacey?"

"She was a hard worker, great with kids, but didn't socialize much with the staff, so nobody knew that much about her life at first. Turns out she didn't know too much about it, either."

"What do you mean by that?"

"Hold your horses," he said irritably. "I'm getting to that."

I didn't think my question was out of line, but I was beginning to understand why he'd summoned me across the bay to Berkeley. He wanted an audience, someone to talk to. I wondered how long he'd been stuck in that closet, ignored by the rest of the staff, craving some attention. I'd just have to be patient and play my part. I could do that.

"I'm sorry, Doctor, please go on."

"All we really knew about Stacey, outside of her work, was that she was married, had a five-year-old daughter, lived in a new house out in Walnut Creek, and took BART into Berkeley every day. Then her husband was killed."

I took the momentary silence as my cue to ask the required question to spur him along. "What happened?"

"His name was Walter O'Quinn and he was an insurance salesman by trade. I only know that, and everything else I'm about to tell you, because of what I read in the papers later. Anyway, he was something of a boating enthusiast, and one weekday morning, while his wife was working and their daughter, Rose, was in school, he took the day off and went out sailing."

As soon as Dr. Long mentioned boating, my pulse quickened. Jack Griffin worked around boats, too. There was a question I was dying to ask, but I forced myself to bide my time, not to jump ahead, to let the doctor spin his tale at his own pace.

"He told some friends at the marina that he was taking a little jaunt out toward the Farrallon Islands, which are about twenty-five miles outside the Golden Gate," Dr. Long continued. "It was a nice day, clear skies, calm seas, no reason for concern. Some fellow sailors he knew saw him trailing a school of dolphins about fifteen miles out. He waved at his friends and had a big smile on his face, a man at peace with the world."

I could guess what Dr. Long was building up to, and it made my question only more urgent. But I bit my tongue. Literally. If I'd bitten it any harder, it would have bled.

"But when he didn't come back by nightfall, Stacey called the coast guard. They mounted a massive search-and-rescue mission, but no sign of the boat was found. No wreckage, no life vests, nothing."

"And no body, either?"

That was the question I was so eager to ask, but I already knew what the answer would be.

"Nope," Dr. Long said.

Call me cynical, but at that moment, I thought I had a pretty good idea who Jack Griffin really was. I wrote *Walter O'Quinn* down on my notepad, circled it, and underlined it twice.

"You said something about Stacey not really knowing who she was," I said.

"No, that's not what I said. Check your notes. What I said was that she didn't know much about her life. There's a difference."

"I stand corrected."

"After her husband drowned, she discovered that his business had gone belly-up, that they were massively in debt, and that their boat and their house were about to be seized by the bank. Her life was a sham, only she didn't know it. The whole story was in the papers."

I made a note to look up the articles on the Internet.

"So Walter committed suicide," I said, though I already knew that wasn't true.

"Nobody could prove it, but whether he did or not, the presumption was strong enough that the insurance company negated his life insurance policy," Dr. Long said. "One day, Stacey simply packed up her things, yanked her daughter out of school, and left."

"To go where?"

Dr. Long shrugged. "Nobody has heard from or seen her since. That was over twenty years ago."

"Do you think she could still be in the Bay Area?"

"Could be," he said. "Or she could be in Madagascar for all I know. What difference does it make now?"

"I'm not sure," I said. "But I think it was important to the man who died a few days ago."

"You think he was Walter O'Quinn, don't you?"

"He was an American with false identification who worked on boats down in Mexico . . . and he was holding this picture when he died," I held it up again to underscore my point. "Either he was Walter O'Quinn or someone with close ties to him."

"It's a mystery," he said.

"Yes, it is," I said and stood up. "Thank you so much for your help, Doctor."

"Will you let me know how it all turns out?"

I smiled. "Of course I will."

But when I did, I'd be sure to take my sweet time revealing the solution.

I was only a few blocks from Julie's dorm, and if I was a good mother, I would have stopped by to see her. But the truth is, I was far too caught up in the case. I wouldn't be able to sit still through a cup of coffee, much less an entire meal, knowing the answers to my questions might be within my grasp.

I'd learned from my experiences with Monk that there's a certain momentum to a case and you need to ride it. If you don't, the clues can evaporate like dew in the morning sun.

I went to my car, keeping my eyes out for Julie or any of her friends, though the likelihood of running into her or any of them was slim. I felt like a cheating spouse and got an inkling why Captain Stottlemeyer's first marriage crumbled. How many days or nights had he done the same thing, and felt the same way, while working a case? How many times did he choose a case over his family?

But I rationalized that it wasn't the same thing for me. My daughter was an adult now. I was single. I was under no obligation to visit her just because I was near her home.

Of course, that rationalization didn't work at all. It would have helped if I'd had some Oreo cookie ice cream to eat at the same time. I've learned that self-delusion is much easier when there's something sweet in your mouth.

Once I got inside my car, I hunched down in the

driver's seat, opened the file that Yuki had given me, and scanned the list of Dalander Homes developments until I found the one that they'd built in Walnut Creek. I jotted down the cross streets that formed the boundary of the development and headed east into the suburban badlands on the other side of the Caldecott Tunnel.

By the 1980s, nearly all of the walnut groves that gave the town its name had been plowed under for housing tracts with names like Walnut Walk, Walnut Acres, and Walnut Grove so people would at least know what had once been there.

By the 1990s, the once quaint downtown was all but demolished, too, replaced with an idealized, decidedly upscale take on small-town America, one where Tiffany, Apple, and Gucci were the local merchants.

The Dalander tract was at the end of Walnut Avenue, where all the streets were inexplicably named after Indian tribes. I drove around the neighborhood, past Kiowa Court and Cheyenne Drive, thinking it would be hard to find the house, but it turned out to be surprisingly easy.

As much as Walnut Creek had changed, the house on the corner of Comanche Court and Cochise Way had not. The O'Quinn residence was still the same color, the bushes and trees planted in the same places where their pots were set in the picture. The only difference was the grass where the dirt had been and the Mercedes SUV parked in the driveway.

I parked my car at the corner and, holding the photo in my hand, stood in the exact spot where Stacey and her daughter posed for the camera, which, I presumed, Walter had been holding.

It was creepy.

I knew a lot more about "Jack Griffin" and the photo

than I had a few days ago, but what I'd learned had only deepened the mystery surrounding his death.

If he was Walter O'Quinn and had faked his own death, was it to avoid his creditors and provide for his family with the proceeds of his life insurance policy? Or did he flee to avoid the shame and responsibility? I was beginning to think it was more about avoiding embarrassment than seeing to it that his family was taken care of. Otherwise, he would have faked his death in a way that looked more accidental than suicidal. But to be fair to Walter, perhaps he just lacked the ingenuity and creativity to do it right. Few of us have the skills required to convincingly fake our accidental deaths.

But assuming he was Walter, and by this point I was convinced that he was, why did he come back to San Francisco to die? Was it to reconnect with the family he'd abandoned? If so, where were Stacey and her daughter now? Did they even know he was here?

"Can I help you?"

The female voice startled me. I whirled around to see a woman standing right beside me, holding a leash that led down to a docile little Jack Russell terrier.

The woman was wearing a faded and paint-stained Northgate High School sweatshirt and an old pair of jeans, her long hair tied into a ponytail that gave her a girlish look that belied her age, which I pegged at about her mid-fifties.

"Sorry, you caught me by surprise," I said.

"I didn't mean to. You did seem pretty deep in thought about something."

"Have you lived in this neighborhood for a while?"

She gestured to the house on the opposite corner of the cul-de-sac. It was an Inglenook floor plan, like the O'Quinn home, but with rock in the facade where the O'Quinn home had brick.

"We built the house in 1979," she said. "It was one of the last empty lots in the development."

"So you must have known the O'Quinns."

"My God, you people never give up. I thought I'd seen the last of their bill collectors years ago."

"I'm not a bill collector. My name is Natalie Teeger. I'm a private investigator." I surprised myself with that remark and hoped it didn't show on my face. I was a PI now? "I'm trying to locate the family of a man who died in San Francisco a few days ago. He had this in his hand."

I held the photo out to her. She stared at it for a long moment. "That's Stacey and Rose. We were putting in our landscaping at the same time, so this must have been taken in the fall of 1979. That station wagon was brand-new. They were so proud of it. You would have thought it was a Rolls-Royce the way they fawned over it."

I suddenly wished I'd had the forethought to bring along Jack Griffin's fake ID to see if she could identify him as Walter O'Quinn. Some private eye I was.

"May I ask you your name?" I asked.

"Gloria Hayworth," she replied.

"Do you know where the O'Quinns went, Mrs. Hayworth?"

She shook her head. "After Walter drowned, the poor woman was grief stricken. It's bad enough to lose your husband, but then the bill collectors swooped down on her like a pack of wolves. It was relentless. They'd come at all hours of the day and night, pounding on her door, demanding money. They even went around to the neighbors, telling us all that Stacey was a deadbeat, hoping we'd shame her into writing them a check. My husband, a very peaceable man, got so upset that he slugged one of them."

"Good for him," I said.

"It's the only time I ever saw Roger raise his hand to anybody. They were despicable people. I didn't blame him for it and I certainly didn't blame her for what she did."

"Did she hit one of them, too?"

"No, but she finally cracked. One night, she and Rose ran off, leaving the front door unlocked and all of her keys, credit cards, and ID behind. I like to think she escaped to somewhere else and started fresh, though some people around believed that maybe she and Rose followed Walter into the sea."

"That's a horrible thing to say."

"Open the newspaper, honey. People do horrible things every day. How many times have you read about mothers strapping their kids into their car seats, then driving off a cliff?"

"But she was a nurse," I said.

"Makes no difference. Everybody has a breaking point." Mrs. Hayworth said it like she had some personal experience to back her statement up, but it was none of my business and I didn't pursue it.

"So what happened after Stacey and Rose disappeared?"

"The bank took the house and sold it. The bill collectors kept coming for a while, then finally gave up. Or maybe they found her somewhere and squeezed every last penny out of her. I don't know."

"Has anyone else come looking for the O'Quinns lately?"

"Not that I've noticed, but I'm not the neighborhood snoop." Mrs. Hayworth pointed to a two-story house across the street that faced the opening of the cul-de-sac. "That'd be Beverly Lundeen. But I have to warn

you, she's two beers short of a six-pack." Mrs. Hayworth waved at the house. "Hello, Bev—I see you."

The living room drapes fluttered as Beverly Lundeen slipped back into the shadows.

"How long has Beverly lived here?" I asked.

"She moved in a month or two before we did." The
dog started whining and tugging on Mrs. Hayworth's
leash. "I'd better go. Rufus wants his walk, and if he
doesn't get it soon, he'll start humping my leg, or
yours."

"We wouldn't want that. Thank you so much for
your help, Mrs. Hayworth. I really appreciate it."

"Good luck with your investigation. If you find Stacey, would you please do me a favor and ask her to
send me a card? I'd love to know how she and Rose are
doing."

"I will," I said.

Mrs. Hayworth wandered up Cochise Way, and I
decided to pay a visit to Beverly Lundeen. I walked
across the street and knocked on her door. She opened
it almost instantly.

Beverly was tall and thin with stringy blond hair,
pale skin, and extraordinarily wide eyes that made her
look perpetually startled. She wore a simple floral sun-
dress and flip-flops.

"Forgive me for disturbing you, but Mrs. Hayworth
thought you might be able to help me."

"What do you want?"

"I was wondering if you've seen any dead men
lately."

She gasped and her wide eyes grew even wider. I
didn't think that was humanly possible. She made E.T.
look beady-eyed.

"How—?" She took a step back from the door and,

for a moment, I thought she might slam it in my face. "I haven't told anyone what I saw."

"When did you see Walter O'Quinn?"

She swallowed hard, and when she spoke, her voice was barely above a whisper.

"It was after midnight, a week ago, under that streetlight." She pointed with a shaky finger to the sidewalk where I'd been standing a moment ago. "He was there, wet and festooned with seaweed, raised from the cold, briny depths. He looked right at me and smiled, his teeth covered with barnacles." She shuddered at the memory. "I hid under my sheets and told myself that it was a waking nightmare, that I'd imagined the whole thing."

"Only the part with the seaweed and barnacles," I said. "He was really there."

"You've seen him, too?"

I nodded. "But you don't have to worry, Mrs. Lundeen. He won't be returning from the briny depths ever again."

# 20

## Mr. Monk Takes It Easy

I went back home, got on the Internet, and pulled up all the articles I could find about Walter O'Quinn's disappearance at sea. The newspaper accounts confirmed everything that Dr. Long had told me and filled in a few more details.

I learned that Walter O'Quinn originally came from the Pacific Northwest and that his father ran a charter fishing-boat business. He met Stacey at the University of Washington in Seattle and they moved to California, where she went to nursing school.

According to the articles, at the time of Walter's disappearance, his bank was about to report him to law enforcement for writing bad checks on accounts he'd already emptied.

His troubles had reached critical mass. It was easy to see why people assumed that he'd killed himself.

"What I don't get is why no one raised the possibility that he'd faked his death—at least not publicly,"

Ambrose said, after I'd gotten both him and Yuki on the phone to fill them in on what I'd learned.

"Because he had nothing to gain from it and neither did his family," I said. "Everybody suffered."

"His family more than him," Ambrose said.

"But he did it anyway," Yuki said.

"He was a coward," I said. "He didn't have the backbone to take responsibility for the mistakes that he'd made, even if it meant that his family had to suffer for them in his place."

"You can't run from yourself," Yuki said. "That kind of cowardice would eat a man alive from the inside out."

"Maybe it did," I said.

"You think the guilt and shame caused his cancer?" Ambrose asked. "That's highly unlikely."

"But it feels poetically right, doesn't it?" I said.

"That doesn't make it so," he said.

"Stress can cause heart attacks and ulcers, so why not cancer, too?"

"Stress can be a contributing factor, but it's not the root cause," Ambrose said. "The presence of high cholesterol in the blood and a helicobacter pylori bacterium infection in the digestive tract are far more indicative of the likelihood of heart attacks and ulcers, respectively, than unethical and immoral behavior."

I thought about O'Quinn, riddled with cancer, standing outside his former home in the dead of night. Why had he dragged himself out there? He had to know his family was long gone. I could think of only one reason—to torture himself with the memories of what he'd lost and the pain that he'd caused.

"Maybe so, but we now know that he was suffering from more than his cancer when he came back here," I said. "I think he wanted to make amends with his family for what he'd done."

"Who cares what that spineless, selfish jerk wanted?" Yuki said. "Good riddance."

"That's awfully cold," I said.

"Not as cold as what he did to his wife and daughter," Yuki said. "Now that you know who he was and what he did, why do you care what he wanted? He's been dead to his family for decades anyway. What difference would it make to them now whether he died then or last week? They are probably better off not knowing the truth."

"I'd want to know," I said.

"Is this about you or about them?" Yuki asked.

I almost blurted out *both*, but I stopped myself.

"Maybe they know already," Ambrose said. "Perhaps O'Quinn was able to contact them before his death."

"We don't know that," I said. "Before I decide whether to drop this or not, I'd like to find Stacey and Rose. Will you help me do that?"

"Of course," Ambrose said, but Yuki was noticeably silent.

"Yuki," I said, "do you think I'm doing the wrong thing?"

"I don't think you know what you're doing or why you are doing it. That's the real mystery, but I can't fault you for trying to figure yourself out. If finding the O'Quinns is what it's going to take, then sure, I'll help."

"Isn't she wonderful?" Ambrose said.

"You both are," I said.

"Now you're just sucking up," Yuki said.

"I'd be a fool not to," I said.

"We'll search local, state, and county databases and see what we can glean from property tax records, marriage licenses, and the like," Ambrose said. "We'll also take a peek at the University of Washington enrollment records. If we have Stacey O'Quinn's maiden name, we can find the present location of any family she might have."

"Thank you, Ambrose, I appreciate that."

"But if Stacey O'Quinn went into hiding and reinvented herself to evade her creditors," Yuki said, "knowing who she once was won't be much help in figuring out who she is now."

"I think it will. You can change your name, but you can't run away from who you are," I said. "I'm sure that's something Walter O'Quinn found out the hard way."

That's when I was struck by the tragic irony of it all. When Walter O'Quinn faked his death and created a new identity for himself somewhere else, he unwittingly forced his wife and daughter to do the same. Perhaps it was having this in common, as well as the knowledge of their prior lives together, that gave him an edge in finding his family again.

But what I still couldn't see was how this would help me find them or, if Yuki was right, help me find myself.

I was writing down everything I knew about the case on index cards, a trick I learned from Kinsey Millhone, when Monk called.

"I thought of a great way for us to relax," he said.

"I am relaxed."

"I've made an appointment with Dr. Bell."

"Have a good time, but I don't see what's going to be relaxing about that for me, unless you emerge as a far less finicky person."

"You're driving me there."

"What am I, your taxi service?"

"Yes," he said.

"So where does my relaxation come in?"

"You get to sit in his waiting room and read magazines," Monk said. "Or you can go get a cup of coffee somewhere."

"I can read magazines and drink coffee at home without going to see Dr. Bell."

"But then I wouldn't be able to see him. So this is a win-win for both of us."

"I thought this was my day off," I said.

"It is," he said. "This is a perk."

I wasn't sure how to proceed with my investigation anyway, so I set aside my index cards, picked up Monk, and took him to see Dr. Bell. On the way, Monk didn't ask me how I'd spent my morning and I didn't volunteer anything. We'd reached the point in our relationship where we were as comfortable in our silences as an old married couple.

While Monk had his appointment, I flipped through *Vanity Fair*, *Esquire*, *People*, *Entertainment Weekly*, and *Psychology Today*, all of which had articles about the latest young female reality-show star and her emotional struggles with sex, substance abuse, plastic surgery, fame, wealth, and her own line of clothing or cosmetics.

My life seemed ridiculously simple and uneventful by comparison, even when I factored in all the homicide investigations.

Monk's session went by in no time, and Dr. Bell escorted him out of the office.

"How's your investigation going?" Dr. Bell asked.

I considered evading the question with a simple "Just fine," but something about the way he asked compelled me to take advantage of the opportunity.

"Do you have a couple minutes free?"

"Sure," he said.

"I mean free as in 'no charge,'" I said.

"You think you need psychoanalysis?"

"She definitely does," Monk said.

"It has been suggested that there's a possibility that this case has more to do with me than the mystery I'm trying to solve," I explained.

"I'm sure that's true," Dr. Bell said. "But that would be perfectly normal. Everything we do is motivated by our own needs, even things we do that appear to be entirely altruistic."

I thought about asking Dr. Bell if we could speak in private, but that would really make it a session, and he'd be justified in charging me for it. I wanted to avoid sharing the details of the case in front of Monk out of fear that he'd solve it out from under me.

But then I realized that I'd solved most of the mystery already and that the questions that remained couldn't be answered just by deduction or by observing something that was uneven, out of place, or asymmetrical. The answer would come from understanding how Walter felt, and I was pretty sure I had the edge on Monk in that department. Besides, what I wanted from Dr. Bell wasn't insight into the case but into me.

So I decided to take my chances and lay the situation out for Dr. Bell in front of Monk.

I told him everything I knew about Jack Griffin, aka Walter O'Quinn, and the family that he'd left behind. I even threw in Yuki's arguments against my continuing to pursue the investigation.

Dr. Bell nodded through my whole story and continued to nod after I was done, crossing his arms under his chest. "It's a fascinating case."

"I think it's a snooze," Monk said.

"Walter O'Quinn was seeking closure, if not for-giveness, before he died," Dr. Bell said. "That much is obvious."

"Painfully," Monk said.

"Closure is something we all seek even though it's often impossible to attain," Dr. Bell said. "We want things tied up, explained, balanced. It's why you solve murders, Adrian."

"It's a good thing these insights are free," Monk said. "Because charging for them would be a crime."

Dr. Bell ignored the dig. "It's also one of the reasons you are pursuing this case, Natalie, despite the fact that you don't sympathize with Walter at all and he might have already achieved the closure and forgive-ness that he sought. You want to know how it turned out. I'm curious about it myself, though that doesn't mean either one of us has a right to know."

"What are the other reasons?" I asked.

Dr. Bell glanced at Monk, then back at me. "Are you sure you wouldn't prefer to discuss this privately?"

No, I wasn't. But I also didn't want to impose on his kindness or get stuck with the bill if he decided not to be kind.

Monk sighed with impatience. "She needs to know whether she's any good as a detective and if she is, whether it's something she actually wants to pursue, or if she's only doing it so she doesn't feel entirely use-less around me."

I looked at Monk, knowing he was right, and aston-ished that he could be so perceptive. Or maybe my mo-tivations were so incredibly obvious that anyone could have told me the same thing.

"I wouldn't have put it quite like that, and certainly not as harshly, but essentially, Adrian is correct," Dr. Bell said. "You're not figuring out who Jack Griffin was and why he was here as much as you're investigating who you are and who you want to be."

I wish I could say that this was a revelation to me, or that it helped me see the case in a new light, but all it really did was make me feel more confused and lost than I did before.

"Is that a bad thing?"

He shrugged. "You could end up causing Stacey O'Quinn and her daughter unnecessary pain merely so you can satisfy your own curiosity about something that's none of your business and prove something to yourself. Or you might bring these two women a priceless gift, giving them the closure they never thought they'd get. Or the result could be something neither one of us can anticipate. Life is messy."

"Don't I know it," Monk said. "But I am doing my best to correct that."

Dr. Bell hadn't made things any easier for me. "So do you have any advice on what I should do next?"

"Of course he doesn't," Monk said. "He just asks questions."

Dr. Bell smiled. "Isn't that how you solve mysteries, Adrian?"

"See? Another question," Monk said. "What did I tell you? He's no help at all. You have to handle your own problems around here."

"Isn't being able to do that one of the ultimate goals of therapy?"

"See? He's doing it again," Monk said. "He can't stop himself. He's incapable of having a simple conversation."

"Thank you for your help, Dr. Bell," I said.

"What are you thanking him for?" Monk said. "He hasn't told you anything you don't already know."

"That's the whole point, Adrian," Dr. Bell said.

"Oh God, he's insufferable," Monk said. "Let's get out of here before I need two more appointments just to cope with the stress of this one."

Monk led me outside and we got into the car. But before I started the engine, he said something to me that made me stop what I was doing.

"You aren't useless, Natalie."

"I didn't say that I was. You did."

"I said that's what you feel like around me, but it couldn't be further from the truth. I need you."

"Anyone could drive you around, give you wipes, and make sure things are symmetrical."

"You do more than that," he said.

"Yes, I do all sorts of menial tasks and I run interference between you and everyone that you meet so that nobody strangles you. But I need to know if I actually contribute anything that's meaningful."

"It means something to me."

"I appreciate that, Mr. Monk. But am I doing anything that's meaningful to anyone else? Like Captain Stottlemeyer, for instance? Or is he just patronizing me, the way Devlin does? I think I'm getting good at detective work, but what if I'm just fooling myself and you're all in on the charade?"

"You were way ahead of me on the Braddock case."

"But I wouldn't have put it all together if you hadn't told me what it was that I already knew."

"We figured out the Sebes case at the same time."

"But would I have solved it if I hadn't been beside you the whole time, essentially shadowing you, looking at what you saw, listening to the answers to the questions that you asked? Could I have done any of it on my own?"

"Why does it matter?"

"Because I want to be good at something besides being your assistant," I said. "What happens if you get hit by a truck tomorrow?"

"You'll make sure that I'm buried in clean clothes that are properly buttoned and that the casket has been thoroughly disinfected," Monk said. "And you'll double-check that I am actually dead before they bury me. You should also clean off the grille of the truck and the pavement where I fell. Better yet, ask Jerry to do it. No offense, but he's more sanitary and thorough than you are."

"What I'm asking, Mr. Monk, is what would I do for a living? How would I support myself? Who would I be?"

"You wouldn't have to answer those questions for at least a year."

"Why a year?"

"That's how long you'll be incapacitated with inconsolable grief, though each day will still be a profound struggle. After all, your whole life revolved around me."

"That's sort of my point. What am I going to do if you're gone?"

"You'll be a great detective," he said. "Would you like me to write you a recommendation so you have it on file?"

"I don't think that's necessary, but solving this case is, at least for me," I said. "So if you already know the answer, keep it to yourself."

"I don't," Monk said. "And I would tell you if I did."

"That's what I'm afraid of."

# 21

# Mr. Monk and the
# Room with a View

I took Monk to his apartment and then went back to my house. I sat down in front of my laptop to check my e-mail. I'd received some replies to the questions I'd posted on the binocular forums about Walter O'Quinn's Jackson/Elite Clipper Model 188.

Someone calling himself "TheLaneSter" wrote:

> On the front bridge of your Clippers, between the objective lenses, there should be stampings on both sides. If you are interested, send me the JE stamping (with one to three digits behind it) and I can tell you which Japanese optical works assembled your finished binocular.

I didn't know if that information would be useful or not, but I wasn't about to turn down any help. So I went to the box of O'Quinn's belongings, removed the old binoculars, and examined the bridge. I found the stamping right where TheLaneSter said it would be and e-mailed the number to him.

The next message that I opened was from Glenn Shaffner, a representative of the company that bought the company that bought the company that bought Jackson/Elite.

Shaffner asked me for the JE stamping, the serial number, and the color of the antireflection lens coatings. He wanted to know if the coating was gold/amber, blue, or green.

I looked at the lenses. They had a gold/amber coating. I was in the midst of sending Shaffner the information when TheLaneSter got back to me. He wrote:

> The binoculars were manufactured by the Kamakura Koki Company, Shimo-Machi, Kita-Ku, Tokyo. Jackson-Elite used that facility for their Clipper line from the late '50s to the mid-1970s. I forgot to ask—what color are the antireflection lens? Amber would place them in the early '60s, blue in the early '70s.

That was useful information. Now I knew that the binoculars were from the early 1960s. I wrote back to TheLaneSter and asked him if the binoculars were valuable or particularly collectible.

He wrote back almost instantly and said that they were mass-produced, and that the same basic model continued to be made through the early 1970s, with some slight regional differences and improvements. The model that O'Quinn owned, he wrote, could be bought on eBay for twenty bucks.

The information only underscored my initial hunch about the binoculars. These were special to him. They might have been the one thing that he'd taken with him from his past life to his new one.

But why?

I thanked TheLaneSter for his help and then put the binoculars back in the box of O'Quinn's belongings—the paperback Westerns, his wallet and fake ID, his shaving kit, the snapshot. It didn't seem like much.

I remembered something I'd said to Ambrose and Yuki about Walter O'Quinn.

*You can't run away from who you are.*

And this was all that he had left behind.

If I was going to solve this mystery, I had to know who he was. I had to see the world the way he did.

I could go to Mexico to see how he'd lived and talk to the people who knew him. Maybe he'd also left some other things behind that could give me some clues.

But what happened in Mexico was Jack Griffin's life. The years there didn't matter. It was his time in San Francisco that did. This was where Walter O'Quinn had died. Twice.

So I picked up the box, grabbed my coat, and headed for the Excelsior Hotel.

I got the key to room 214 from the squirrelly manager and went upstairs, carrying the box and a grocery bag. I could feel the eyes of all the transients in the lobby on me as I walked up the stairs. If the room didn't have a sturdy dead bolt, I'd have to wedge a chair under the doorknob.

The stairwell and hallways reeked of chlorine, but when I opened the door to room 214, I was hit with the strong odor of Jerry's solvents and cleansers. I hoped the stuff killed only germs and not people.

The room was neat and orderly, the way Jerry and

Gene had left it. The mattress and box spring had been replaced, and someone had managed to find another threadbare, sun-bleached bedspread to put on top of it. At least this bedspread wasn't covered with suspicious stains and cigarette burns.

I closed the door, locked it, and then set the box and grocery bag on the bed. I unpacked the bag, arranging the canister of Pringles, the cans of mixed nuts, and the bottles of water where I'd seen the original items before. I did the same thing with all of O'Quinn's belongings. When I was done, I had a fair re-creation of the room as we'd found it when O'Quinn died. The only things missing were the pill bottles, the vitamins, and O'Quinn himself.

I sat down on the edge of the bed and looked around the bleak room.

Why would a dying man want to spend his last days in here? I could think of many more pleasant places to die. It might as well have been a prison cell.

Maybe the symbolism was intentional. He took the trip out to Walnut Creek to revisit the scene of his crime, and then he'd sentenced himself to this death-row cell to atone for what he'd done.

But why this hotel?

Why this room?

Why not someplace in Walnut Creek?

Maybe because there wasn't a hotel miserable enough out there to match what he thought he deserved.

I parted the moth-eaten drapes and looked out the window at the street below.

It was dark now, so the only people out were the hookers, drug addicts, muggers, and drunks who emerge at night from wherever they've been hiding all day to forage in the Tenderloin.

The bar at the corner was open and attracted the

nocturnal crowd like a bug light. All that was missing was the electric crackle of death.

The wannabe Starbucks across the street was called Brewster's Mug. It was closed, the windows and doors protected with corrugated metal covers that were spray-painted with graffiti and resembled roll-down garage doors. The coffee shop was on the ground floor of the office building that had been renovated into loft condos.

The building was a beachhead on the leading edge of the gentrification invasion.

I wouldn't want to live there.

Only a few units were completed and occupied, their windows lit behind closed drapes or blinds. But the drapes were open in one corner unit, and I could see a young couple in their kitchen, making dinner.

I was curious about those brave tenants, so I picked up the binoculars and spied on them.

They looked like models in a model home, a living advertisement for the good life. They were perfectly coiffed and designer clothed, and radiating a self-conscious elegance and grace that was more pose than poise. It was as if they knew I was watching. Me, and the whole world, too.

There was nothing salacious enough to keep my attention, so I scanned the rest of the building for activity. Most of the windows revealed vast, empty floors, the walls open to the I beams and studs, wires dangling from the open ceilings, the spaces illuminated by the occasional glowing, naked bulb.

I wondered if O'Quinn did this, too.

Was that why he was here? To spy on the residents of the building across the street? Could one of them be Stacey or Rose?

It was something to think about. Maybe Ambrose

and Yuki could find out who owned the units from property tax records or other real estate–related databases.

I wasn't entirely sure what to do next, but I knew that Ambrose and Yuki were looking into Stacey O'Quinn and her daughter, so the investigation was moving forward even if I wasn't, which was reassuring.

Now I understood why so many fictional detectives had sidekicks to do their busywork and beat people up. Sidekicks gave the detective some freedom to think.

I probably provided the same service for Monk, even if I wasn't much good to him as a researcher or as muscle.

I opened the can of Pringles, picked up one of the Westerns, and laid back on the bed to read.

At least this was something I was reasonably sure that O'Quinn had done.

The bedspread was rough and the pillow crackled as I put my weight against it, as if I were resting on a bag of Ruffles potato chips.

But it wasn't long before I got caught up in the tale of a tough cowboy, wandering the endless prairie in search of desperados and his own redemption.

I rode off with him, losing myself in the tall grass.

The sunlight woke me up at about eight a.m. I was startled and disoriented, but after an instant of panic, the adrenaline cleared my head and I remembered where I was.

I didn't awake with any revelatory new understanding of Walter O'Quinn or the case, but I still felt my stay in his hotel room had been a valid approach to immersing myself in his final days. Sleeping in his bed, however, was probably more than was necessary.

As I lay there, collecting my thoughts, I made a mental note to get a morgue photo of O'Quinn that I could show to local merchants. The cancer had taken a toll on his face by the time he'd arrived in San Francisco, and he had no longer been the same man who was in the picture on his fake IDs. I was hoping that perhaps someone would remember him. But that was a project for another day.

There was no way I could see Monk without a shower and a change of clothes, so I'd have to make a stop at home before work, which would mean I was going to be late.

Monk wouldn't like that.

I decided to keep O'Quinn's things in the room, put a "Do Not Disturb" sign on the knob, and left, taking the key with me.

I was headed toward my car, which I'd parked in the red zone in front of the Excelsior with the police department placard on the dash, when I was lured across the street to Brewster's by the aroma of fresh coffee.

It was packed inside with young professionals who looked very much like the living mannequins I'd spied on the previous night. I wondered what they were all doing there.

My clothes were wrinkled, my skin was sticky, my hair was a mess, and I still had the smell of Jerry's solvents in my nose, so I wasn't surprised when people kept their distance. They treated me like I'd slept in the alley all night under a cardboard box.

When I got to the counter, the fresh-faced, twenty-something female barista gave me a surprisingly authentic-looking smile, even though she was both harried and disapproving. The name on her apron was "Alyssa."

"Good morning, how may I help you today?"

I ordered a big cup of straight-up black coffee and then asked her, "Where do all these people come from?"

"What do you mean?"

"They certainly don't live in this neighborhood," I said.

"There's a cheap parking lot a few blocks up, so they leave their cars and walk to Union Square, the Civic Center, and the financial district. They come here for a pit stop."

"Define cheap."

"Under twenty-five bucks a day," she said.

I was glad I had my police parking placard or I doubted I could afford to drive a car in the city.

I took my coffee and was on my way out the door when my cell phone rang.

It was Jerry Yermo, calling to firm up our date for that night, assuming that no murders, suicides, or decomposing corpses ruined our plans. I envied people who didn't have to regularly factor death into their social lives.

We decided to get together early, around six p.m., at the Ferry Building, grab a coffee there, and then take a casual stroll along the Embarcadero to the Grinder, a smoky, working-class dive bar–cum-steakhouse in a back alley that's been a local fixture for a half century.

The Grinder used to be a hangout for the dockworkers, but now that the docks had become upscale shops and cafes, they were serving a new clientele. I'd never been there, but I'd heard that their drinks were strong enough to be used as cleanser and that the steaks were huge, served rare or medium rare with massive helpings of potatoes topped with slabs of butter as thick as a dinner plate.

It was exactly my kind of place. And I thought it was a very good sign that somehow Jerry seemed to know this after only one date. It boded well for our relationship.

I ended the call quickly, before the flirtatious banter could start. I wanted to conserve my flirting energy for the date, and I didn't want to take the risk that I'd embarrass myself by saying something stupid in a lame attempt to be clever. If I was going to do that, I wanted it to be with a drink in front of me that I could blame.

I got in the car, put my coffee in the cup holder, and was about to head home when my phone rang again.

It was Captain Stottlemeyer.

"Don't do this to me," I said as I answered the phone.

"Good morning to you, too," he said.

"Is it a murder?"

"It usually is," he said.

"Does Mr. Monk have to be there right away?"

"How long does he need?"

I quickly calculated how long it would take me to get home, shower, change, and then pick up Monk. And that didn't even include the travel time to the crime scene, wherever it was.

"Never mind," I said, resigned to my fate. "Give me the address."

# 22

## Mr. Monk and the Clean Freak

"You're wearing the same clothes you wore yester-day," Monk said as he got into my car.

"Yes, I am," I replied and drove off.

He cocked his head and tried to wink at me. It looked like he had a scratched retina. "I thought your date with Jerry was tonight."

"It is. I wasn't with him."

"So where have you been that you couldn't bathe or change your clothes? Were you being held hostage in a cave?"

"I spent the night in a hotel room," I said.

"This is Ambrose's fault," Monk said.

"What is?"

"He shacks up with some motorcycle mama he met on the highway and now you're picking up strangers off the streets for sordid one-night stands. He's in-fected you with his reckless immorality."

"It's not what you think. I was in Walter O'Quinn's

room at the Excelsior, trying to immerse myself in his world, and I fell asleep."

"Of course you did. This case is so boring that I can barely stay awake when you talk about it. What did you learn from your night in the hotel?"

"Nothing, but I found out earlier that his binoculars are from the 1960s."

"It's a wonder you can even stay conscious with exciting developments like that."

"Is that sarcasm?" If it was, it was a first for him.

"I'm stating a fact," he said. "You could have picked a more interesting case for your first solo effort."

"It may not have the urgency of a triple murder, but it's still an emotionally compelling story."

"Apparently not enough to keep you awake."

The crime scene was a two-story, wood-shingled, Cape Cod–style house at the corner of Rayburn and Liberty, on a hill overlooking Castro and Noe streets, the fog-shrouded Sutro Tower, and the Twin Peaks to the west. Where the two streets intersected, Liberty became a terraced, garden stairway leading down to Noe Street. The houses along Rayburn, between Liberty and Twenty-first streets, had unobstructed views that were to die for. Maybe that was the motive for the homicide we'd come there to solve.

Rayburn was very narrow, little more than an alley, and was clogged with official vehicles, which were all in a neat line, parallel to the cars already parked on the street. It wasn't done to satisfy Monk, because there was no other way to park, but he seemed pleased anyway, nodding with approval as we walked past the vehicles.

Stottlemeyer was waiting out front for us.

"This is a big week for murder," he said. "I can't remember the last time we had so many of them."

"And all of them within walking distance of my house," I said. "Maybe I should move."

"Any luck finding Rico Ramirez yet?" Monk asked.

"Not so far," Stottlemeyer said. "Devlin is on it. So I'm taking this case myself, though I'm hoping you can help me speed the investigation along."

"You mean you'd like him to solve it on the spot," I said.

"That would be nice," Stottlemeyer said.

"Who is the victim?"

"Stuart Hewson, fifty-two, an engineer working with the Bay Area Rapid Transit District. Every morning he goes power walking with a couple of his neighbors before work. When he didn't answer the door, they were concerned because he's had some heart trouble, which is why he does the walking. One of the guys had a key, opened the door, and found the body."

Stottlemeyer stepped aside and beckoned us into the house. Monk led the way, and Stottlemeyer and I followed.

A miniature railroad track ran along the tops of the walls and into each room like crown molding. But the train that rode those tracks wasn't a replica of a locomotive or steam engine—it was a distinctive silver electric BART train. The track continued on over the picture windows and out to the kitchen and the rooms beyond.

I was so busy looking at it that I didn't notice the side table in the entry hall and banged against it, nearly knocking over Stuart Hewson's car keys and his neatly stacked mail.

The entire house was neat. In fact, it was the neatest house I'd ever been in besides Monk's. Everything was straight and clean and even. The floors, tabletops, and counters gleamed. There was no disarray, nothing the slightest bit out of place, except for the corpse in the middle of the living room floor.

Stuart Hewson was a big man, barrel-chested and thick-necked, with a military buzz cut. There were four bullet holes in his upper body. He was in his stocking feet and wore jeans and an untucked red lumberjack shirt.

"The ME says the time of death was around one a.m., but no one heard any gunshots," Stottlemeyer said. "These homes are packed pretty close together, so the killer must have used some kind of silencer."

Monk squatted beside the body and examined the wounds. "That's odd."

"What is?" Stottlemeyer asked.

"The killer was experienced enough to fit his weapon with some sort of silencer, but his aim was terrible. He shot up Hewson when one well-placed bullet in the chest or head would have done the job."

"Could be he wanted Hewson to feel some pain before he died," Stottlemeyer said.

"How did the killer get into the house?"

"The back door was jimmied open," Stottlemeyer said.

"Maybe Hewson startled a burglar," I said, "who panicked and shot him."

"That would explain the four wild shots," Stottlemeyer said, "but not the silencer. You don't bring that unless you're planning on trouble."

Monk got to his feet. "This is a heinous crime."

"Murder always is," Stottlemeyer said.

"Stuart Hewson was a pillar of the community, an upstanding citizen, and a truly decent human being."

"Really?" Stottlemeyer said. "How well did you know the guy?"

"I didn't, but his sterling character and moral integrity are obvious."

"Because he was a clean freak," Stottlemeyer said.

"There's nothing freakish about cleanliness and order. It is the norm. The fact that so few follow the norm is what is freakish and very, very wrong."

"If hardly anyone is so clean, then how can you call it the norm?" Stottlemeyer said. "Isn't what most people do, by definition, considered the norm?"

"Only if you're looking up the definition in the Dictionary of Aberrant Behavior. I've lost a kindred spirit today. I shall avenge this crime and bring the perpetrators to their knees."

Monk turned his back to us and began to move around the house, doing his thing, hands in front of him, framing his view.

"That was an extreme reaction, even for Monk," Stottlemeyer said.

"I'm not a shrink, but my guess is that he's latching onto Hewson because he feels his values are under attack."

"But he always feels that way."

"Ambrose has a girlfriend," I said.

"Is she virtual or inflatable?"

"She's flesh and blood and she's living with him. She's Yuki Nakamura. You met her in Yosemite. She was Dub Clemens' researcher."

"The Asian woman with the tattoos?"

"That's her," I said. "She's Ambrose's assistant, too."

"How does that make you feel?"

"I'm happy for him," I said.

"You're not even a little bit uncomfortable?"

"Why should I be?"

"Because it could give Monk ideas about the two of you."

"Don't be ridiculous," I said. "We don't see each other in that way."

"Yet," he said.

"Ever," I said.

"Well, all things considered, I'd say Monk is handling it well."

"Only because he's had the Ramirez killings, the crime scene cleaning, and now this as a distraction. If he stopped to think about it, he'd fly off the rails again."

As I said that, the miniature BART train zipped past me on the track over my head, which probably explained why I'd used that cliché to describe Monk's mental state. I had railroad tracks on my mind.

Stottlemeyer and I both instinctively ducked, even though the train was on a stationary track several feet above our heads.

"Speaking of distractions," Stottlemeyer said, straightening up again. "How goes your investigation into Jack Griffin?"

"It's not a distraction," I said. "I am taking it very seriously."

"Sorry," Stottlemeyer said.

"I've identified him. His name is Walter O'Quinn, and he was presumed dead, lost at sea years ago," I said, telling him the rest of the story as Monk surveyed the scene.

"I'm impressed, Natalie," Stottlemeyer said when I finished. "You found out who he was and you managed to close a cold case that's been unsolved for decades. I'll dig up those files from storage, update everything, and officially close the case. I'll also notify the morgue to hold his body for a little while longer."

"You could show your appreciation by getting me a crime scene or morgue photo of O'Quinn."

"Will do," he said.

"You could also run a background check on Stacey O'Quinn and her daughter, Rose."

"I'll be glad to. If we can find them, I'll notify them of his death."

"I'll do that," I said.

"Are you sure?"

I nodded. "That's the fun part, bringing it all to an end. I need to be there for that."

"You may be in for a disappointment. In my experience, it's never pleasant telling a person that a loved one has died."

"They thought he died years ago, so that's not going to be a shock to hear," I said. "The news is that he was alive all of these years and that he came back here to find them."

"I'm just saying that you never know how someone is going to react. It may not go the way you expect," Stottlemeyer said. "I'll come with you, if you like. You can use me for my badge or for moral support. Or for both."

"That's very nice of you, Captain."

"You've earned it," he said.

Monk crouched on the hardwood floor beneath one of the picture windows. I went over and joined him, mostly so I could look out at the view. He was studying three indentations in the wood that formed the points of a triangle.

"Could you please step back?" Monk said. "You smell like a hobo."

I sniffed myself. "Do I? I can't tell. The solvents in that hotel room have burnt the lining off my nasal passages. All I can smell are cleansers."

Monk stood up suddenly and backed away from me.

"Okay, you've made your point, Mr. Monk, I'll take a shower as soon as we leave."

But Monk wasn't listening. He made a beeline past me and Stottlemeyer to the kitchen, where he opened the cupboard under the sink and began sorting through the cleansers. Stottlemeyer and I shared a look.

"Do I really smell that bad?" I asked.

"I've smelled worse," he said.

"That's not the reassurance I was looking for."

Monk closed the cupboard, then moved to a utility closet in the adjacent laundry room. He opened the door and examined the broom, mop, and vacuum inside the closet, then hurried past us again to the entry hall as if we weren't there. We followed him.

"C'mon, Mr. Monk, you're overdoing it," I said.

"Natalie's hygiene can wait," Stottlemeyer said. "We have a murder to solve."

Monk picked up the set of keys on the side table and opened the front door.

"What are you doing?" Stottlemeyer asked.

Monk pointed the key fob at the street and pressed a button on it. A car alarm started to wail. He followed the shrill, electronic whine to a pickup truck parked midblock. We hurried after him.

"You're not seriously thinking about driving off in the dead guy's car, are you?" Stottlemeyer shouted.

"You stay, Mr. Monk, I'll leave," I said as we caught up to him. "I'll go straight home and shower."

"I haven't been to the hotel," Monk said, "but I smelled cleansers in the house, too."

"So did I," Stottlemeyer said. "Because the guy is a clean freak."

That's when we got to the truck. It was covered with

a fine layer of dirt. The space between the dashboard and the windshield was stuffed with yellowed papers and invoices. The seats were stacked with files and there were loose papers and empty soft drink cans on the floor.

"So why is his truck a rolling trash bin?" Monk said. "His cleaning tools are filthy, too."

"I'll be damned," Stottlemeyer said. "Whoever killed Hewson cleaned up the crime scene afterward."

"Thoroughly and professionally," Monk said. "He used the same cleansers as crime scene cleaners do. He didn't want to leave a trace of forensic evidence behind."

"Why didn't Stuart Hewson's friends say anything about how much cleaner the place is than usual?" I asked.

"Because they didn't notice," Stottlemeyer said. "When you see your friend pumped full of bullets on the floor, you don't pay attention to the housekeeping."

"I would," Monk said.

"You're the exception. But I'll bring Hewson's friends back to look at the scene now. You did good work, Monk."

"Thank Natalie," Monk said. "If she didn't reek so horribly, I might not have noticed the discrepancy."

"I'll take that as a compliment," I said.

"I'd prefer you take a shower," Monk said.

# 23

## Mr. Monk Sees the Answer

I did as Monk asked.

We went straight from the Hewson crime scene to my house, which was only a few blocks away. I was reluctant to bring him with me, since my place was a mess, but then I saw the upside.

"Please forgive the clutter," I said. "And make yourself comfortable. I won't be long."

"Be long," Monk said. "It's a big job."

"It's a shower, Mr. Monk."

"It's more like decontamination at this point."

I went to my bedroom for a change of clothes. I cringed when I saw the unmade bed and overflowing hamper. Monk wouldn't like that. So I made sure to leave my bedroom door ajar so he could see it.

I knew Monk couldn't forgive the clutter. And I knew exactly how Monk would make himself comfortable: He'd clean my entire house.

So why fight it? I not only gave in, I made the job irresistible for him.

Besides, Monk was right. It had been a while since the house had been thoroughly cleaned, and on the off chance Jerry might be coming back with me tonight, I wanted the place to sparkle.

You could say I was taking advantage of Monk.

Or you could look at it from another perspective and say that I was making him happy by letting him do something that he loved.

Either way, I was sure there would be some misery involved for me, so I wasn't getting out of this without paying a price. But the pluses outweighed the minuses.

I began with a scalding shower and then segued into a long, hot bubble bath, giving Monk plenty of time to indulge himself.

As I lay there soaking my cares away, I thought about Stuart Hewson and wondered what he'd done to make someone sic a hit man on him. Perhaps he'd uncovered some sort of conspiracy inside the Bay Area Rapid Transit District and the bad guys wanted him silenced.

But if he was killed by a pro, why was he shot four times? Was it to throw us off? Or was it, as Stottlemeyer suggested, because the killer wanted Hewson to experience agony before his death?

It was idle speculation, since I didn't know anything at all about Hewson yet. We'd get into that investigation once both my house and I were clean.

I was also eager to get back to the O'Quinn case, though I was at a standstill until I had some more facts to go on or O'Quinn's photo to show around. That reminded me that I had to call Ambrose and Yuki and ask them to look into who owned those condos across the street from the Excelsior.

I got out of the bathtub, opened the drain, and began to dry off. I could hear Monk vacuuming so I took my time brushing my teeth, shaving my legs, putting on skin cream, and doing my hair.

By the time I was done, Monk had cleaned most of the house and there were three bulging trash bags lined up at the front door. He was wearing my pink dish gloves, my apron, and a surgical mask.

"Where did you get that mask?"

"I never leave home without one," Monk said. "You should know that by now."

"My mistake," I said and motioned to the trash bags. "What's in those?"

"Toxic waste," he said. "This entire house should be on the EPA's hot list."

I walked past Monk and peeked into my bedroom. The bed was made and I noticed my hamper was open. But I didn't hear the washer or dryer running, which made me very nervous.

"Did you throw out all of my laundry?"

"Not all of it," Monk said.

I turned around and saw him in the bathroom, picking up my dirty clothes off the floor with a pair of kitchen tongs and holding them at arm's length from his body.

"You really need to get an incinerator," he said, walking my clothes to one of the bags.

"You are not throwing out my clothes or burning them," I said and glanced toward the kitchen. The sink was empty, and so was the strainer, and the dishwasher wasn't running. "Are my dishes in one of those bags, too?"

He dropped my clothes into a bag and threw the tongs in, too, as if they were red-hot. "Just the ones that were soaking in swill, lost beyond all hope of recovery."

"I appreciate the cleaning that you've done, Mr. Monk, but you can leave the bags where they are. I'll sort through them later."

"Do you have a Tyvek suit?"

"No, I don't," I said.

"You should ask Jerry for one tonight," Monk said. "And if you bring him back here for a romantic interlude, he should put on his first."

"That's taking protection a little too far," I said.

"There's no such thing," Monk said. "I could use one now."

"Why?" I said. "You're done cleaning."

"There's still the bathroom."

"Don't worry about it," I said. "I'll do it later."

"That's what they said about the leak at Chernobyl." He took deep breath to fortify himself. "I'm going in."

And with that, he marched into the bathroom.

I took it as an opportunity to call Ambrose and Yuki. They told me that they'd been able to find all of Stacey O'Quinn's relatives, but no trace of the woman herself or her daughter. Most of the family still lived in eastern Washington State, around Spokane and Walla Walla.

"You'll have to grill the family," Ambrose said. "I'm sure they know her new name and where she is."

"Try to talk to them in their homes," Yuki said. "They may have some family photos in plain sight that will give you some clues."

"I'm hoping I won't have to make a trip to solve this," I said. "I have another possible lead closer to home."

That's when I asked them to find out who owned condos across the street from the Excelsior. They agreed to do it and told me that they'd e-mail me the results.

After the call, I opened up my laptop and checked

my e-mail. I had a message from Glenn Shaffner, the representative from the company that now owned the discontinued Jackson/Elite brand of binoculars.

He told me that the antireflection coating dated the binoculars from the early 1960s, which I already knew. But what I didn't know was that the serial number placed it among the stock of the now-defunct chain of Valu-Mart discount stores in the Seattle region.

Now, *that* was big news.

"Why do you have that dopey grin on your face?" Monk asked, looking over my shoulder.

"You're done already?"

"Far from it. I needed some fresh air to gird myself for more battle," Monk said.

"You make it sound like the bathroom is fighting back."

"Have you seen what's growing between your shower tiles?" Monk asked. "You have nothing to be grinning about."

"Yes, I do. I just found out that Walter O'Quinn's binoculars came from a store in Seattle in the early 1960s."

"So?"

"That's where Walter O'Quinn lived. His father had a charter fishing-boat business up there."

Monk looked at me. "My God, that's amazing."

"You're ridiculing me."

"No, I'm genuinely amazed that you are so stupefied by this dull case that you think it's a revelation that people buy items in the places where they live."

"I think it was Walter O'Quinn's father who bought those binoculars and that Walter kept them because they had enormous sentimental value to him."

"Okay," Monk said. "So what?"

"Walter brought them to San Francisco," I said. "I

think he was using the binoculars to spy on people in the building across from the hotel."

"So he was a pervert, too."

"What if Stacey or her daughter lives in that building? That could be the answer to the mystery."

Monk stiffened from head to toe. "It is."

"You think they live there?"

"I'm not talking about them," he said, rolling his shoulders. "I'm talking about Stuart Hewson."

"Well, I'm not," I said.

"I know why he was killed." Monk peeled off his gloves and tossed them in one of the trash bags.

"And who killed him?" I asked.

But Monk didn't answer that question. He untied his apron and dropped it in the trash bag, too. "Call Captain Stottlemeyer and tell him to meet us at Hewson's house right away."

If Monk was willing to leave my bathroom behind only half-cleaned, this had to be big.

Monk didn't say a word during our short drive back to the Hewson crime scene. Rayburn Street was clear this time—only Captain Stottlemeyer's car was out front. He was leaning against it, smoking a cigar as we arrived.

"You got here fast," I said.

"I have a loud siren and I was only a few blocks away, having lunch," Stottlemeyer said. "I showed Stuart's friends the place again. You were right, Monk, it was never that clean before."

"Why are you telling me something we already know?" Monk asked.

"I thought you'd appreciate the confirmation."

"I didn't need confirmation. I have confidence in my own conclusions."

"Too much, sometimes. Are you going to tell me why we're here?"

"I'm going to show you," Monk said. "We need to go inside."

Stottlemeyer snubbed out his cigar on the hood of his car, tossed the stub through the open window onto his passenger seat, then went up to the door. He took Hewson's keys from his pocket, cut the yellow police seal sticker on the door with the edge of the key, and let us in.

Monk rushed inside and started opening closets.

Stottlemeyer turned to me. "Do you know what he's looking for?"

"Nope," I said. The BART train zoomed over my head, startling me. "Why did you leave that on?"

"Couldn't figure out how to turn it off."

"You could shoot it," I said.

"Do toy trains irritate you that much?"

"Only when they are running nonstop around my head."

Monk emerged from a back room lugging a telescope on a tripod, which he carefully set in front of the big picture window. The legs fit right into the indentations left on the hardwood floor.

"This was here until the killer moved it," he said.

"Why did the killer do that?" Stottlemeyer asked.

"So we wouldn't see why Hewson was killed."

"For his view," I remarked.

"Exactly," Monk said.

"I knew it," I said. Both men turned to me. "I mean, I *thought* it. The moment we drove up, I thought, 'Hey, this is a view to die for. I wonder if that's why he was killed.' And it was."

"You would have saved us a lot of time and trouble if you'd said it instead of thought it," Monk said.

"I didn't say anything because it seemed silly. It was a facetious thought. I mean, really. He was killed for his view?"

"Real estate is worth a lot of money," Stottlemeyer said. "If you want a house bad enough, you might kill for it."

"That's not why Hewson was killed," Monk said.

"You're the one who said it was for the view," Stottlemeyer said.

"Yes, I did," Monk said. "It was for what he saw."

He stepped back from the telescope and beckoned us over. Stottlemeyer bent down and peered through the viewfinder first. When the captain looked up again, he appeared bewildered.

"I'll be damned," Stottlemeyer said, stepping aside so I could have a look.

I bent down and took a look. What I saw was Mark Costa's bedroom in his house below us on Castro Street. The drapes were open and I could see every inch of the room. It was a powerful little telescope. If someone had been standing in the room, I could have seen the color of their eyes and the blemishes on their skin.

"Mark Costa was a womanizer," Monk said. "I think Stuart Hewson enjoyed watching him and his partners fornicating."

"I guess Hewson wasn't such an upstanding citizen after all," Stottlemeyer said.

"I believe we've already established that I was operating from a false assumption when I made that statement."

"We certainly have," Stottlemeyer said.

"Wait a minute," I said. "I don't understand. Are you saying Rico Ramirez killed Stuart Hewson because he witnessed the murder?"

"No, I'm not," Monk said.

"Then who killed him?" I asked.

Monk looked down at his feet and hesitated. "It pains me to say this, Natalie, more than you can possibly know."

"Spit it out, Monk," Stottlemeyer said.

"I don't spit," Monk said. "Ever."

"It was a figure of speech," Stottlemeyer said.

"It should be banned," Monk said. "It's coarse and ugly and certainly shouldn't have been used in a solemn moment like this."

"Solemn?" Stottlemeyer said. "The way you're acting, you'd think it was the pope you're about to accuse of murder."

"Close," Monk said.

It wasn't until I saw the hurt on Monk's face, the genuine and unmistakable sadness, that I knew who the killer was, even though I couldn't imagine what the motive could be. I felt queasy and light-headed just thinking about it.

"No, Mr. Monk," I said.

Monk nodded, a grim expression on his face. "It was Jerry Yermo."

"Who?" Stottlemeyer asked.

"The crime scene cleaner," Monk said.

# 24

# Mr. Monk Is Disappointed

"You're not making any sense," Stottlemeyer said. "What possible motive would a crime scene cleaner have for killing Hewson?"

"A fortune in diamonds," Monk said.

"You've lost me," Stottlemeyer said.

"If you take a look in the telescope again, you'll see that Jerry and his crew tore up Costa's bedroom floor and replaced it."

"Of course they did," I said. "It was soaked with blood."

"But they also replastered and repainted the bedroom walls," Monk said. "And there was no blood on them. So why do you think they did that?"

I peered into the telescope. Monk was right. The walls appeared to be freshly painted. I stepped aside and let Stottlemeyer have his turn. He bent down, closed one eye, and looked through the viewfinder.

"I don't know," I said.

"Jerry overheard us talking about something valuable being hidden in the couch. He assumed Costa found the valuables and hid them somewhere in the house," Monk said. "Cleaning up the crime scene gave Jerry free rein to tear the place apart."

"That's why Jerry wouldn't let you stay to help clean," I said. "He'd already decided what he was going to do."

"Meaning he'd ransacked a dead person's home for valuables before," Stottlemeyer said, straightening up. "Or the decision wouldn't have come so quickly and easily for him."

Monk nodded somberly. "Here's what happened: Stuart Hewson saw all the police activity at Costa's place and was naturally curious. He kept the scene under constant watch and he saw Jerry find the diamonds."

"How did Jerry know what Hewson saw or didn't see?" Stottlemeyer asked. "We're a couple of blocks away. There's no way Jerry could have known he was being watched."

"That was Hewson's fatal mistake. He called Jerry and demanded a piece of the action," Monk said. "So Jerry had to silence him."

"Wait a minute," I said. "Jerry wasn't alone. He had his whole crew with him. I don't see how he could have done any of this without them knowing about it."

"You're right," Monk said. "They were in on it, too."

"That's pure speculation," Stottlemeyer said.

"I wish it was," Monk said. "But Stuart Hewson's body proves it."

"I don't see how," Stottlemeyer said.

"That's why he was shot four times," Monk said. "Each member of the crew took a shot so they would all be equally culpable."

"That's not proof, Monk, that's guesswork."

"My guesses are as good as fact," Monk said without the slightest trace of modesty. In this case, though, his words carried a palpable sadness.

Jerry's fall from grace undoubtedly represented a deep and painful betrayal for Monk. I wasn't too happy about it, either, or what it said about my taste in men.

But the realization that Corinne, the clean and dependable med student, had participated in a theft and a murder had to rub salt and cayenne pepper in the wound.

Stottlemeyer sighed and paced back and forth across the living room. "It could just as easily have been Rico Ramirez who did this. I could make a convincing argument."

"But it wasn't him," Monk said.

"We don't know that," Stottlemeyer said.

"I do," Monk said.

"You're missing my point."

"Because you haven't made one," Monk said.

"There's just as much evidence pointing to Rico Ramirez as there is pointing to Jerry Yermo," Stottlemeyer said. "Which is to say, there is no evidence at all."

"I just gave you the evidence," Monk said.

"You gave me a theory, but nothing that would stand up in court," Stottlemeyer said. "I couldn't even justify an arrest warrant based on what you've given me."

"You know I'm right," Monk said.

"What I know and what I can prove are two entirely different things," Stottlemeyer said. "There's no physical evidence and there won't be. Cleaning up this stuff is what Jerry does best. He left nothing incriminating behind."

"Except the lingering scent of his cleansers and solvents," I said.

"Yeah, that'll convince a jury," Stottlemeyer said.

"It convinced me," Monk said.

"Anybody could have used the same chemicals to clean this place," Stottlemeyer said. "Jerry is not the only crime scene cleaner out there. And those chemicals are widely available. Hospitals use 'em, too."

"What about Hewson's view? You saw it for yourself," Monk said. "He can see right into Costa's house."

"And a hundred different other homes, too. Or maybe he used his telescope to study the stars and wasn't a Peeping Tom at all."

"Why else would the killer move the telescope?" Monk asked.

"Maybe the killer didn't," Stottlemeyer said. "Maybe Hewson put it in the closet. Face it, we've got nothing."

"You know Mr. Monk is right," I said. "So the maybes don't matter. The question is what are we going to do now?"

Stottlemeyer paced some more and tugged absentmindedly on the corner of his mustache.

"If Jerry has done this before, he must have a network in place to fence the goods that he plunders. The diamonds aren't worth anything in his pocket. He'll have to take 'em to the street, and that's when he'll be vulnerable. He's in the same bind that Rico's in."

"But Rico doesn't have the diamonds," Monk said.

"We have to assume they both do and take it from there," Stottlemeyer said.

"Why?" Monk asked.

"Because you could be wrong, Monk, and the diamond-fencing angle is all we have right now on either one of these killers."

"So, in effect, you're waiting for one or both of them to make a mistake," Monk said.

"You got any better ideas?" Stottlemeyer asked.

"Yes," Monk said. "Natalie can go on a date."

Monk had me take him to a hardware store to get a fresh set of masks, gloves, and goggles before going back to my house to finish cleaning my bathroom.

I wasn't surprised that he was intent on finishing the task. For one thing, he couldn't leave the job incomplete; it would have nagged at him. But that wasn't the big reason. He found comfort in cleaning—it was how he put himself and the world back in balance.

So I didn't argue. I took him to the hardware store and then back home.

I let him scrub for a while in peace before I joined him in the bathroom, sitting on the edge of the tub while he cleaned the tiles.

"What is the world coming to, Natalie?"

"You've been deceived before, Mr. Monk."

"But if you can't trust a crime scene cleaner, who can you trust?"

"There are bad people in every profession," I said.

"But crime scene cleaning is a calling," Monk said. "Jerry took an oath."

"I wasn't aware that crime scene cleaners had to take an oath."

"He had a professional obligation to leave every place he went clean and disinfected. He violated that. And what about Corinne Witt? She's a medical student. Not only did she break her oath as a crime scene cleaner, but the Hippocratic oath as well."

"Not to mention a couple of commandments. But is that really why you're so disappointed?"

"Isn't that enough?"

"I think there's more to it than that."

He intensified his scrubbing. "I admired Jerry and

the principles he stood for. He was out there on the front lines of the war against dirt, decay, and disarray, confronting the worst filth there is head-on, with unrelenting dedication. He cleaned with a depth I can only aspire to."

"I thought he was a nice guy," I said. "Understanding, funny, considerate."

"It wasn't just him, it was his whole crew. Corinne, Gene, and William. They were people who shared the same core beliefs as me, who put those beliefs into action, who appreciated the beauty and balance of cleanliness and order. They let me be a part of that. I didn't feel alone anymore."

"You aren't alone," I said. "You have me."

"I'm talking about people who live by the same principles that I do. You live like an animal."

"Okay, what about Ambrose?"

"He's shacking up with an ex-convict biker chick," Monk said. "Before you know it, he'll be drinking water from the tap. I've lost him."

"No, you haven't, Mr. Monk."

"I'm so alone," he said.

"Stop whining. If anything, what Jerry has done should make you appreciate the people you already have in your life."

"No one I know cleans as thoroughly as he does."

"Look at the conclusions you jumped to about Stuart Hewson's character just because you thought he kept a clean house. There are more important measures of character than how clean someone is, or whether someone lives their life exactly the way you want them to. Ambrose, Captain Stottlemeyer, Randy, Sharona, Julie, Molly, and I may not always meet your expectations, or your high standards, but we are always there for you."

"We don't clean together," Monk said.

"I'm letting you clean my bathroom, aren't I?"

"It's not the same thing," Monk said. "Not like it was with Jerry, Corinne, Gene, and William. I had a posse. I've always wanted a posse."

"I know, Mr. Monk."

"I was betrayed," Monk said.

"So was I," I said. "I suppose that gives us one more thing we can share."

"The pain," he said.

I nodded. "Sometimes I think that binds people together more than the good times do."

"I wouldn't know," Monk said. "I have so few good times."

"Yes, but it's your positive attitude that carries you through."

Monk glanced at his watch. "What time are you meeting Jerry?"

"We were supposed to get together at six, but given what we've learned today, you can't really expect me to keep my date with him tonight."

"Why not?"

"Because he's a killer. I have a strict rule: I don't eat with murderers."

"You have rules?"

"Of course I do," I said.

"How come you've never given me a copy of them?"

"They aren't written down."

"Then how do you expect others to follow them?"

"I don't," I said. "I am the only one who has to, so I keep them to myself."

"So who is there to catch you if you break a rule?"

"I am," I said.

"That sounds like a flawed system to me," Monk said. "There are no checks and balances."

"There's my conscience," I said.

Monk waved that off. "I have no faith in that."

"Gee, thanks."

"Give me some more of your rules."

"Never date a man who has more hair on his shoulders than I have on my head. Don't wear tops that show my bra straps. Never eat a Jell-O mold that has fruit or anything else floating in the center. Don't trust anyone named Scooter or Skip. Don't go grocery shopping on an empty stomach."

"You call those rules?"

"What would you call them?"

"Inadequate. It's a wonder you're still alive," Monk said. "You should keep your date with Jerry."

"And you think going on dinner dates with murderers is good for my survival?"

"You want to be a detective, don't you? This is your chance to play cat and mouse."

"I don't know how to play cat and mouse," I said. "And I'm not entirely sure who would be the cat and who would be the mouse in this situation."

"You heard the captain. The only way this investigation is going to move forward is if Jerry makes a mistake. Right now, he is feeling secure. You need to shake him up."

"It may not be safe," I said.

"He's not going to hurt you, especially if you stay in crowded, public places," Monk said. "Besides, I'll be watching you."

"You will?"

"You won't even know that I'm there," Monk said. "I will become one with the night."

# 25

## Mr. Monk and the Night

Whenever I see the Ferry Building, I always remember that scene in the movie *It Came from Beneath the Sea* when a giant octopus, enraged by atomic bomb blasts at sea, swims into San Francisco Bay and begins attacking architectural landmarks, as monsters of all kinds love to do.

First the octopus goes for the Golden Gate Bridge, then sets his sights on the iconic, and very phallic, 245-foot clock tower in the center of the long, broad Ferry Building. He wraps one of his tentacles around it, snaps it in half, then goes off looking for Coit Tower, or Ghirardelli Square, or some other historic landmark to destroy.

Before the bridges were built, most people traveled to and from the city through the Ferry Building's terminal, except for those few who made the trek up the peninsula. But after the bridges, there wasn't much use for those ferries anymore, and the building eventually fell into disrepair and disuse. It was renovated in 2003, the grand nave restored and transformed into an upscale marketplace lined with gourmet takeout. It was usually packed with tourists and long lines, which sort of killed the whole point of running in for a quick bite.

But I was thankful for the crowds that night. If Jerry Yermo wanted to kill me, he'd have to do it in front of thousands of witnesses, not to mention Adrian Monk.

Jerry was waiting outside the main entrance, a big smile on his face. He didn't look like a cold-blooded killer, but cold-blooded killers seldom look the part. A bitter wind was blowing off the bay, and the chill went through my skin and into the marrow of my bones.

Or maybe it wasn't the wind. Maybe it was Jerry.

For a moment, I wished that octopus would attack, grab Jerry with his mighty tentacle, and drag him into the depths. The sentiment must have shown on my face, because his smile faltered at the edges.

"Is everything okay?" he asked.

I didn't have a script, or a plan, or a clue. I was going entirely with my gut, which was cramping, and that didn't give me much direction. I gathered my coat tight around myself and shivered.

"I just need a coffee," I said. "It's been a long day and I could use the jolt."

He led me to the overpriced coffee place and got us both piping hot tall ones, and we started walking south on the Embarcadero, in the general direction of Cupid's Span, a big sculpture of a bow and arrow stuck in the grass of Rincon Park.

The coffee helped. I don't know whether it was the caffeine or the simple, creature comfort of having something hot in my cold hands.

"What's your day been like?" he asked.

"The usual. Another day, another corpse."

I glanced across the street and saw Monk in a dark overcoat, the collar pulled up, tapping parking meters as he kept pace with us. He missed one, doubled back, and then hurried to keep up.

"It's what keeps us in business. Sad to say, but someone has to do the dirty work."

"Actually, this murder was surprisingly clean," I said.

"Strangulation? Poison? Suffocation?"

"Four gunshots to the upper body."

"That doesn't sound very clean," Jerry said. "You can't shoot someone four times and not leave a lot of blood."

"Oh, there was blood. But other than that, the killer wiped the place down. He didn't leave a trace behind."

"That's what you get with all those CSI shows on TV nowadays," Jerry said. "All the criminals are forensics experts."

"I mean really, seriously clean. He used the same specialized solvents and cleansers that you would."

"That is odd," Jerry said. "Who was the victim?"

"A BART engineer named Stuart Hewson. He lived up on Rayburn and Liberty."

"Isn't that over by your house?"

"And Mark Costa's, too," I said. "In fact, you can see Costa's house from Hewson's living room window."

"That's a killer view," he said.

"It certainly is."

I glanced across the street. Monk had fallen behind. He was helping someone parallel park their car. He had his tape measure out. Adrian Monk: one with the night.

I stopped and turned my back to the street, as if to admire the view of the Bay Bridge and the East Bay.

What I really wanted to do was keep Jerry from seeing Monk.

"This one isn't bad, either," I said.

"I agree," he said, giving me a not-too-subtle once-over. A day before, his look might have flattered me. But at that moment, knowing what I did about Jerry, it gave me the creeps. It was like he was a mortician sizing me up for a casket.

"Hewson had a telescope and liked to spy on people," I said. "He saw a burglary being committed, and that got him killed."

"Sounds like a variation on Alfred Hitchcock's *Rear Window*."

"Except in that story, the witness survived and was trying to do the right thing. Hewson contacted the burglar and tried to cut himself in on the deal."

"Then it's hard to feel much sympathy for him. From the way you've described the situation, if he'd done the right thing and called the police, he'd still be alive."

"So he deserved to die and the murderer should walk?"

"I'm just saying that maybe nobody would have died if Hewson hadn't escalated the situation. It was a victimless crime until then. Sounds to me like he brought it on himself and forced the burglar to do something he wouldn't have done otherwise."

"There was an alternative," I said. "The burglar could have paid Hewson off instead of killing him."

"That's easy for us to say now, looking at it from the outside, but I'm sure when you're in the moment, weighing all the options and possible long-term problems, you would go with the option that offers the quickest, most definitive resolution."

"Murder is certainly definitive."

"Do you have any leads on the killer?" Jerry took a sip of his coffee and looked across the bay, trying a little too hard to be casual with his question.

"We have more than that," I said. "We know who it is."

"So he's been arrested."

"Not yet," I said. "But very soon."

He looked at me and smiled. "What's holding them up?"

"A few procedural details," I said, smiling right back at him. This cat-and-mouse stuff was fun. But he was far too relaxed and confident. I wanted to see him sweat and it suddenly occurred to me how to make that happen. "But the clock is ticking. We aren't the only ones going after this guy."

"Other law enforcement agencies are getting into the act, too?"

"Oh no," I said. "The case isn't that big of a deal."

"Then who else is there?"

"You know those other killings, the really bloody ones you've been cleaning up over the last couple of days?"

"It would be hard to forget them," he said. "It's how we met."

"Rico Ramirez, the guy who butchered those people, is hunting for Hewson's murderer, too."

"What's the connection?" Jerry said.

"Whoever killed Hewson took something that belongs to Rico," I said. "And Rico wants it back. He won't ask for it nicely."

"I don't see how Rico is going to tie that engineer's murder to his missing item."

"We're talking about diamonds, the ones that were hidden in Costa's couch."

"This is getting very complicated."

"It's actually very simple," I said. "Whoever has the diamonds now is living on borrowed time. He's going down. The only question is who will get to him first— the police or Rico Ramirez. In one scenario he lives, and in the other he dies a really horrible death."

"Maybe the killer will cleverly elude them both."

"We don't think the killer is that smart. If he was, we wouldn't be onto him so quickly, would we?"

"But you haven't been able to arrest him," Jerry said. "That tells me that there's a big gulf between what you think you know and what you can prove."

"That might be true," I said. "But that legal distinction isn't going to mean anything to Rico Ramirez. You've seen what the man can do with a knife."

Jerry took a big sip of his coffee and tipped his head toward the street behind us.

"Would your chaperone like to join us for dinner?"

I turned and saw Monk measuring the space between two parked cars with his tape measure, while a woman, presumably one of the drivers, stood behind him, gesturing angrily at the sidewalk. I couldn't hear what she was saying, but I got the impression she wanted him to get the hell away from her and her car.

I faced Jerry. "I've lost my appetite tonight. I'm going to pass on dinner."

"I am sorry to hear that," he said. "I was really looking forward to seeing you again."

"You will," I said. "You can count on it."

"I thought you said you'd be one with the night," I said as Monk and I walked back to my car. I'd just finished telling him all about my conversation with Jerry.

"I was," he said. "I blended right in."

"You were double-checking the gap between parked cars with a tape measure."

"Just like any other parallel parker in the city would do."

"People don't use tape measures when they parallel park," I said.

"You mean that you don't."

"I mean that nobody does. You stood out."

"Only because you knew I was there," Monk said. "You were hyperaware of me."

"Jerry saw you, too."

"Only because he knew that you knew that he was the guy and that I would never let you meet him unprotected," Monk said. "Plus you probably blew my cover by looking at me all the time. Do you think you rattled him?"

I shrugged. "Who knows? The whole thing about Rico Ramirez was pure improvisation on my part. He probably saw right through it."

"I don't see why he would," Monk said. "It's a credible threat."

"I'm not sure that Jerry thought so."

"So we'll try someone else," Monk said.

# 26

## Mr. Monk Tries Again

The medical school at the University of California, San Francisco, is tucked between the southeastern edge of Golden Gate Park and the tall woods at the northern slope of Mount Sutro.

We met Corinne Witt in front of the statue of Hippocrates on Parnassus Avenue. I thought that was a little symbolically heavy-handed on Monk's part, but I didn't say anything about it.

Corinne was wearing a bulging backpack, the zipper unable to close over all the textbooks that she was lugging. She wasn't the bubbly, enthusiastic girl I remembered. She looked pained. Who wouldn't, carrying that backpack, along with a big, guilty secret that could send her to prison for life?

All that considered, I was surprised that she'd agreed to meet us. Then again, saying no might have made her appear as if she had something to hide.

Surely Jerry had warned her, and everyone else on

the crew, that Monk and I were onto them in the hour since I'd met with him on the Embarcadero. I'm sure he'd assured them that we had nothing but theories and that they had to hang tough, because if one of them went down, they all did.

"Hey, Adrian, Natalie, what's up?" she said, forcing a smile that still looked more like a grimace.

"Thank you for seeing us," Monk said.

"Sure, no problem, but I don't have much time," she said. "I've got to cram for a big test."

"I'm here about the big test you had yesterday," Monk said. "The one that you failed miserably."

"I don't understand," she said. "I didn't have any other tests this week."

"You were presented with a choice and you made the wrong one," Monk said. "You betrayed the man behind you."

She glanced over her shoulder at the statue of Hippocrates, draped in his robes, staring down at her.

"What are you talking about?"

"In purity and according to divine law will I carry out my life and my art," Monk said in an oratory manner. "Into whatever homes I go, I will enter them for the benefit of the sick, avoiding any voluntary act of impropriety or corruption, including the seduction of women or men, whether they are free men or slaves."

"I haven't seduced anyone except my boyfriend."

It might have been less confusing if Monk had quoted only the relevant portions of the Hippocratic Oath and left the other stuff out, but it didn't seem like the right moment for me to say that.

"You're a medical student, sworn to uphold the Hippocratic Oath," Monk said, "and yet you committed an act of the highest impropriety and corruption. You took a life. Stuart Hewson's."

"I don't know what you're talking about," she said.

"I know everything that happened, Corinne. You found diamonds hidden in a wall at Mark Costa's house. Instead of turning them in to the police, the four of you divvied them up amongst yourselves. But Stuart Hewson saw you, and he demanded a share. You had a choice at that moment. You could have walked away, no harm done. Instead, the four of you broke into Hewson's house and killed him. You each shot him once with the same gun. How can you ever hope to become a doctor living with that?"

"You're creeping me out, Adrian," she said. "You're not making any sense at all."

"What makes no sense is what you've done," Monk said. "You're a cleaner, dedicated to cleanliness and order, and yet you made the worst kind of mess. You spilled another person's blood. And for what? Some glittering stones?"

"I really have to go." She started to walk away, but I blocked her path.

"Are you an organ donor?" I asked.

"What?"

"Do you have one of those stickers on your driver's license that tells the authorities that, in the event of your death, your organs should be harvested and donated to others?"

"Yes, I do," Corinne said. "What does that have to do with anything?"

"You might as well peel that sticker off," I said. "Because when Rico Ramirez is done hacking you up, there will be nothing left of you to save."

"I don't know anyone named Rico Ramirez."

"You will, Corinne. You took his diamonds. And some night very soon, he'll come introduce himself. He'll be the last person you ever meet on this side of hell."

She pushed me aside and marched off. Monk and I watched her go.

" 'This side of hell?' " Monk said.

" 'Whether they are free men or slaves?' " I said.

"Mine was a direct quote," Monk said. "Yours was melodrama."

"You're talking to me about melodrama? You're the one who told her to meet us in front of the statue of Hippocrates. I was taking my cue from you."

"I think we made our point," Monk said. "We played on both her guilt and her fear."

"But she didn't crack," I said.

"Yet," Monk said. "Guilt and fear are a kind of rot. It spreads unless it's cleaned. And there's only one way to do that."

"I suppose there's a reason they say that confession is good for the soul."

And that made me think about Walter O'Quinn again, who thought he could run away from who he was and what he'd done. He couldn't do it, and Corinne Witt wouldn't be able to, either. The question was whether she'd carry that guilt with her as a free woman or in a prison cell.

I dropped Monk off at his apartment and then headed home. There was an e-mail waiting for me from Ambrose and Yuki with a list of the people who owned condos in the building across from the Excelsior.

If one of the homeowners was Stacey O'Quinn or her daughter, Rose, neither of them had been courteous enough to buy property under her real name.

Ambrose and Yuki assured me they were in the midst of running background checks on the homeowners to narrow down the field of suspects.

I e-mailed them a thank-you note, told them I was

in their debt, and went to bed. But I had a hard time falling asleep. I couldn't stop thinking about Jerry Yermo.

It was one thing to steal items left behind by the dead—more a crime of opportunity than of premeditation. You lift up a floorboard, or rip open a mattress, and find a stack of cash or gobs of jewelry—it's like stumbling upon buried treasure. Who is going to know if you take it?

But this time was different. Jerry had been caught in the act.

Why didn't Jerry just tell Hewson to go to hell, turn the diamonds in to the police, and consider the whole incident a frightening wake-up call? Wouldn't that have made more sense than murdering the guy?

Jerry would have been free and clear. Even in the unlikely event that Hewson called the police and accused Jerry of initially intending to keep the diamonds, what evidence was there? It would have been a Peeping Tom's word over that of a respected crime scene cleaner. Both Monk and I would have probably stood up for him, too.

So what had made Jerry decide murder was the better approach? And how did he convince Gene Tiflin, William Tong, and Corinne Witt to go along with him?

But the biggest question that nagged me was how I could have been so wrong about Jerry. He was a thief and a killer and I had no inkling of it at all. If Monk hadn't uncovered the truth, I probably would have had another wonderful date with Jerry that night. And who knows where that might have led?

How could I have not sensed, on some level, his profound moral and ethical weakness?

My inability to see Jerry's true character might not have bothered me so much if it had been the first time that I'd been attracted to a man who later turned out to be a murderer.

But it wasn't. If you've stopped keeping track, I'm not going to remind you how many there have been. It's too embarrassing.

I had to wonder, though, if there's something about a murderer, particularly a confident one, that gives him a certain charisma or charm that I, in particular, am susceptible to.

I mean, there's a reason more women are attracted to Dracula than repelled by him.

I made a resolution to myself. From now on, I'd assume that every man I was attracted to was a murderer until proven otherwise.

Perhaps it wasn't the most promising strategy for starting a relationship, but I might live longer.

There had been four murders in almost as many days, and all in roughly the same neighborhood. I suppose it was foolish to think that nobody would notice a murder spree like that.

Stottlemeyer had done his best to keep things quiet, but by Saturday morning, reporters were hounding the department's public information officer for details. More than one reporter raised the question of whether there was a serial killer on the loose.

That chilled the chief of police's blood, so he immediately dispatched one of his deputy chiefs, Harlan Fellows, to Stottlemeyer's office for a briefing. Stottlemeyer summoned us and Lieutenant Devlin for the meeting.

When we arrived, Stottlemeyer was behind his desk, Devlin was leaning against the wall, and Fellows was sitting in one of the guest chairs.

Monk and I had never met Fellows before. He was a

thin man in a crisp white shirt, black tie, silver cuff links, and suspenders. His shoes were polished like glass, and the crease in his slacks was sharp enough to qualify as a deadly weapon.

Fellows rose to greet us with his hand outstretched and a smile on his face.

"I'm Deputy Chief Fellows," he said. "It's a pleasure to finally meet you, Mr. Monk."

Monk turned his head away, repulsed, and would have reared back if Fellows didn't already have his hand firmly in his grasp. That's because Fellows' smile revealed a row of crooked, overlapping front teeth that were all jammed together.

"Likewise," Monk said, still looking away.

Fellows looked confused. "Is something wrong?"

"The glare from the window behind you—it's right in our eyes," I said, wincing as if the sun were in my eyes as well, though we were both completely in shadow. "Could you please lower the shade, Captain?"

"Of course," Stottlemeyer said, rising from behind his desk.

I offered my hand to Fellows. "I'm Natalie Teeger, sir, Mr. Monk's assistant."

He shook it. "Thank you for coming."

Monk took a seat on the couch and I joined him, handing him a wipe.

"I'm sure you appreciate the chief's concern about this case and the potential for the media to blow things all out of proportion," Fellows said. "We need to know exactly where things stand so we can determine the best strategy for handling press inquiries."

Monk wiped his hands, gave me the wipe, and then directed his gaze to his feet.

"The good news is that we've solved the crimes and identified the perpetrators," Stottlemeyer said.

"That's marvelous and, I must say, a tremendous relief," Fellows said. "It would be enormously helpful if you have them in custody in time for the evening news."

"I wish we could," Stottlemeyer said. "But we aren't ready to make any arrests yet."

"What are you waiting for?"

"Evidence," Stottlemeyer said.

"Let me get this straight. You know enough to be able to identify the killers and yet you are allowing them to remain free?"

"I wouldn't put it quite like that."

"How would you put it, Captain?"

Stottlemeyer sighed. "I'd say that we're screwed, sir."

"I don't see how you can have enough evidence to know who the killers are but not enough to arrest the bastards," Fellows said. "And I've been doing this a long time."

"Explain it to him, Lieutenant," Stottlemeyer said.

Devlin stepped forward, her hands behind her back. "It begins with a couch, sir," she said.

Fellows gave her a withering look.

"A couch," he said.

# 27

# Mr. Monk and the Apocalypse

Devlin walked Fellows through the case, step by step. She explained how Rico Ramirez hid his stolen diamonds in Cheryl Strauss' couch, which she gave away to a thrift shop, which in turn sold it to Mark Costa.

"When Rico got out of prison and discovered his couch was gone, he tracked it down, killing the thrift shop manager, Mark Costa, and finally Cheryl Strauss."

"How did you determine that the couch was the common denominator in these killings?" Fellows asked.

Monk raised his hand but kept his head down. "It was obvious."

"How so?" Fellows asked.

Monk lifted his head, looking only at Stottlemeyer as he spoke.

"Cheryl Strauss had a matching living room set that was missing the couch," Monk said. "The same couch that was in Mark Costa's house. The couch was ripped apart."

"I asked the question, Mr. Monk," Fellows said.

"Yes, I know," Monk said, looking at me.

"Our electronic forensics team confirmed that sales records for that couch were accessed by the killer from the thrift shop computer," Devlin said. "Once we discovered that Cheryl Strauss was romantically involved with Rico Ramirez, it all fell together."

"What physical evidence or eyewitnesses do you have linking Rico Ramirez to these three killings?" Fellows asked.

"None at all," Stottlemeyer said.

Fellows turned around in his chair to face Stottlemeyer. "You can't place him in Strauss' apartment, the thrift shop, or Costa's house?"

"No, sir," Stottlemeyer said.

"No fingerprints, no hairs, no nothing?"

"That is correct," Stottlemeyer said.

"Then what the hell makes you think he's the killer?"

"Because he is," Monk said, addressing Devlin.

Fellows turned back to Monk. "And you know this based on what?"

"What I feel. The pieces all fit where they are supposed to," Monk said. "It's orderly, like a row of normal teeth. It's unquestionably, without a doubt, certifiably him."

"If you're so certain," Fellows said, "why can't you even look me in the eye when you say it?"

"Could you please close your mouth?" Monk asked.

Fellows glared at Monk. "What did you just say to me?"

I spoke up quickly. "Forgive Mr. Monk, he doesn't handle confrontation well."

"You've never gone with your gut before, sir?" Stottlemeyer asked Fellows.

"Of course I have, Captain," Fellows said. "My own,

not the feelings of individuals whose psychological stability remains highly in doubt."

Monk held his hand out in front of him, blocking out the lower half of Fellows' face from his view, and looked Fellows in the eye.

"Rico Ramirez is the guy," Monk said. "I am never wrong about homicide."

"I agree with him," Devlin said, then quickly added, "That it's Ramirez, not that Monk is never wrong."

"I also believe it's Ramirez," Stottlemeyer said. "Monk is never wrong about this stuff. He's the best. That's why the chief has him under contract."

Fellows sighed and shifted his gaze to Devlin, much to Monk's relief. Monk lowered his hand and looked at the floor again.

"I just wish we had some evidence to sink our teeth into," Fellows said.

Monk groaned and rolled his shoulders. I patted his knee.

"Do we even know if Rico Ramirez is still in the city?" Fellows asked.

"He's gone to ground," Devlin said. "We've got all his known associates under watch, but he hasn't showed. And from what I'm hearing from my sources, the diamonds haven't shown up on the street, either."

"What about this other killing? The BART engineer?" Fellows asked. "What do you have on that?"

"It's related," Stottlemeyer said. "The victim, Stuart Hewson, spied on people with his telescope. He was watching Costa's house when a crew of crime scene cleaners, led by a guy named Jerry Yermo, uncovered the diamonds and kept them. Hewson tried to blackmail the cleaners and they killed him."

"How do you know that's what went down?" Fellows asked.

"Because it is," Monk said, holding his hand in front of his face again.

"Based on what?" Fellows said.

"Hewson's home was thoroughly cleaned and smelled strongly of crime scene cleaning chemicals," Stottlemeyer said.

"And Hewson was shot four times," I said. "That's one for each crime scene cleaner on Yermo's crew. And Hewson had a telescope facing Costa's house."

"That's it?" Fellows said. "That's all you have?"

"We pulled the victim's phone records," Devlin said. "We know that he called the crime scene cleaners a few hours before he was killed."

"That's hardly a smoking gun," Fellows said. "What physical evidence or eyewitnesses do you have linking these crime scene cleaners to the BART engineer?"

"We don't have any," Stottlemeyer said.

"What evidence is there that the crime scene cleaners recovered the diamonds and Rico Ramirez didn't?"

"There is none," Stottlemeyer said.

"I had a date with Jerry Yermo last night," I said. "And we were talking around the whole thing, but I knew that he did it and he knew that I knew that he did it, and it was just right out there. He's the guy, no question about it."

Fellows stared at me. "Who are you again?"

"Natalie Teeger, Mr. Monk's assistant."

Fellows sighed and looked at Stottlemeyer. "This is a farce, Captain. Can't you see that?"

"What I see, sir, is that we have more work to do if we are going to make these cases stick."

Fellows shook his head and turned to us. "Could the captain and I have a moment in private, please?"

Devlin, Monk, and I walked out of the captain's office, the lieutenant closing the door behind us.

"This isn't good," she said.

"Thank you for standing up for Mr. Monk," I said.

"I wasn't standing up for Monk," she said. "I was defending our case."

"Still, we appreciate it." I glanced at Monk. "Don't we?"

"Did you see that man's teeth, Lieutenant?" Monk said. "That's why you need to floss."

The door to Stottlemeyer's office opened and Fellows emerged, acknowledged us with a nod, and continued on his way. The three of us filed back in and stood in front of the captain's desk. He looked up at us.

"Deputy Chief Fellows has ordered us to start the investigations into these four murders from scratch and to abandon all of our previous conclusions, which, as he put it, have no credibility whatsoever."

"He's wrong," Monk said. "Just look at his teeth."

"He went on to say that if we feel we are incapable of conducting a professional and competent investigation, he will find homicide investigators who can."

"We're giving Ramirez and Yermo a free pass," Devlin said. "You know that, Captain."

"It doesn't matter what I think," Stottlemeyer said. "We have our orders. If you don't think you can look at this case with fresh eyes, Lieutenant, I will be glad to hand it off to Jensen or Baker."

"Give it to them," Devlin said. "Because I won't pretend I don't already know who the killers are."

"Leland," Monk said. "You can't do this."

"You're done, Monk. It's not your problem anymore." Stottlemeyer handed me a file. "You can help Natalie with her case. Here's the picture of Walter O'Quinn and the other information that you wanted. You've got plenty of time to work on it now."

*       *       *

Monk was depressed.

He couldn't even muster up the energy to clean. He just sat on his couch and stared at the wall.

I sat down beside him. He didn't bother to acknowledge my presence. I put my hand on his. At least he didn't flinch.

"Is there anything I can do, Mr. Monk?"

He shook his head.

"How about a nice glass of water? Or a wipe?"

He shook his head again.

"There's no amount of water or disinfectant wipes that can solve this."

"The police will get the evidence," I said. "No one is going to get away with murder."

"It's bigger than that," Monk said. "The balance of the universe has been disrupted."

"You mean your universe," I said.

"There's only one."

That was pure Monk. The universe revolved around him and he was totally unabashed about saying so. But I wasn't going to hit him while he was down. I decided to take a gentler approach.

"Don't you think you might be blowing things slightly out of proportion?"

"Am I?" He turned to me. "Here's how it's supposed to work. I solve a murder, the police make an arrest, the killer is convicted, and order is restored. But that's not happening now. I solved the crime, but police with crooked teeth are declining to make an arrest, and the killers are walking free. It's anarchy."

"It's an isolated incident, Mr. Monk. It will be fixed."

"Will it? Open your eyes, Natalie. My brother is shacking up with an ex-con biker chick. Crime scene cleaners are spilling blood instead of wiping it up. And now the complete collapse of our justice system. I saw the signs five days ago and I was right. The apocalypse is nigh and the first horseman rode in on a Harley."

"Would you like me to call Dr. Bell?"

"What can he do about this?"

"Maybe he can help you feel better."

"Can he change anything that's happened? Can he restore the order that's been lost?"

"No, but he might be able to help you put things into perspective."

"No matter what point of view you look at this with, the reasonable and inevitable conclusion is going to be the same," Monk said. "It's the end of civilization as we know it."

I sighed. There was no point in trying to argue with him now. He was too upset.

"Are you sure there isn't anything I can do to make you feel better?"

"Maybe there's one thing," Monk said. "Do you still have those trash bags I left at your house?"

"Yes," I said.

"Burn them," he said.

# 28

## Mr. Monk and the Plan

It wasn't until I got home that Saturday afternoon that I finally opened the file that Captain Stottlemeyer had given me in his office.

He'd printed out four photographs of Walter O'Quinn taken on the bed in the Excelsior. They would be much less awkward to show around than photographs of a corpse on a morgue slab.

I set the photos aside and turned to the rest of the pages, which I hoped would reveal who Stacey O'Quinn and Rose were, and where I could find them.

But the papers contained no information about the O'Quinns at all. What Stottlemeyer had given me were dossiers on Jerry Yermo, Gene Tiflin, William Tong, and Corinne Witt.

What was Stottlemeyer trying to accomplish by slipping me the material? Was this his way of saying he wanted Monk and me to continue investigating an angle that he'd been ordered to drop?

I stuck a pepperoni Hot Pocket in the microwave, added hot water to a cup of Folgers crystals, and sat down with my instant, late lunch to go through the material.

What I soon discovered was that the four of them had a common motive for keeping the diamonds for themselves: They were all in deep financial trouble.

Jerry had bought property and cars, creating a lifestyle that was well beyond his means. Death in San Francisco simply hadn't kept up with his spending. But rather than downsize, he kept right on buying more and more, compulsively adding to his credit woes. It made no sense.

Gene Tiflin was in debt even before the economy devastated the construction business in California. He had a wife and three teenage kids to support and was paying a steep mortgage on a house in the East Bay that was now worth two hundred thousand dollars less than he'd paid for it.

William Tong had lost his teaching job two years ago. If that wasn't bad enough, his wife had left him for a woman, emptied their savings account, and moved to Sweden. Bill collectors swarmed him and picked his wallet clean. He'd been forced at age thirty-five to move back in with his mother. He had a net worth of zero and his self-esteem was probably hovering at about the same level.

Corinne Witt was living frugally in a studio apartment in a former motel that now rented its drive-up rooms to UCSF students by the month. But she was carrying enormous student debt from college and was in arrears on both her rent and her medical school tuition. She was facing imminent eviction or expulsion. Something had to give.

And that was when they found the diamonds.

Now that I knew the financial pressure that they were all under, I could better understand why they'd killed Stuart Hewson.

After the euphoria of finding the diamonds, their salvation, it must have seemed like a bitter, brutally unfair twist for Hewson to come along and demand a share.

What had he done to earn it? They didn't weigh the pros and cons of murder. They simply reacted out of anger and possessiveness. They were a team, they had a bond forged by gore and heavy debt, and Hewson was an opportunistic, greedy outsider threatening their safety and financial security.

Killing him wasn't one of several options. It was the *only* option.

As much as I may have understood what they had done now, it didn't bring me any closer to finding a way to prove everything that Monk had so brilliantly deduced.

We were still, as Captain Stottlemeyer had so eloquently put it that morning, screwed.

It was early evening, and I was still sorting through the garbage bags, rescuing my dirty laundry and washing my clothes, when there was a knock at my front door.

I dropped the load of clothes I was carrying on my coffee table, peeked through the front door peephole, and was surprised by whom I saw staring back at me as if she were facing a security camera.

It was Lieutenant Amy Devlin.

I opened the door. "It's not polite to look directly at the peephole when you knock at someone's door."

"Why not?"

"Because it's aggressive," I said.

"Why pretend that you aren't aware that you are being watched?"

"It's called a social nicety," I said and beckoned her inside. "Sort of like bringing a bottle of wine or flowers or a pastry when you visit someone's home for the first time, especially when you show up uninvited."

Devlin reached into the pocket of her leather jacket. "I think I've got a mint from a restaurant in here somewhere."

"It's okay," I said. "Never mind."

She walked around the living room, examining my shelves, artwork, and furniture.

"Your place feels very lived in," she said.

"I'll take that as a compliment."

"How do you do that?"

"Take a compliment?"

"Make a place feel lived in?"

"You live in it," I said. "What can I do for you, Lieutenant?"

She looked at the file on the table and sorted through the pages that Stottlemeyer had given me. "I see you've read my report on Yermo's crew."

"Did you know that the captain gave that to me?"

She nodded. "I recognized the file when he handed it to you. That's my coffee cup ring on the cover."

"Is that why you're here, to pick up the file?"

"No," she said. "Monk solved these two cases. He's right about who the killers are. It was our job to make the arrests and we didn't."

"Monk isn't blaming you, Lieutenant. Or the captain."

"I don't care what Monk thinks. I've got a problem being told to stand down when I know who the killers are."

"None of us are happy about it," I said.

"Until recently, I was an undercover cop. I'm not used to being part of a team, working in an office under direct supervision, having to deal with rank and politics. I'm used to being on the street, working from within the criminal organization, going with my instincts and manipulating the people and the situation so it plays out my way."

"You can't do that now."

"I think I can," she said. "I've got an idea how we can bring down Yermo's crew and nail Rico Ramirez, too."

"So tell the captain," I said.

She shook her head. "My approach is unorthodox and a career killer if it goes wrong. Probably even if it doesn't. But I don't care."

"Why tell me?"

"Because I can't do it alone," she said. "I've called in a lot of markers on this, but I still need your help."

I thought about it for a moment. Devlin hadn't told me a single detail about her plan, but the fact that she had one, and that she was sharing it with me, someone she didn't like much, revealed the depth of her commitment to seeing that the right thing was done.

It was a big step for her. It also told me a lot about who she was beneath that hard skin of hers.

"How dangerous is it?" I asked.

"The first stage, not at all," she said. "The second stage, potentially fatal. But you don't have to worry about that part. I'll be doing that solo."

"If we do this together," I said, "we do it together to the end."

"Let's see how stage one goes," she replied. "Because if that fails, there won't be a stage two and we might both be in jail."

"Jail?" I said.

"Do you still have a key to that room at the Excelsior?"

"How did you know I have a key?"

"I'm a cop," she said. "Do you have it?"

I nodded.

"Good." She looked at my laundry on the coffee table. "Do you have anything sexy to wear?"

Devlin explained her plan to me as she rummaged through my closet and my dresser. I didn't think her idea was unorthodox at all. I thought it was insane.

I also thought it just might work.

It would also be the most daring thing I'd ever done, and that had a certain appeal.

Apparently, none of my clothes were right for the job. So she went out to her car, a 1990 Firebird, and rooted around in a suitcase that she kept in the trunk.

She came back with two sheer, black, skintight minidresses, one sleeveless and one strapless, and two pairs of high-heeled shoes.

"We're lucky we're about the same size," Devlin said.

"Those dresses are too small and too tight for either one of us."

"Exactly," she said. "Take your pick."

The vast, seventeen-story atrium lobby of the Hyatt Regency Hotel, with its glass elevators, huge spherical sculpture, and glittering lights, always made me feel like I'd stepped into a 1970s science fiction movie like *Logan's Run*. That night with Amy Devlin, I felt that way more than ever before.

That's because in *Logan's Run*, the future offered the "perfect world of total pleasure," a life of nonstop sex and partying with just one little catch: No one was allowed to live past the age of thirty. If you didn't shuffle off voluntarily to the death chamber, you were chased down and killed by cops called Sandmen.

When we showed up at the lobby bar, the place was packed with young professionals in their twenties mingling with the business travelers, conference attendees, and other hotel guests looking for action on a Saturday night.

I felt every one of my thirty-and-then-some years. I half expected a team of Sandmen to come rushing in after me, laser-cannons blasting.

*It's time for you to die, old lady. Step aside for the young. You've had your time.*

"Relax," Devlin said. "You're a hot, single lady looking for a good time."

"Easy for you to say. You don't look like a grandmother trying to pretend that she's twenty-one."

In fact, Amy Devlin looked dazzling in her strapless minidress. She'd transformed herself into another person entirely.

The way she moved, the way she spoke, the way she wore that dress, were all completely different from the Amy Devlin that I knew. The tough, streetwise, cynical cop without a trace of femininity was gone. This Amy Devlin exuded casual self-confidence, a mischievous nature, and raw, unabashed sexuality. All the eyes in the bar—the eyes of men and women alike—were on her.

"How you look is only part of it," she said. "It's what you're thinking. It's the way that you move. It's what you express with your eyes. That's what people see and respond to. Don't dress the part, become it."

It was true. She hadn't done much to her hair and almost nothing to her face, beyond adding a little makeup. And yet, she was a new woman. I wouldn't have recognized her myself, especially out of the context of a police station or crime scene.

"Ignore the twentysomethings," she said. "They are set decoration. He may lust for them, but he knows they are out of his league."

"So are you," I said.

"Which is why this is going to be so easy," she said. "You just be there when I need you."

I tried to match her walk and confidence. I tried to think of myself as a sensual creature, living only for the night and the pleasure I could find in it.

And then I tripped on my high heels.

Devlin caught my elbow, saving me from a fall, and gestured toward an empty table.

I took a seat and watched her as she continued on without me, moving with feline grace to the bar and William Tong.

# 29

# Mr. Monk and the Missing Head

Tong's attention was so totally fixated on Amy Devlin that I doubted he'd even seen me. And if he had, he clearly didn't make the connection between Devlin's friend in the black minidress and the frumpy detective's assistant that he'd seen briefly at two crime scenes.

I hadn't believed Devlin when she said that's what would happen, but she was right. She apparently knew more about how men looked at women, or at least what they remembered about women, than I did.

I couldn't hear what she and Tong were saying to each other, but I watched the seduction with fascination—the way she arched her body toward his, allowing herself to brush against him in the tight crush of people, and how she always looked him in the eye and smiled, licking her lips every so often.

Tong didn't stand a chance against her, not that he'd

even attempted to resist. It was probably all he could do not to weep with gratitude at his good fortune.

But we knew that before we got there.

We were depending on it.

"The man has been neutered," Devlin told me as we were heading to the Hyatt. "He lost his job, his wife left him for a woman, and he's living with his mommy. The guy probably sits down to pee now."

"That's an image I could have lived without, thank you."

"Tong is desperate to reaffirm his manhood any way he can. So every night, he's at the bar, itching to score. Any woman with a pulse will do, but they can smell his insecurity."

"How do you know?"

"I've been watching," she said. "I've been looking for our way in."

"There are a lot of bars in the city. Why the Hyatt?"

"Because he can't take a woman to his room in Mommy's house. How pathetic would that be? If the woman he picks up isn't a guest at the Hyatt, or doesn't want to take him back to her place, he can probably get a room there at a cut rate," she said. "Jerry's got a deal with the hotel to handle their unattended deaths and any messes where lots of bodily fluids are involved. They keep him pretty busy."

"I don't even want to think about it," I said.

"The man just scored a fortune in diamonds and killed a man," Devlin said. "For the first time in months, he's feeling like he's taken charge, like he's tough, like he's a man again. He'll want to prove it with a woman. And that's going to be me."

"Lucky you," I said.

"Unlucky him," she said.

And now it was going just the way she knew it would. He was so distracted by her cleavage that he never saw the roofie that she dropped in his drink. I didn't see it, either, but I knew when it happened because she gave me the signal—she tugged at her earlobe.

I waited until I saw him take a sip of his drink. I knew we didn't have much time to get him out of there before the drug took effect.

She whispered something to him. He quickly paid for their drinks. Devlin took his arm in hers and they started to leave the bar.

I caught up with them. "Leaving me behind, Trixie?"

"I saw him first, Brittany," she said.

"You two are friends?" Tong asked me, no recognition at all in his eyes, a dopey smile on his face.

"Bosom buddies," Devlin said.

"But she has all the luck," I said. "I've struck out tonight. Plenty of boys around, but so few men."

Devlin nibbled on his ear. "Do you mind if Brittany and I share you?"

"Just this once," Tong said, trying to appear nonchalant, but his wide eyes betrayed him. "I'm feeling charitable tonight."

I took his other arm and we led him out of the hotel.

We went to the Excelsior in a taxi and by the time we got Tong up to my room, he was disoriented and barely conscious, but his dopey smile hadn't waned.

We dropped him on the bed and told him to take off his clothes. He gladly complied and managed to get down to his underwear before he passed out, his pants bunched around his feet.

Devlin put on a pair of rubber gloves from her purse, removed his watch and rings, and then bound his hands to the bedpost with his belt, tight enough to secure him but loose enough so that he could free himself with some effort.

While she did that, I put on gloves, too, and sorted through his pockets, extracting his wallet and keys. I left his breath mints, condoms, and Gas-X pills behind.

We put Tong's valuables in evidence bags, gathered up all of O'Quinn's stuff, and dumped everything in the file box that I'd left behind before.

We gave the room a quick once-over, picked up the box, and walked out, leaving the "Do Not Disturb" sign behind on the doorknob.

"I gave him a big roofie," she said. "That should give us about eight hours before he comes around and wonders how he ended up naked in a dive hotel."

"Are you sure he won't remember anything that happened?"

"He'll be lucky if he still knows his own name," Devlin said. "And whether he does or not, he's going to be so ashamed of himself, he'll want to forget the night that he forgot."

"Well, we know that's not going to happen," I said.

Her car was parked around the corner from the Excelsior. She got inside and changed clothes while I stood watch, and then she did the same for me.

We drove to the Embarcadero and the dark back alley where Tong illegally parked his old VW Passat every night, accumulating scores of tickets that he never paid.

The alley was narrow and a dead end, leading to the loading dock of an empty warehouse. It was strewn with trash and reeked of urine and stale beer.

It was a good place for killing.

Devlin had a lot of work left to do and not much time to accomplish it. I handed the evidence bags containing Tong's belongings to her and took the box of O'Quinn's things back to my car, which was parked a few blocks away in an underground garage across the street from the Hyatt.

I drove to Monk's house, parked in a red zone, and waited anxiously for Devlin's call.

It came thirty minutes later.

"I'm ready to send the black-and-white for Corinne," she said. "Are you sure we need Monk for this?"

"She'll expect him," I said. "If he's not there, it's not going to look right. It will play stronger with him than without him."

"Unless he ruins everything," she said.

"That's a definite possibility."

But she knew as well as I did that we really didn't have any choice. I hung up on her and called Monk. He didn't bother to say hello. Nobody else called him in the middle of the night except me.

"Who died?" he asked.

"William Tong," I replied.

The alley was harshly lit by two tall halogen utility lights and was sealed off with bands of yellow police tape that fluttered in the cold night air. The light washed over Tong's car, illuminating dark splashes of blood on the dashboard and windshield. Numbered yellow cones marked spots where evidence had been recovered at various places on the alley floor.

Monk and I stood at the mouth of the alley watching Devlin, who was crouched beside the open driver's side door, carefully picking up a bloody wallet and dropping it into an evidence bag as two police officers led Corinne Witt to the car.

"Who are you?" she asked Devlin.

"I'm Lieutenant Amy Devlin, homicide. I believe

you already know Adrian Monk, who advises us on murder cases, and his assistant, Natalie Teeger."

Corinne cast a nervous glance in our direction, then shifted her attention back to Devlin.

"Am I under arrest?"

"Nope," Devlin said.

"Then why have you dragged me out of bed in the middle of the night and brought me down here?"

"To show you your future. Or maybe it's your tragic end. I'm like the last ghost in *A Christmas Carol*, only with an attitude and a badge. Do you know what happened here?"

"No, of course not," Corinne said.

Devlin looked past her to Monk. "What can you tell us, Monk?"

He cleared his throat and rolled his head. "The way the blood has been splattered on the windshield and dashboard, it appears that someone has been garroted or decapitated."

It was an artful answer. He'd stated the truth. There was no lie to catch him in. He wasn't responsible for any implications or misinterpretations that Corinne drew from his words. Devlin and I might be, though.

Devlin reached into the car and handed Corinne an evidence bag containing Tong's watch and rings. "Do you recognize these?"

The color drained from Corinne's face and she looked at the car again, seeing it in a new light. "I'm not sure."

"Maybe this will help," Devlin snatched the bag from her and handed her the one containing the bloody wallet, which was opened to reveal William Tong's driver's license.

Corinne let out a little whimper and shook her head. "No, this can't be."

"We think Tong tried to sell his share of the diamonds to a fence," Devlin said. "Word got back to Rico Ramirez, and he hunted Tong down."

Corinne shuddered. "Where's William now?"

Devlin shrugged and glanced at me. "What do you think Rico did with the body, Natalie?"

"He's keeping it so he can deliver it in pieces to the others as a warning," I said. "You know, like the horse in *The Godfather*. Who knows what Corinne might find in her bed when she gets home?"

Devlin nodded and looked at Corinne. "You'll be sure to let us know, right? A head, a pinkie, an earlobe, whatever. You give us a call and we'll come get it."

"You can't be serious," she said.

"Thank you for confirming that these were Tong's things. It spared us from having to bring his mother down here," Devlin said. "The officers will take you home now. You have a good night."

"How long will they be staying?" she asked.

"They won't be," Devlin said.

"But what if Rico comes for me?" Corinne asked. "What if he's there already?"

Devlin shrugged. "Call the police. We'll send a patrol car down as soon as we can. But with all the budget cuts, we're spread pretty thin. It might be twenty or thirty minutes."

"You can't leave me alone to die," Corinne said. "I need protection."

"Stay with friends," Devlin said. "Or adopt a dog."

Corinne turned to Monk. "Tell her, Adrian."

Monk shook his head. "The police have limited resources, Corinne. If you want police protection, you will have to give the lieutenant a compelling reason why you think your life is in danger from Rico Ramirez."

Corinne pointed to the car. "That's it, right there. That's why I need protection."

"You will have to do better than that," Devlin said. "What's your connection to Rico Ramirez? Why would he be angry with you? What do you have that he might want? You will need to make a strong case if you want me to allocate manpower for you."

"I have a Fifth Amendment right against self-incrimination," Corinne said, her eyes welling with tears.

"Yes, you do," Devlin said. "You have the right to remain silent. Anything you say can and will be held against you in a court of law. You have the right to an attorney, and if you can't afford one, one will be provided for you."

"Am I under arrest?"

"No," Devlin said. "I am just informing you of your rights so there's no question that you understand them before you decide whether or not to convince me that you need help."

Corinne closed her eyes and tears rolled down her cheeks. "This is a nightmare."

"One of your own making," Monk said.

She opened her eyes, took a deep breath, and faced Devlin. "We took Rico's diamonds."

# 30

## Mr. Monk and the Endgame

Captain Stottlemeyer didn't like being called into the station hours before dawn on a Sunday morning. He came in surly and irritable in wrinkled clothes, his hair a mess. But when he saw Corinne Witt in the interrogation room and was given her signed statement, he didn't seem to mind so much that his good night's sleep had been rudely interrupted.

Devlin, Monk, and I were in the observation room, directly adjacent to the interrogation room, keeping the captain company as he went over Corinne's statement. While he read, we looked at Corinne through the one-way glass. She sat alone, her eyes bloodshot from crying, staring vacantly at the metal tabletop.

By confessing and agreeing to testify against the other crime scene cleaners, she'd get the lightest sentence. She'd confirmed that Yermo was the ringleader, that finding the diamonds and killing Hewson had been his idea. But that didn't make her and the others that much less complicit in Hewson's murder. They'd all fired a shot into him. That was Yermo's clever idea, too, to spread the guilt evenly among them. Even so, Corinne might actually see the outside of prison before she was fifty. It probably didn't offer her much solace, not that she deserved any.

When the captain was done reading, he narrowed his eyes at Devlin and then looked skeptically at Monk and me.

"The Hewson case was blown wide-open just because a couple of patrolmen spotted a bloody car in an alley," the captain said. "And you happened to be the homicide detective on call."

"Yes, sir," Devlin said. What she didn't say was that she'd made the anonymous call that sent the officers there in the first place. "When I ran the plates and realized the car belonged to William Tong, one of the crime scene cleaners, I called in Monk."

"You can't stand Monk," Stottlemeyer said, then turned to Monk. "No offense."

"None taken," Monk said.

"I have a hard time believing that your first instinct was to call him in on this," the captain continued.

"It was an apparent homicide without a body, and I thought it was damn strange," Devlin said. "We call Monk on the strange ones. Besides, he's responsible for every major development in this case."

"And they have been summarily dismissed with prejudice by Deputy Chief Fellows," Stottlemeyer said.

"Now we know how wrong the DC was, don't we?" Devlin said. "You have the proof right there in your hand, sir."

"Yeah, and it's all nice and tidy."

"That's the goal," Monk said.

"Yes, it is, Monk," the captain said. "But it bothers me when it comes so easily."

"You're the one who told us that we'd have to wait for one of our suspects in this case to make a mistake," I said. "Well, that's exactly what happened. You should be patting yourself on the back and feeling smugly superior instead of complaining that it all worked out."

Nobody likes having their face rubbed in their own words, especially not when they've been yanked out of bed in the middle of the night on a weekend.

Stottlemeyer glowered at me for a moment, then shifted his gaze to Devlin. "Did you hear any word on the street today about anybody trying to hock some impressive stones?"

"No, sir, but I wasn't out there asking. You took me off the case, remember?"

That was twice in less than two minutes that he'd had his own words thrown back at him. Now he was glowering at her, too. "What have we got on Tong's disappearance?"

"The forensic team is going over his car for clues right now," Devlin said. "We have officers canvassing the area for his body, and we're checking area hospitals for anyone who might have come in matching his description."

She didn't look at me, and I didn't look at her out of fear that my face might betray something. If Stottlemeyer noticed that we were making a point of avoiding each other, he probably chalked it up to our established animosity.

"So you saw the bloody car as an opportunity to put a scare into Corinne and get her to confess," Stottlemeyer said.

"Absolutely," Devlin said. "Wouldn't you?"

Stottlemeyer sighed and tossed the report on a table.

Something was hinky about all of this and he knew it—he just couldn't put his finger on exactly what was wrong. He turned to Monk.

"What do you make of all this, Monk?"

"You could say it's the natural order of the universe," Monk said. "Greed made the crime scene cleaners into killers and greed now appears to have been their undoing."

"What goes around comes around," Stottlemeyer said.

"I like to think of it as the natural balance," Monk said. "Everything eventually becomes level, symmetrical, and even."

Stottlemeyer turned back to Devlin. "Go arrest Jerry Yermo and Gene Tiflin for murder. I'll wake up a judge while you're on the way and get you search warrants for those diamonds."

I found a place in the station hallway for Monk and me to sit so that Jerry Yermo had to be led past us in handcuffs on his way to be booked.

I looked Jerry right in the eye as he went by, escorted by two uniformed officers, shortly after sunrise on Sunday.

"I told you we'd see each other again," I said.

"Yeah, you're always going to be alone, you miserable bitch."

"At least it won't be in a cell on death row," I said.

"She won't be alone," Monk said. "She'll always have me."

"Then she's going to wish she was on death row," Jerry said as he was taken through the door into the booking area.

Monk looked at me. "What did he mean by that?"

"He thinks you're insufferable."

"Do you?"

"Of course not, Mr. Monk," I said. "Do you want to stay for Gene Tiflin's booking?"

He shook his head. "It was satisfying enough just to see Jerry arrested. Balance has been restored. I was in despair that it might not happen this time. Or ever again."

"You can thank Lieutenant Devlin," I said. "This was all her doing."

"She must have started flossing," Monk said.

We got up and went back into the squad room. Devlin was at her desk, writing up her reports. Stottlemeyer saw us and waved us into his office.

"William Tong is still missing, but I just got a bizarre preliminary report from the lab," Stottlemeyer said. "The blood in Tong's car wasn't human. It was from a pig."

"That is odd," I said and tried very hard to keep my face expressionless, which, I suppose, was a form of expression itself. The truth was that I knew that Devlin had gotten the blood from a butcher in Chinatown.

"That's an understatement," the captain said. "What do you make of it, Monk?"

"It's obviously some kind of prank," Monk said.

"One that worked out conveniently well for us." The captain looked out his open door at Devlin, who was concentrating too hard on her typing but was obviously listening to every word. "I wonder who pulled it off and why."

"Whoever it was and whatever the reason, it wasn't illegal," Monk said. "Unless William Tong registers a vandalism complaint."

"He would have to be alive for that, and since we're dealing with pig blood and not his, I'm hopeful he's gonna turn up breathing," Stottlemeyer said. "Maybe he'll have an explanation for all of this."

"Have you searched his house?" Monk asked.

Stottlemeyer nodded. "His mother's house. And we found the diamonds, the same number of stones that were hidden in the homes of the three other crime scene cleaners. They divvied up the loot evenly."

"My faith in humanity is renewed," Monk said.

"Because the killers divided their stolen diamonds into equal shares?" I said.

"It proves that even in man's darkest moments, the duty to protect the natural order of the universe prevails. It was what ultimately led to Hewson's doom."

"How do you figure that?" Stottlemeyer asked.

"They knew it was impossible to divide the diamonds evenly by five."

"Or they were just too greedy to share," Stottlemeyer said.

"That's the cynical view," Monk said.

Devlin rose from her desk and joined us, handing Stottlemeyer her report. "I'm done with all the paperwork. I'm ready to be Corinne Witt."

Stottlemeyer went to his desk, opened a drawer, and tossed her a leather pouch.

"Don't lose these," he said.

She opened it up and spilled four diamonds into the palm of her hand. They were beautiful. She put them back in the pouch and put it in her pocket.

"What are you going to do with those?" Monk asked her.

"I'm going to hit the street as Corinne and try to fence them."

"Rico will come after you," Monk said.

"That's the idea," she said.

That was stage two of her original plan, the fatally

dangerous part that she wanted to handle on her own. At least now the captain and, presumably, the rest of the force were in on it, too.

"He'll kill you," Monk said.

"He can try," Devlin said with a smile.

She'd be disappointed if he didn't. In fact, I was willing to bet that the bigger the knife, and the closer it got to her throat, the happier she'd be. She was practically giddy at the prospect of facing a violent death at the hands of a multiple murderer.

"Don't worry, Monk, we'll have her under constant surveillance," Stottlemeyer said.

"You don't have to," she said. "I can handle myself. I'm used to being undercover without backup."

"Then you'll appreciate the extra support this time," the captain said.

For the first time in months, she was back in her comfort zone. And Monk, Stottlemeyer, and I were about to be as far from ours as we could get.

# 31

# Mr. Monk and the Killer

I hadn't slept in more than twenty-four hours, so I dropped Monk off at home around noon, had something to eat, and went to bed, intending to take a nap. I set the alarm for three p.m.

Big mistake.

I woke up at two a.m. to find the alarm clock on the floor in pieces. I must have swatted it off the nightstand pretty hard.

So there I was, wide-awake, in the wee hours of the morning with nothing to do, not that I felt like doing anything anyway. My twelve-hour nap left me feeling lousy and out of step with the world. I ate a bowl of cereal, watched reruns of *Maverick*, *Gunsmoke*, and *Bonanza* on TV Land, and then forced myself back to bed again, where I eventually fell into a light sleep around six.

I woke up again at about ten a.m. on Monday morning feeling jet-lagged even though the only distance I'd traveled was between my bedroom and the kitchen.

Meanwhile, Devlin spent her Sunday transforming herself into Corinne Witt, while the SFPD tech unit hid cameras in Corrine's apartment and wired it for sound.

William Tong finally showed up at his mother's house, dazed and disoriented, late Sunday afternoon. He was even more stunned when the two cops who were staking out the house appeared, arrested him, and brought him down to headquarters.

Stottlemeyer interrogated him for more than an hour. Thankfully for me and Devlin, Tong had no memory of what had happened to him. All he knew was that one minute he was at a bar having a drink and the next he was tied to a bed in a dive hotel, his wallet, jewelry, and car keys missing. He couldn't even remember where the hotel was, not that he really cared. Tong was much more concerned about the diamonds, the murder, and spending his life in prison. And who could blame him for that?

As far as bad days go, Tong was having one for the record books.

On Monday morning, Devlin hit the streets as Corinne, visiting the fences that Jerry Yermo usually did business with. She showed off the diamonds, argued about the prices they gave her, and told everyone she'd think about their offers.

Devlin also visited a few pawnshops just to be certain that word got around. She was careful to make sure that everybody could see the name and address on the tag that dangled from her backpack full of textbooks.

Then she returned to the UCSF campus, had a yogurt, and settled down in the library to study, all under the watchful eyes of the plainclothes cops who were shadowing her at all times, much to her displeasure, which she conveyed to Stottlemeyer via her Bluetooth earbud.

Monk and I heard her rant over the speaker in the mobile command center, a retrofitted motor home that had been gutted and filled with banks of monitors, where we were parked with Stottlemeyer a few blocks away.

The command center was high-tech, but it was also cramped and smelled like a men's locker room, a Chinese restaurant, and a pack of wet dogs all rolled into one.

Monk held a handkerchief over his nose and mouth and made little gagging noises.

"These are the worst undercover cops I have ever seen," Devlin said over the speakers. "They might as well be in uniforms."

"They are there for your safety," Stottlemeyer said.

"Get them the hell out of here. Rico isn't going to attack me in public, but he might be watching to learn my movements. If he sees these clowns, they'll blow my cover."

Stottlemeyer groaned. "Fine, I'll pull them back. We'll patch into the library security cameras instead."

"Thank you," she said.

He got on another radio frequency, ordered the plainclothes cops on campus to withdraw, then turned to one of the two technicians in the command center and told them to get the library cameras up.

Within a moment, the six monitors showed different angles of Devlin in the library. I was astonished by how thoroughly and convincingly she'd transformed herself. She wasn't physically very similar to Corinne, and yet she perfectly mimicked the manner in which the girl carried herself, her attitude, even the way she smiled.

Monk cocked his head. "Remarkable."

"I bet she could even do you, Monk," Stottlemeyer said.

"She's obviously a woman," Monk replied.

"She could hide that," Stottlemeyer said.

"The gums would be a dead giveaway."

"It's not the gums or physical features that count," I said. "It's all about the attitude, what you project of yourself from inside, that sells character more than makeup or hair or prosthetics ever could."

Stottlemeyer turned in his chair to look at me. "Where did you hear that?"

"*Maverick*," I blurted out. It was the first thing that popped into my head, which was still pretty foggy from sleeping through most of Sunday.

"The old Western?" Stottlemeyer asked.

"They were undercover cowboys."

"What were they when they weren't undercover?" the captain said.

"Real cowboys," I said. "It was a complex show."

Actually, it starred James Garner and Jack Kelly as gamblers and grifters, but once you're stuck in a lie, you've got to go with it. Lucky for me, Stottlemeyer wasn't an expert on old TV Westerns.

Monk reached into my purse, took out a wipe, and began rubbing down the command console.

"What are you doing?" the captain asked.

"I'm buying us some time," Monk said. "How long has it been since this command center was cleaned?"

"I have no idea," Stottlemeyer said.

My guess was years.

"We need some cleaning supplies delivered right away," Monk said.

"Cleaning the van can wait until after we're done

with our surveillance," Stottlemeyer said. "We have bigger priorities right now, like catching a psychopath who has murdered three people."

"We aren't going to be much good to Devlin if we're dying in here of some gangrenous pestilence when she's being butchered by Rico Ramirez."

"I'm with Mr. Monk on this," I said.

Stottlemeyer stared at me. "You're concerned about gangrenous pestilence, too?"

"Maybe not that specifically," I said. "But you have to admit that it smells awful in here."

"What do you expect a mobile command center to smell like, Natalie?" Stottlemeyer asked. "When we're on a case, men are in here around the clock, without a bath or fresh clothes, eating nothing but fast food and coffee, trying to stay alert while—" He stopped himself, looked at the two of us, and sighed. "Give me a list of what you need."

I was thankful to be cleaning the command center. It relieved the tension and, most of all, the boredom of being in that confined space for hours on end.

And although Stottlemeyer and the two technicians would never admit it, I think they were glad we were cleaning, too.

The place smelled better almost immediately, and maybe it was my imagination, but it seemed brighter and even more high-tech. A more commanding command center.

Monk was meticulous about disinfecting and polishing every dial, button, and light, accidentally turning off a monitor, speaker, or recorder every now and then, but he was forgiven. Every surface gleamed.

He even took it upon himself to clean the small

bathroom, an unspeakable hellhole that no other man on earth would have tackled alone. For that, the entire department owed him a debt of gratitude.

I scrubbed the floors and deep cleaned all of the seats, which meant that the captain and the techs had to spend some time standing, but it probably did their circulation some good.

While all this was going on, night had fallen and Devlin went back to Corinne's studio apartment, a second-floor room in a converted motel. The conversion was really nothing more than replacing the word "Motel" with "Apartments" on the building's facade, adding flower boxes under the windows that were full of blooming geraniums, begonias, and alyssums, and charging tenants by the month instead of by the day or week.

The front door of every room faced the street, where we were parked with a clear view of the building from the tinted windows of the mobile command center. We could also see the inside of Devlin's one-room unit from several camera angles on our monitors.

Her apartment had the basic layout of a billion other motel rooms. The front door opened into a bedroom, with the bed on one side and a desk, dresser, and TV on the other. There were two chairs and a table under the front window. The doors to the bathroom and closet were against the back wall.

The Special Weapons and Tactical Unit officers were suited up, armed, and waiting in position in vans parked on adjacent streets.

Devlin lay on her bed, eating ramen and watching Hong Kong action movies. At around ten p.m., she opened the bathroom door, had a glass of water, and returned to bed, turning off the lights.

"She's bunking early," Stottlemeyer said.

"Maybe it's just an act for Rico's benefit," I said. Considering how many hours she'd been up without sleep, I was surprised that she'd lasted that long. Two minutes after she turned out the lights, she began to snore.

"She didn't brush her teeth," Monk said.

"It's okay, Monk," the captain said.

"We're supposed to be protecting her life."

"From Rico Ramirez," he said.

"Ramen is loaded with salt, and if she goes to bed without brushing, it's going to erode the enamel right off," Monk said. "Meanwhile, the bits of food between her teeth will rot, the bacteria and germs seeping into her bloodstream through her inflamed gums. She'll welcome Rico's blade as sweet release from her slow death."

"One night without brushing won't kill her," Stottlemeyer said.

"You could call her," Monk said.

"No," Stottlemeyer said.

"At least alert the SWAT team," Monk said.

Stottlemeyer swiveled around in his seat to look at Monk. "And tell them what?"

"That they should be ready to swarm in with guns and Listerine," Monk said.

"I'll take that under advisement," Stottlemeyer said and turned back around to watch the monitors.

A few minutes later, Monk sprayed the command center down with Lysol air freshener and sat in his seat with a weary sigh. It was his finishing stroke. All that was missing was taking a bow.

"My job is done," he said.

Stottlemeyer and the two techs applauded.

"I have to hand it to you, Monk, the unit has never looked better," Stottlemeyer said. "When this is over,

I'm calling the editors of *Mobile Command Center Beautiful* to do a photo spread."

But the night ticked on and we soon missed Monk's cleaning. It had been a welcome distraction. Now there wasn't anything to do except watch Devlin sleeping on her back on top of the bed, her body illuminated by the streetlight seeping through the thin drapes. The rest of the room was dark and still.

It was almost as exciting as watching paint dry, though that was an activity that Monk actually enjoyed. He also liked to sit and watch Fantastik's scrubbing bubbles work on his bathroom tiles.

One of the techs slapped his computer monitor.

"What is it?" Stottlemeyer asked.

"A heat signature fluctuation," the tech said. "Some bonehead set the sensors too high."

"Why do you say that?"

"Because it's reading two people in the room instead of one."

"There's only one person," Stottlemeyer said. "We can all see that."

"I know, sir," the tech said. "It's just a glitch."

We were all looking at the screen when the glitch, big and dark and shaped like a man, rose from under the bed, a butcher knife in his hands.

I screamed, though not nearly as loud as Monk did.

"Move in!" Stottlemeyer yelled into his microphone. "Go! Go! Go!"

But it was too late.

Rico Ramirez plunged his knife down toward Devlin's chest. At the last instant, she rolled away, the knife sinking into the mattress where she'd been.

He was a huge man, with a bald head and pockmarked cheeks that looked like they'd been clawed by a bear. He yanked the knife out of the mattress and raised it for the kill once more, snarling with rage.

Devlin rolled back at him with a spin kick in the face that flattened him against the closet, his eyes wide with shock and rage.

Before he could recover, she jumped to her feet and drove her fist deep into his gut, doubling him over, and then rammed her elbow down on the back of his neck.

Rico dropped to the floor as the SWAT team broke open the door and spilled into the room, their guns out.

It was all over in less than a minute. I was suddenly aware of myself again, and then of all of us in the command center, and then of the shocked silence.

It had happened so fast it was hard to believe, much less absorb.

But Devlin was completely relaxed. She sat down on the edge of the bed and calmly watched the SWAT officers drag Rico away.

Stottlemeyer sighed with relief. Monk tapped him on the shoulder.

"Yes, Monk?"

"Now would be a good time to remind her to brush her teeth."

# 32

# Mr. Monk and the Flower

"How the hell did he get in the room?" Stottlemeyer asked.

We were standing on the long landing outside the open door to Corinne's apartment while a forensics unit processed the scene, taking pictures and gathering evidence.

"He climbed in through the bathroom window in the back of the building," Devlin said.

"Who left the window open?"

"I did," Devlin said.

"Why did you do that?" the captain asked. "It was like inviting him to come kill you."

"I was," Devlin said. "He wasn't going to walk up and knock on the front door, was he?"

Monk rolled his shoulders and shifted his weight between his feet. "The bathroom door was closed throughout the early evening as you watched TV and ate dinner. You went into the bathroom to take a drink of water, and then you went to bed, leaving the door open."

"This isn't about her teeth again, is it?" Stottlemeyer said. "Because she's brushed them. Twice."

"What I'm saying is that Rico was already in the apartment when Lieutenant Devlin got that drink of water," Monk said. "She knew he'd snuck in while the bathroom door was closed and that he was hiding in the shower. But instead of apprehending him at that moment, or alerting us that he was there, she turned out the lights and went to bed, and left the door open for him. She gave him the opportunity to crawl out and try to kill her as she slept."

That was why we didn't see him on the monitors. It was pitch-dark in the room and he was on the floor until the last moment, when he rose into the light from the streetlamps.

Stottlemeyer looked angrily at Devlin. "What possessed you to do that?"

"I didn't want there to be a question in anyone's mind about what he came there to do," she said. "And I wanted to kick his ass."

"You could have been killed," Stottlemeyer said.

"So could've he," she said. "It was lucky for him the SWAT team came in when they did."

The captain stepped up close to her. "You ever pull a stunt like that again and I will have your badge. Do we understand each other, Lieutenant?"

"No," she said, "but I understand you, sir."

She walked off, brushing past Monk on her way to the stairs. He gestured to me for a wipe. I reached into my purse and gave him one, banging my elbow on the flower box outside Corinne's window in the process.

"She scares me," he said, wiping his sleeve.

"Me, too," Stottlemeyer said.

"But the good news is that we've apprehended Rico Ramirez, recovered the diamonds, and closed the book on four murders," I said.

"And disinfected the mobile command center," Stottlemeyer said.

"And Natalie's bathroom, too," Monk said.

"Well, we can't do much better than that, can we?" Stottlemeyer said. "We can go to bed tonight knowing that, for the moment, all is right."

"Not quite," Monk said. "Ambrose is still shacked up with an ex-con motorcycle chick."

"You can't have it all, Monk," Stottlemeyer said.

That reminded me that there was still the O'Quinn mystery left for me to solve, and with these cases behind us, there was no reason I couldn't devote the next few days to the task.

Stottlemeyer started to leave and we followed. It was a tight fit on the landing, and I banged my arm on the flower box beneath Corinne's window once again as I walked past it.

I glared at the box, as if it had intentionally misbehaved, and was distracted by the pleasant flower arrangement, a colorful assortment of blooming geraniums and begonias ringed with bunches of white alyssums. I leaned down to smell them.

"You shouldn't do that," Monk said.

"Why not?" I asked. "They say you'll see the world in a whole new way if you stop and smell the roses."

"It's suicidal," Monk said.

"Flowers won't kill you, Mr. Monk."

"You could inhale an excessive amount of pollen, have a severe sinus reaction, and drown in your own mucus. Or a bee could fly up your nose, sting you, and cause your esophagus to swell shut, ensuring your death from anaphylactic shock."

"I don't have sinus problems and I'm not allergic to bees," I said.

"As far as you know," Monk said. "This would be a horrible way to find out that you're wrong. Is the sniff really worth it?"

"Yes," I said, closing my eyes and smelling the flowers again. And when I opened them, I saw more than just the flowers.

"What they say is true," I said.

"Your sinuses are filling up?"

"I see things in a whole new light," I said. "I've just solved the mystery of Walter O'Quinn."

"Tell me," he said.

But I didn't.

Monk didn't handle the frustration well. He called me twice during the night asking me to tell him what I'd figured out, but I refused.

"I thought you said the case was too boring to be interesting to you," I said.

"It is," Monk said. "But if there's a solution, I need to hear it."

"You will," I said. "Tomorrow."

"I need to know now," he said.

"Then solve it yourself," I said. "You have the rest of the night."

"What's left to solve?"

"You can find his family," I said. "Like I have."

"How did you do that?"

"You're the detective," I said. "Detect."

But to be fair, Monk was at a big disadvantage. He wasn't privy to the same information that I was, nor had he been able to make the same observations that I had, not that I was going to concede any of that to him.

I picked Monk up in my car at eight the next morning and we drove to the Tenderloin. It was a thrilling change for me to be the one who knew all the answers and for Monk to be the one tagging along, completely in the dark. I wanted to make the experience last, but I was also eager for the conclusion, to reveal what I knew and to satisfy my curiosity about what I didn't.

I parked in front of the Excelsior, got out of the car, and opened the door to the backseat, taking out the box that contained O'Quinn's fake ID, the binoculars, the old snapshot of Stacey and Rose, the Western novels, and the photo taken of O'Quinn on his deathbed.

Monk joined me and I carried the box across the street with me to Brewster's, the coffee place.

"What are we doing here?"

"I'm getting a cup of coffee and something sweet to start off my day. Can I get you something?"

"Do they have Fiji bottled water?"

"They might, but coffee is their specialty. Why not try a cup?"

"Drink hot liquid muddied with the effluent of crushed beans? No, thanks."

"How about a cup of hot tea?"

"Drink boiled leaves? Oh sure. Maybe I can sample a cup of hot mud, too."

"You eat meat, Mr. Monk. And you eat fruits and vegetables. I don't see how coffee or tea is any worse."

"Even a dog knows better than to drink something that isn't clear," Monk said.

"I've seen dogs drink beer."

"That's supposed to be a convincing argument?"

"You're the one who brought dogs into this," I said, and we went into the coffeehouse.

It was filled with the same crowd of young professionals as before, and the baristas were scrambling to keep up with the demand. The girl who'd served me on Friday, Alyssa, was there again, too.

"What can I get for you?" she asked when I approached the counter.

"A coffee and cinnamon roll for me and a bottle of Fiji water for my friend."

"Coming right up," she said and asked for my name, which she wrote on the side of an empty paper cup.

I found a table by the window for Monk and me, put my box on the floor, and took out the binoculars.

"Is this a stakeout?" he asked.

"No," I said, setting the binoculars in the center of the table.

Monk gestured to the binoculars. "Then why do you have those out?"

"You'll see," I said. "Be patient."

Alyssa called out my name and I went up to get our order. She handed me a tray with the coffee, water, and pastry.

"You have a beautiful name," I said.

"Thank you."

"I like names that come from flowers," I said. "Like Rose."

I turned and went back to our table. I felt Alyssa's gaze on me the whole way. When I took my seat, I looked back just in time to see her glance at the binoculars.

"The girl was staring at you," Monk said.

"I know. She'll find an excuse to come over in a minute."

"Why would she do that?"

"Because she won't be able to help herself."

A minute or two later, she picked up a tray and a

couple of wet towels and stepped out from behind the counter to clean tables. She worked her way over to us.

"Those are nice binoculars," she said.

"What? These old things?" I said.

"My father used to have a pair just like them."

"These are his, Rose," I said.

She froze, and for a moment I thought she might faint. Monk nodded at me with approval.

"A woman in her twenties named for a flower and working right across the street from the hotel," Monk said. "Very observant. I'm impressed."

"Thank you," I said.

"Who are you?" Alyssa asked. "What do you want?"

"You have nothing to be afraid of," I said. "My name is Natalie Teeger and this is Adrian Monk. We work with the police. We're helping them investigate your father's death."

"That was over twenty years ago," she said.

"It was last week," I said and pulled out a chair.

I could see her mind working in the expression on her face. She was following the implications of my remark, which cast her past, and everything she'd been through, in a new and not very pleasant light. It was dizzying. She took a seat and looked at the binoculars.

"May I?" she asked.

"Of course," I said. "They're yours now."

Alyssa picked them up and held them. Focusing on the binoculars seemed to steady her. "I never thought I'd see them again. My father loved these and kept them on his boat. They were a gift from my grandfather. When I think of Dad on that boat, I picture him with these binoculars, looking at the sea ahead. How did you get them?"

"Your father had them with him when he died."

"I know," she said. "They were on his boat when it sank."

I shook my head and pointed to the Excelsior. "He died in that hotel across the street, in a room on the second floor with a view of this coffeehouse. He brought these binoculars with him so he could watch you down here."

She shook her head. "No, that's not possible."

"He'd been living in Mexico all these years, crewing on fishing boats and yachts, under the name Jack Griffin. He came back again because he had terminal cancer and, I think, because he wanted to make things right with his family." I reached into the box and took out the snapshot. "He had this in his hand when he died."

She looked at the picture and wiped a tear from her face. Monk motioned to me for a wipe. I reached into my purse and handed it to him.

"Not for me, Natalie, for her."

"People don't use disinfectant wipes for tears, Mr. Monk." I gave her a napkin instead. She took it and dabbed her eyes.

"I remember the day this was taken," she said. "I was so proud of that bike. He was so proud of the house. Mom was so proud of him. We were all so damn proud. We thought that's what killed him."

"I know that he went out to the house in Walnut Creek a few days before he died," I said. "One of the neighbors saw him. I thought he might have approached you, too."

"I think I would remember that," she said. "I guess he was a coward to the end."

I took out the photo that Captain Stottlemeyer had given me of O'Quinn lying on the bed and I set it on the table in front of her. "This is what he looked like. Maybe he bought a coffee from you."

She touched the photo and shook her head. "I never saw him, or, if I did, his face meant nothing to me." Fresh tears rolled down her cheeks. "How sad is that?"

I wondered for whom. For her? For him? Or for all of them?

"How long have you been back in the Bay Area?" I asked.

She pushed the picture away from her. "Only for a few months."

"Where were you living before?"

"Vancouver," she said. "My mother and I went up to Canada after Dad's boat sank to start a new life."

"Away from the bill collectors," I said. "But still close to your mom's family in Washington."

She nodded and handed the snapshot back to me.

"You can keep the pictures," I said.

"I don't want them," she said and handed over the binoculars, too. "Or these."

"What am I supposed to do with them?"

"Has he been buried yet?" she asked.

"No," I said.

"Put them in the casket," she said. "Or in the trash. I don't care."

"Maybe your mom would like them," I said.

Alyssa shook her head. "I'm never telling her about this and I'm begging you not to, either. It took her so long to get past the pain, the anger. She finally got re-married to a very nice, dependable man who would never leave her. I have two stepbrothers. That's her life now. I'm not sure what mine is."

"Maybe knowing the truth about your past will help you figure that out," I said.

She glared at me and I knew that I'd crossed a line.

"It's his life that was a lie, not mine. There's nothing false about my past or who I am. Everything I felt, everything I lost, was true."

"You don't have to worry, Alyssa. I won't disturb your mother," I said. "I promise. Nobody will."

"How did he find me?" she asked.

"I don't know," I said.

"Why did you come looking for me?"

I glanced over at Monk for help, but he had nothing to say. I was on my own.

"I was with the police when your father's body was found. He'd died of natural causes, had false identification, and his fingerprints weren't in the system. The police were going to drop it and let him be buried as a John Doe. I thought someone out there might care that he was dead."

"Well, you were wrong," she said, then got up and walked away, turning her back to us.

I sighed.

"Congratulations," Monk said.

"More sarcasm?"

"Why do you keep accusing me of being sarcastic? I'm not that kind of person. I meant what I said. You did a good job on this case."

"This wasn't the way I expected it to turn out."

"What were you expecting?"

"To feel like a hero," I said.

"Is that why you solved the mystery?" Monk asked. "For praise and gratitude?"

"Why do you do it?"

"Because I have to. I don't have a choice. But you did."

"Maybe not," I said.

"You don't know?"

"I felt compelled to investigate, but maybe not in the

same way that you do or for the same reasons. It's not clear to me now."

"Perhaps it will be next time," he said.

"What makes you sure there will be a next time?"

"My work is never done."

"So neither is mine?"

"You're my assistant, aren't you?"

"Yes, I am."

"Then you're doomed," he said.

The Victorian house at the corner of Cole and Hayes streets was listed for sale at two million dollars, which was a fair price considering that it was newly remodeled, immaculately maintained, and only a short walk from the University of San Francisco, Golden Gate Park, and Haight-Ashbury. However, it was going to sell for a lot less than the asking price, if it ever sold at all. I wasn't a real estate expert like the dead woman on the entry hall floor, but I knew that murder always brought down property values.

The dead Realtor's name was Rebecca Baylin. She was twenty-seven years old, shirtless, and her head was caved in. Ordinarily, Adrian Monk wouldn't be able to look at a topless woman, but there he was, framing the scene between his hands and tipping his head from side to side to examine her from different angles.

Monk would be repulsed by someone with a bit of lettuce stuck between his teeth, or a missing button on his shirt, or a single pierced ear, or zit on his chin, and yet he had no qualms about staring at bodies with all manners of horrific violence perpetrated on them.

It made no sense to me, but then again, there was a lot I didn't understand about my obsessive-compulsive boss, even after all my years as his underpaid and over-worked assistant, agent, driver, shopper, researcher, publicist, and all-around emotional punching bag.

I'll make a guess, though. Maybe the reason he could look at Rebecca Baylin was that her nakedness was negated by her lifelessness. He didn't see her as a woman anymore, or even as a person. She'd become something that was out of place, disorder that had to be made orderly, a mess that had to be cleaned up, a question that had to be answered. And he wouldn't be able to rest—and by extension neither would I—until he'd figured out what had happened to her, caught her killer, and restored the balance that had been disrupted by her murder.

And I knew that Monk would. He always did.

This was a fact that Captain Leland Stottlemeyer had come to rely upon. It was why Stottlemeyer fought countless political battles to employ Monk as a consul-tant. It was why he found the patience to tolerate and forgive all of Monk's aggravating eccentricities. And it was why he called us down to that open house on that foggy Saturday morning to meet with him and Lieu-tenant Amy Devlin.

"This home was Baylin's listing," Devlin said. "She was supposed to host an open house here this morn-ing. A couple came by at ten a.m. to see the place, found the door unlocked, and walked in on this."

Devlin gestured to the body on the floor.

"We've got the couple sitting in the backseat of a black-and-white, if you'd like to ask them a few questions," the captain said, standing beside me and chewing on a toothpick, the tip tickling the hairs of his bushy mustache as he watched Monk work. Stottlemeyer wore a wrinkled off-the-rack suit and a tie that had gone out of style with disco.

"That's not necessary," Monk said. "You can send them home. They didn't do it."

"How do you know?" Devlin stood across from us. She had short black hair that looked like she'd had her gardener trim it with a weed whacker, and wore faded jeans and a gray hoody under a leather jacket.

"It's obvious from the rigor mortis and other physical indications that she's been dead for at least eight hours."

"That doesn't mean they didn't kill her last night and then came back this morning so they could discover the body and rule themselves out as suspects," Devlin said.

She watched Monk with obvious impatience, her hands on her hips, parting her jacket to reveal the badge and gun that were clipped on her belt, not that there was anyone around at the moment who'd be impressed by them. She'd transferred to homicide recently after a long string of undercover assignments, and I think on some level she enjoyed advertising that she was a cop instead of working so hard to hide it.

Or maybe she just wanted easy access to her gun so she could shoot Monk if he continued to irritate her.

"That sounds awfully convoluted to me," Stottlemeyer said. "Almost Disher-esque."

"Disher-esque?" she said.

The captain was referring affectionately to Randy Disher, the cop she'd been brought in to homicide to replace after he took a job as the police chief of Summit, New Jersey.

"Never mind," Stottlemeyer said. "Were you serious with that theory about the couple who found the body?"

"Of course not," Devlin said. "But it's exactly the kind of ridiculous conclusion that Monk usually comes to."

"Except that when he comes to a conclusion," I said, "he's always right."

Stottlemeyer gave me a cold look. He hated it when I brought up Monk's perfect record in front of them. It only stoked Monk's ego and Devlin's animosity toward him. But defending Monk was a reflex for me.

If Monk heard the compliment, he didn't acknowledge it. He turned his back to us, walked around the body one more time, then drifted off into the adjacent living room.

Devlin sighed with frustration. "I don't see what the big mystery is here."

"How about who killed her?" Stottlemeyer said.

"Beyond who the actual perpetrator is," Devlin said, "the circumstances of her death don't strike me as a mind-boggling puzzle that requires outside assistance."

She had a point, not that I would give her the satisfaction of admitting it.

It used to be that Stottlemeyer called Monk for only the most difficult, unusual, or high-profile murder cases. But ever since the captain had remarried, he'd begun bringing Monk in on more and more of the routine homicides, particularly if they happened on weekends, just so he could get home sooner. That's because Monk often solved cases on-the-spot, while an average detective would take a day or two to sort out the same job.

Monk's amazing eye for detail used to rile the captain. But nowadays, Stottlemeyer didn't have as much ego invested in proving that he and his detectives were capable of doing the job without Monk's help.

The same couldn't be said for Amy Devlin. She never denied Monk's abilities. But she found him enormously irritating and wanted to do her job herself, even if it took a little while longer for her to close the case.

Since Monk was busy wandering around the living room, Stottlemeyer focused his attention on Devlin. "So, what do you think happened, Lieutenant?"

"Baylin stopped by last night to prep the house for today's showing and either left the door unlocked or encountered someone who came by pretending to be interested in the house. Whoever it was tried to sexually assault her. When she resisted, he brained her with a heavy object and fled."

Monk turned around, nodding to himself as he drifted back in our direction.

"You agree with her, Monk?" Stottlemeyer asked.

"No," Monk said. "I need to meet the owners of this house right away."

Nobody had mentioned them at all, so it was a surprise to me that something about the crime had led Monk to them. "You think that they might have something to do with this?"

"Of course not," Monk said. "They are people of class, distinction, and impeccable moral character. They would have nothing to do with a murder."

"You don't know their names and you've never met them," Devlin said, "so how can you possibly make any assumptions about their character?"

"Look at how they live, Lieutenant. Everything is clean, orderly, and tastefully organized. They are a remarkable family, and I want them in my life," Monk picked up a framed family photo from the coffee table.

It showed a young couple on the beach with their two children and their two golden retrievers. The whole family was dressed in jeans and white shirts. "Look at them, so balanced and symmetrical. If more families followed their example, we'd have fewer divorces, a lower crime rate, and far less gum on the sidewalks."

"It's not going to happen," I said.

"I don't see why not," he said.

Monk had an incredible eye for detail, but because he was clueless about the nuances of basic human interaction, there was still a lot that he missed, which was why he was lucky to have me around.

"Because those people are models," I said.

"For all of us," Monk said. "Everybody should follow their extraordinary example. They are true Americans."

"What I mean, Mr. Monk, is that the family does not exist. They are professional models who were hired to pose for those pictures. This whole house is staged."

Monk looked around, seeing everything anew. "You're saying that this Realtor was perpetrating a massive fraud? How do you know?"

I started to reply, but Devlin cut me off, eager to take the opportunity to trump Monk.

"Because it's too orderly, too clean. Everything is perfect," she said. "It's an idealized version of a home. Nobody actually lives like this."

"I do," Monk said.

"This was a spec home," Stottlemeyer explained. "The owner bought it, remodeled it, then hired a company to dress it like a movie set to maximize its features, hide its shortcomings, and make it more attractive to buyers."

Monk regarded the picture again, this time with sadness. "I wish they were my family."

"That's the point," I said. "To make this house, and

the idea of living in it, as alluring as possible on every level. What we buy is often based more on emotion than on practical considerations anyway."

"No wonder she was murdered," Monk said. "Think of all the people she's tricked with this elaborate ruse."

"You're the only one," Devlin said. "Nobody is fooled by this. It's like a commercial. We all know it's fake."

"But it could be real," Monk said, "if everybody made just a little effort."

"The only thing that's real in this house is the dead body on the floor," Devlin said.

"Speaking of which, could we please focus on the murder?" Stottlemeyer said. "Tell me you have something, Monk."

Monk set the photo down on the coffee table. "Someone wants us to think that the murder happened exactly the way Lieutenant Devlin thinks it did. But it didn't."

"What makes you say that?" Devlin said.

"The murder weapon, a heavy object of some kind, is missing. And because everything is orderly and in place, it's clearly not an object that was already here, within immediate reach, that was grabbed in the heat of the moment. Everything is where it is supposed to be."

"Because he brought the weapon with him," Devlin said. "And left with it, too."

"Wouldn't it be more likely that an assailant would bring a knife or a gun rather than a brick or a bat?"

"Yeah, but I wouldn't rule it out," Devlin said. "Maybe clubbing women over the head and then molesting them when they are unconscious is his thing."

"Then why was she bashed multiple times?" Monk asked. "And why didn't the assailant complete the assault?"

"Maybe he didn't mean to kill her and walked away because he's not into necrophilia," Devlin said. "Or maybe this is exactly how he gets his jollies, and he doesn't complete the act with the victim."

"Yuck," I said.

"Perhaps you're right," Monk said to Devlin. "But where's the blood? Her hair is thick with dried blood, but there is only a little on the floor. Scalp wounds bleed a lot. There should be a large puddle of blood, not to mention some spatter on the walls from the force of those blows. But there isn't any. The place is immaculate."

"Because he's seen *CSI* and cleaned up after himself," Devlin said.

"I don't smell any cleansers," Monk said.

"Your nose could be wrong," Devlin said.

Stottlemeyer shook his head. "There are bloodhounds that could take lessons from Monk."

"She was definitely killed somewhere else and dumped here," Monk said. "The murder is as staged as everything else in this house of lies."

"Then we'd better go get ourselves some facts," Stottlemeyer said.